CW00864777

The
Dogged Desire
of
Lindy Styre

VICKI WILLIAMS

Tellwell Talent
www.tellwell.ca

ISBN
978-0-2288-1873-1 (Paperback)
978-0-2288-1872-4 (eBook)

In memory of Al

and,

as always, for Lorne

.

CHAPTER ONE

The Mad Woman of Chaillot

That's when the money started to make sense.

That's when Lindy decided to spend it on something unexpected.

Something exhilarating.

Something terrifying too.

A doggington bark. A doggington woof. A doggington growl...

More than a year had passed since Dad had died. The standard ecumenical service he'd arranged for himself had been held. A withered handful of old neighbours and surviving civil service colleagues had attended. Lindy and her older brother Greg had dumped his ashes into the Ottawa River so they'd drift downstream to eventually toss with Mom's in the Atlantic seas.

The retirement residence and the funeral parlour had been satisfied. The accountants and the taxmen had taken their cuts. The bankers had indicated that the remaining inheritance could be disbursed. The lawyers had asked Lindy and Greg to come to their office today to sign off on the final documents.

Naturally, Dad had been definite about where his legacy should go and to whom.

Greg was getting the lion's share of the family fortune. Dad knew that his only son would take good care of the money that he'd shrewdly invested in stocks and bonds and barely tapped for over fifty years. His only daughter, Lindy, was getting the house, the furniture, the car and, for reasons known only to Dad, a relatively small cash bequest.

Greg was happy. Lindy was happy. It was all good.

A paid-up mortgage and robust health meant Lindy could easily stay in the home where she'd lived for sixty-two years. Well—except for that brief moment when she and Malcolm had tied the knot. But, of course, with Malcolm being Malcolm—and Dad's blessing—their student marriage had quickly fallen apart. Long before the wedding guests had time to wonder what to buy the happy couple for their paper anniversary, Lindy had once more found herself sleeping alone in the second bedroom at the end of the upstairs hall.

"Nice women don't get divorced," her mother had whispered, as Lindy returned to the routine of serving her tea and toast. "You're lucky your Dad's letting you back in under his roof..."

That was one way to see it, Lindy supposed, but perhaps it might have been a very good thing if Dad had thrown her out. He was awfully quick to dismiss Mom's daily help once his daughter was back to cook and clean, and she'd never gotten up the gumption to leave the family compound again.

So she'd never moved past the government clerical position Dad had arranged for her by finding an equally dull job in his own department for the Colonel's dopey son next door. And she'd never gone back to school to get her Masters of Library Science degree...

But—"water under the bridge," Lindy's pragmatic brother would say.

Water under the bridge.

Leave the past in the past.

What's done is done.

Easy for him to say, of course. At eighteen, he'd left for the University of Toronto and rarely been back...

"Come visit us sometime soon," offered retired actuary Greg, as he drew his stylish raincoat over his thin stooped shoulders and gave Lindy a quick dry hug.

But he didn't say when, and Lindy wasn't expecting to see her brother and his wife, Nan, at least until next Christmas. And only then if she took the train down to Oshawa to stay in their Louis-Quinze guest room with the Lawren Harris iceberg print over the bed.

Which might be a pleasant adventure for some, thought Lindy, but she wasn't sure that she, a dollar store decorator, would ever feel comfortable in the midst of their vintage blown glass festivities. Last Christmas—while visiting her brother's house for the first time in twenty years—she'd spent many an anxious moment trying not to shatter any of the fragile treasures artfully strewn about their tasteful home.

Now that she thought of it, that was probably why Lindy had been given the house and not Greg. Dad would have been suspicious that Nan would be eager to ply her paintbrush, coating his dark oak trim with a subtle off-white…

Dad had also been probably pretty confident that—with the weight of his family's history and his ghostly eye on her—Lindy would never dare. She wasn't the type to rearrange furniture, much less set out on major paint jobs, and Dad knew that his daughter would simply make do with what he'd determined should already be there.

Home improvements, no.

Self improvements, even less so.

Under Dad's hypercritical gaze, Lindy had never even considered painting her nails or putting highlights in her hair. Pierced ears? Not a chance. A tattoo, like the ones girls now embroidered all over their bodies with such flare? Unthinkable.

As Malcolm had once gently teased her, Lindy was what his birder friends would call a 'Little Brown Jobbie' or 'LBJ'—a small, common bird, indistinguishable from the rest of its kin. By which he meant that, as a short and slightly pudgy, brown-haired, brown-eyed, white woman of Anglo-Saxon descent, Lindy would be quite unremarkable in a Canada Day crowd on Parliament Hill.

Nan, on the other hand, was aesthetically tall and slender, black-haired, blue-eyed and striking in an Eastern European way. Lindy always felt unsophisticated, plain and frumpy in her sister-in-law's presence and a gawky bungler in her elegant home.

No, she really didn't want to go visit Greg and Nan in Oshawa.

And, besides—there was Paulie.

Shrugging into her light fall jacket, Lindy suppressed a shudder.

A doggington woof. A doggington yip. A doggington snarl...

Paulie the Doberman was definitely a doggington snarl, and Nan had been so peeved last Christmas when she and Greg had been forced to keep her darling fur baby out of whichever room Lindy was in. Not that she'd ever said much about it, but Lindy could tell from her brittle smile that Nan had regarded Lindy's heart-shredding fear of Paulie as a personal insult.

"You're right, of course, Lindy," Nan had murmured, casting a critical eye over their spotless family room where Paulie quivered on the Persian rug, raring to sink his fangs into Lindy's throat. "We'll never get on top of all the dog hair as long as Paulie's in here relaxing with the rest of the family..."

"I—I—I'm sorry..." Lindy had croaked, frozen with dread in the doorway.

And then, with a nod to the Festive Season, Greg had become awkwardly jovial, merrily chiding, "Hey, cut the dramatics, little sister. No one would guess you'd grown up with a dog."

"Just 'til I was nine," Lindy had faintly objected through clenched teeth.

"No, we had Buddy longer than that—"

"Well, that's when Mom had her first cancer—"

Lindy vividly recalled Dad complaining that he didn't have time for a sick wife and an ugly mutt. And Mom getting the raw side of his tongue for how much the vet had charged to put the old dog down.

"Besides—it was your chore to walk and feed him," she'd added shakily. "Buddy always growled at me. He even bit me once," —she'd still blenched at the memory—"and it took forever for my arm to heal. I guess, after that, I was always pretty scared of him..."

Greg had rolled his eyes, asking the gods for strength. But, even so, he'd dragged their rumbling Cerberus into the butler's pantry where Paulie had howled blue murder until Nan had caved in and let his slavering jaws loose again to—Crack!

At the government-funded mental health group Lindy had once attended—until Dad had discovered she'd been "belly-aching in public"—an overworked therapist had advised her to head off negative thoughts by snapping an imaginary elastic band on her wrist. This Lindy had done with regularity ever since. Although it hadn't kept the downward spirals into gloom and doom away in the first place—and it sometimes hadn't worked at all—snapping her elastic had become a useful tool to abruptly marshal her thoughts and lead her back to reason.

Therefore—Crack!

Be sensible, Lindy scolded herself. Paulie is four hours away in Oshawa with Nan.

What you really need to do right now is beetle off to your bank with that cheery little cheque.

Before she hipped opened the law office's outer door, Lindy donned her protective sunglasses. Dogs, she truly believed, wouldn't attack quite so often if they couldn't see the terror in your eyes. Then, standing in the doorway, she scoped out the sunlit October streetscape. Noting that, presently, the busy downtown sidewalk seemed to be dog-free, she flipped her greying bob behind her ears and scurried down the block to the nearest bus stop, sheltered beneath the flaming leaves of a caged city maple tree.

Lindy could drive a car—of course she could. Getting her licence through the high school driver education course was one thing she could thank Dad for pushing her into, even if it was because he "didn't have time to be your mother's goddam chauffeur." So, from the age of seventeen, Lindy had spent hours driving Mom to the grocery store or to the hairdresser or to church or to one of her numerous medical appointments. In fact, a lot of what was supposed to be Lindy's sick leave and vacation time over the years had been used up dealing with Mom's chronically rotten health.

But—at Dad's insistence—Lindy had always frugally bussed to work at her downtown Ottawa government building and, even as a retiree, she'd kept her bus pass paid up. The bus still ran right along her Avenue, after all. So it was far more convenient for her to use public transit than to fight the traffic and search for a paid parking spot in the bustling inner city.

And—as she'd confided to Malcolm over a friendly beer at the Royal Oak Pub last week—buses only allowed the politest dogs to ride. Serious dogs with serious jobs, laying subdued beside their owners with never a woof. Although, there was that one time when she'd been crowded into the aisle by a portly seatmate and an in-coming harnessed black lab had given her exposed hand a featherlight lick—Crack!

Lindy's bus arrived before any dogs walked by and, thankfully, she snagged a window seat near the middle door.

A cheery cheque, yes, but not so little, reckoned Lindy as she stared fixedly out at the passing scene so that the college girl who'd sat beside her wouldn't think she was a snoopy old woman with nothing better to do than sneak looks at her smartphone screen. Twenty-six thousand and change. Not enormous, she mused, but big enough for a bit of a—a what?—a bit of a splurge perhaps? A new car? No, she thought, I'll never use Dad's old Ford enough to wear it out.

Her bus left behind the high-rises and storefront businesses of centretown and bumbled past the boutiques and cafes of the affluent Glebe. Past Lansdowne Park—no longer host to the thrilling candy apple and horse show summer exhibition of Lindy's youth—lurched her bus. Then up and over the Rideau Canal bridge and into Lindy's neighbourhood, it rumbled.

It passed Mom's greystone United Church, where Dad had argued so bitterly with the minister about the fees due for conducting Mom's funeral that Dad had forbidden Lindy to ever set foot in its sanctuary again—Crack!

It passed the public library, where the most recent renovations had erased the garage that used to house the bookmobile. It passed the vintage movie house, still operating but now chiefly showing indie films and 'Rocky Horror' at Halloween. It passed the giant big-box pharmacy, a recent replacement for the long-gone druggist who'd plied his trade on the opposite corner where the dollar store now stood.

Ghost businesses and phantom buildings haunted Lindy's mental map of the neighbourhood where three generations of Styres had lived for the past ninety years. The firehall with its clanging pumpers had morphed into a community centre, the long term care hospital, into a seniors' residence, and the bus timeyard at the end of her

one-way Avenue, into a low-rise apartment building. The

tall red brick elementary school that Lindy and her brother

had walked to, however, was still there.

A child of the nineteen-fifties, Lindy was old enough
to remember when the breadman and the milkman had
made home deliveries. When she or her brother could be
sent alone to the confectionary to pick up cigarettes for
Dad and penny candy to share with Mom. Then, their
neighbourhood had been mostly inhabited by working or
middle class folk. But now doctors, lawyers and government
ministers had bought in, and the Styre's modest house was
one of the few largely unimproved properties left on her
Avenue.

Shaking off her memories, Lindy rang the bell, and her
bus rattled to a stop. Stepping into well-known territory,
she slipped through a gap in the traffic to cross to her bank.

"Hi, Ms Styre," smiled the perky young clerk who'd
been dealing with Lindy's accounts since Dad died. "What
can we do for you today?"

Once the cheque was safely deposited into her savings
account, she re-crossed the street at the traffic light, strode
quickly past the bicycle shop and kitty-cornered through
the convenience store parking lot to her leaf-littered
Avenue. There she paused to peer narrowly down the two
and a half blocks toward her house.

Way down the Avenue, a bus was just pulling out after
picking up a passenger at the Brewer Park stop and, near
the closest cross street, a spritely English setter was towing
his owner down the sidewalk in her direction.

Abruptly, Lindy backtracked through the parking lot to stride up Bank Street to the Starbucks coffee shop across from her former elementary school. Soon, with an English Breakfast tea in hand and nowhere else to be, she was settling into a small table by the window for a luxurious muse.

As a penniless undergrad when their marriage tanked, Malcolm hadn't been required to pay alimony. But Lindy was still nicely situated for a retired single divorcee. Despite never being too comfortable speaking conversational French, she'd consistently passed the written comprehension exam and so been grandfathered in her supposedly bilingual Federal job. Consequently, she now received a solid government pension from her thirty plus years as a civilian library clerk at the Department of National Defence.

Furthermore—being at Mom's beck and call for most of her working life—she'd spent very little of her salary beyond her room rent, the purchase of necessary clothes and shoes, or the price of an occasional office lunch or movie matinee. And most of her subsequent savings had been stashed in a fat Dad-approved blue chip investment portfolio.

And now she owned the Styre's house and all of its furnishings, too. And a car. And a cat. And a...well, she'd think of what else she owned but, the truth was, she had lots. She really didn't need anything else...

Maybe she should just give away her bequest to the people who did?

But, then again, she did give to charity pretty regularly. To the kitties and puppies at the SPCA. To the Third

World poor. To the homeless men's shelter. So she was well within her rights, she thought defiantly, to spend her windfall on a treat. Like a trip to Europe...or some diamonds from Birks or...well, whatever she wanted, really.

But what did she want?

About to take a cautious sip, Lindy noticed that she'd forgotten to put milk in her tea.

Damn.

If she left her jacket on the seat while she scooted over to the jug, would someone dump it on a bench and take her table? She could leave her purse—that would make it clear that she was coming back—but what sort of idiot would leave their purse? People steal purses. They steal jackets too, for that matter. Maybe she should just drink her tea without milk today.

But I like milk in my tea, thought Lindy stubbornly.

So, after checking that no one in the Starbucks looked particularly predatory, and leaving her jacket to fend for itself, she swiftly grabbed her cup and purse and scuttled over to the jug. With a minimum of fuss, she accomplished her mission and, trundling straight back, nestled triumphantly into her chair. Feeling highly adult and supremely independent, she took a swig of her milky tea and began to ponder anew.

She had $26,278.00 to spend on a spree. Not a princely sum, but a substantial amount. And she would blow it— and be damned!—on whatever she wanted. And what she wanted was...?

Nothing came.

Damn.

If her best-friend-since-forever, sometime-retail-clerk, sometime-jewelry-designer, sometime-lady-of-leisure, always-floating-aristocrat, Madelyn Cesky, had received a lovely little legacy, she would certainly know how to spend it.

A cruise to Singapore. Or a fabulous custom gown. Or tickets, perhaps, tickets to the Paris Opera...or, maybe, she'd bankroll an opera here...or finance one of those strange and wonderful productions at the Fimbria Festival that Madelyn had taken Lindy to last June...

Smiling at the memory, Lindy drained her cup, stood up to put on her jacket, smoothed her coif and replaced her sunglasses. As she left the cafe, she routinely scrutinized her surroundings and observed that currently the street seemed to be populated solely by humans.

What a relief.

Here, in her own neighbourhood, she was painfully aware that almost every third tree-shaded residence housed some breed of canine. In about an hour—when the school bell rang—the streets would be thick with doggington barks and doggington woofs. Right now, however, as long as her Avenue seemed clear when she reached the convenience store parking lot, she could afford to concentrate on her thoughts as she walked along.

Ever since I was a teenager, Lindy thought, I've been fascinated by plays...

In grade nine, Maddie had bullied her into auditioning for a part and, unexpectedly, she'd ended up rehearsing in the chorus of *Brigadoon* for six weeks—until Greg had snitched to Dad and she'd had to quit. But that had aroused her curiosity and, by the time she'd graduated, she'd dipped into all six play collections in her high school library. She'd majored in History at university, but she'd enjoyed reading the plays in both her Shakespearean Comedies and Twentieth Century Literature courses. And over the years she'd attended at least twenty theatrical productions, including that time she'd gone on a university sponsored trip to the Festival Theatre in Stratford—the town in Ontario, not the one in England.

But, until Maddie took her to the Fimbria, Lindy had always assumed that the Shakespeare and Shaw, the Beckett and Ionesco that they'd seen at the National Arts Centre while Dad and Mom were away on their annual two week winter trek to Florida were the height of creative theatre, thoroughly modern and edgy. Those 'absurd' ones, especially, and that Greek one she'd puzzled over, with its 'Cuckoo-cloud-land,' certainly seemed so.

Modern? Maybe.

Edgy? Ha!

She'd been totally unprepared for the giddy buffet of performances served up by the Ottawa Fimbria Festival.

Madelyn had tried to alert her, advising: "Maybe this isn't going to be your cup of tea, hon. Some of it can be pretty bizarre. Just give me a nod if you want to trot home..."

But Lindy hadn't wanted to leave.

She'd had a few collywobbles, it was true, when Maddie had first escorted her to the central box office upstairs at the Victorian-era Arts Court building. As she'd admitted in the elevator, a lot of the shows she'd read about on the Fimbria website sounded way out of her comfort zone.

Also, she'd confessed as they'd inched forward in the box office line, she hadn't been entirely sure that the theatre venues, most of them within a few blocks of the building where she'd served out most of her government career, would be completely unleashed-dog-free.

Nevertheless, when they'd arrived at the box office window, she'd gone ahead and bought their Fimbria passes—the buttons they'd wear throughout the eleven day festival to indicate that they were supporters—and two ten-ticket packages to the shows.

And once she'd surged to her feet to applaud Madelyn's first option—a rollicking Polish sex comedy—and sat bemused and vaguely repelled through Maddie's second—an angry young man's murky recital of his grandmother's gory folk tales—Lindy had become a born-again Fimbria fan, impatient to leaf through the official program to pick out which shows to patronise next.

Some of the shows had been slick and professional, a laugh riot, as they say, or a moan fest, sweeping the crowd along with a sure hand. Some had been raw and amateurish, boorish or embarrassingly ham-handed. But most had seemed to be a mixed bag, with dramatic gems glittering amid uninspired dross, all tumbled together on stage.

And every single one had been performed at strange times in peculiar theatre spaces for large or small or middling crowds. Crowds who had waited, greyhounds in the slips, for venue doors to be thrown open, seats to be snagged, house lights to dimmed and unpredictable live shows to be unveiled.

Afterwards, loose-lipped over alcohol in the warm June night, Madelyn and her arty friends had sliced and diced some of the clumsier productions into bleeding piles on the Festival beer tent floor.

But Lindy had never joined in the slaughter.

For in each case—without fail—she'd loved them all. The fancy pants English clowns whose descent into heartbreak brought their huge audience to tears. The wild-eyed Australian raconteur. The super-earnest local high school kids who did a breathless fifty minute 'Twelfth Night.' The awkward family drama. The cheesy one-woman Walmart mime. The tragic Inuit saga. The hysterical rubber chicken puppet show. The burlesque lesbian musical review...

For Lindy, every show had been a true snowflake, the ephemeral crystallization of someone's good, bad, or indifferent idea, and not a single show had disappointed her. Not a single show, she had assured skeptical Maddie on the Fimbria's closing night, hadn't been worth the price of admission.

They had all been unique. So bold. So free...

And Madelyn had kindly informed her that, at the Fimbria Festival, anyone could put on a show. You just had to name your company—which could be just you—and, after winning the Fimbria lottery, pay the fees. And then, miraculously, you would be given a theatre space, a technician and six time slots for your show.

And anyone could do it.

Anyone who won the Fimbria Festival lottery. Anyone with cash for the fees. Anyone who had anything to perform.

Anyone. Anyone at all...

As she scuffed through the vivid fallen leaves on the final half block to her driveway, Lindy was deep in reverie.

So deep, in fact, that at first she did not notice the fluffy brown spoodle, off-leash after its run by the river.

And then she spotted it—a doggington ruff—trotting down the sidewalk straight toward her.

Lindy froze.

Sensing that the human in front of her was terrified, the spoodle froze too. What could be so scary? Nostrils wide to sniff the autumn air, the spoodle could pinpoint nothing that she'd consider a threat—no ferocious dogs, no menacing wild animals, no sinister people...

The spoodle's owner, the A-one leader of her dog and human pack, was quickly approaching from behind, chatting to invisible friends as he so often did. Had her owner sensed this panic-stricken female? From the even timber of his voice, the spoodle thought not. So, knowing instinctively that frightened animals are the deadliest, and absolutely certain that it is a dog's sacred duty to protect its pack, with a raspy snarl the fluffy brown spoodle bared its fangs and leapt.

You're going to die! screamed Lindy's brain. Her heart raced, the skin on her palms and the back of her neck went clammy and dank. Facing extinction, but, uncertain whether to fight or fly, her muscles spasmed and, with a final spontaneous thrust of arms across the delicate sense organs on her face, she collapsed into a dead heap on the sidewalk.

As her owner shouted, "Taffy!" and quickened his pace, the spoodle backed off and circled, barking madly at the flaccid lump on the ground. It took the owner a moment to grab his dog's collar and get the leash fastened back on, but eventually he dragged her away, quieting her with a stern command. Then, swallowing his laughter at this stupid old woman's gormless reaction to his family's goofy playmate, he inquired after Lindy's well-being.

"Are you okay, ma'am? She's really a very friendly pup. Do you need a hand up?"

Her panic ebbing once the dog had calmed down, Lindy felt her body begin to firm as her brain clawed back from the brink of the grave. Regaining a modest amount of muscle control, she managed to look up and shake her head, all the while despairing, oh damn, my panties are wet...

They always say their dogs are 'very friendly,' she thought grimly, as the owner and his now securely leashed dog watched her painfully stagger up off her knees. Greg and Nan always describe Paulie that way too. Even while he unsheathes his daggers and growls in my face...

Still, for Taffy's owner, she managed to plaster on a sickly smile and protest much too loudly, "Oh, I know she is. I'm just an idiot. Please don't blame your doggie." Your doggie that you allow to run in the streets unleashed, she added bitterly to herself. "Really, I'm fine."

And she was, actually. Merely shaken, bruised, damp— and deeply humiliated.

Satisfied that she was okay—of course she's okay, he grinned to himself, Taffy's an angel and all the neighbours know that woman's nuts!—the owner and his spoodle resumed their jaunty walk home.

Mechanically, Lindy dusted leaf mould off her knees and turned toward her house.

Down her maple-strewn driveway, past the flagstones leading to the painted wooden steps of her wide front veranda, she marched.

Along the red-bricked wall to the sticky wooden side door where the family had always entered their two storey Craftsman house, built in the mid-1920's by Grandpa Styre from a mail order plan.

Down the basement steps to take off her shoes and hang up her coat on the row of hooks that Grandma Styre had hammered into the wallboard to keep Grandpa's and Dad's messy outdoor clothes away from the formal front vestibule.

Up two flights of stairs past the cracked stained glass window to tidy herself in the main bathroom, last renovated with harvest gold fixtures in the nineteen-seventies.

Across the hall into what had been for the last year Lindy's bedroom, the biggest bedroom of the three—the one her parents had shared for three days short of their fifty-eighth anniversary—to fish in the drawers and closet for a change of pants.

Down the creaky oak stairs again to the floral-wallpapered kitchen where her silver-grey cat, Phyllis, yawned a greeting and wound herself around Lindy's legs as she automatically put the kettle on to brew some tea.

Into the dark oak-trimmed living room to plunk herself down onto the podgy brown sofa with her steaming china cup.

Inevitably now, anger began to swamp Lindy's shock.

Not anger at the doggington growl or her supercilious owner, however.

Anger at herself.

Idiot! she berated herself. Useless, sniveling coward!

And then, right on schedule, the nasty badgering voice seeped in—

Disgracing yourself in front of all the neighbours, it hissed, that's not how you were brought up...not how I tried to teach you...

With a trembling hand, Lindy put down her tea.

You think you're so smart with that university degree and that government job?

Let me set you straight, girl.

I paid for those classes. I got you that job. There's nothing that you know that I don't know. Nothing that you've done that I couldn't have done with one hand tied behind my back.

So don't give yourself airs!

Lindy balled up her fists. She bit her lip and bowed her head beneath the coming onslaught.

Hey, kid! Are you listening to me? You may have been born ugly, but did you have to be a moron too—?

By Jeezus, it makes me sick just to look at you!

You're nothing!

You're nobody!

And, you know what, kiddo?

You're beggin' for a bruisin'—yeah, I'm going to tan your hide!

Lindy shrank from what had always came next—

Buddy! Fetch me your leash!

But, strangely, for once the nasty voice wasn't winning. For once, Lindy didn't feel compelled to make herself feel normal by slapping pain onto her cheeks. For once—fed by more than a year and a half of making independent choices while she'd lived alone—defiance sparked in her heart, ignited her courage and roared through her soul.

Leave me alone, you evil old man! cried the renegade fire.

It was a cry of mutiny, of insurrection unthinkable while he still breathed.

Who are you—you vicious ghost!—to make me cringe like that little nobody, cowering beneath your thrashing arm?

Yes, spoke the rational side of Lindy's brain—freed by her long humbled spirit's rebellion—there's no need to punish yourself.

Dad's dead.

You were there at the hospital. You saw him die. You went to his funeral with Greg.

Dad's dead, and you're still alive and, if you don't allow it, he can't make you shrink any more.

Picking up her cup of tea with a consciously steadied hand, Lindy took a defiant gulp and set it down again.

I am neither a moron nor a defenceless child, she told herself firmly.

And I am certainly not a nobody.

I am a bright and independent woman of means. A woman with a hard-earned bonus of twenty-six thousand dollars to spend.

And I deserve to spend my windfall on anything that I want.

And what I want—what I know I want—what you can't take from me now, Dad!—is a Fimbria show of my own!

"Yes!" shouted Lindy, leaping up, spilling her tea and startling her cat. "Yes, that is what I want! And, Dad, you're not here to tell me that I'm too dumb or too boring or too ugly or too—I don't know what else you would have said

I was too much of, but I do know that you're not here to bully or shame me out of it! So I am going to write and I am going to direct and I am going to put on a Fimbria show—and you can't stop me now!"

At which point Lindy noticed that Phyllis had skittered through her puddle of milky tea, so she forced herself to calm down and clean up, and then hied herself to her laptop to send Madelyn an e-mail.

'I've come into a little pot of money, so I'm going to put on a Fimbria show. Want to join me? Come have tea at my house tomorrow afternoon. Lindy.'

Then, just as she was about to hit 'send,' she reconsidered and, pushing her hair behind her ears, sent it to Malcolm too.

"And the great thing about putting on my own show—" she explained to her patient cat as she brewed herself a fresh cup of tea, "—is that I get to say whether there are any dogs in it."

CHAPTER TWO

The Birds

She did the intelligent thing and hid.

But the doorbell kept ringing and, figuring that it was probably just Madelyn arriving inexcusably—but predictably—late, eventually she answered it.

"For gawd's sake, Lindy!" laughed Maddie, as she pushed her way into the front vestibule, hung up her cruelty-free tote and proceeded to unwrap. "You know I never bring Helmutt with me. Although he wouldn't hurt you if I did...he's very friendly...all Alsatians are...it's one of the primary characteristics of the breed."

Yes, thought Lindy, winding her friend's lively cotton scarves over the hooks on the antique mirror frame, Helmutt, a true doggington bark, seems very friendly—when he isn't making that low grumbling noise in his throat at me.

Undraped from her cloak, The Empress Madelyn, a stately white brunette who had always carried herself taller than her height and now appeared younger than her sixty-two years, sailed into the living room and alit with a jangle of silver bracelets on the sofa next to Phyllis.

Being a feline, and sensing that Madelyn loved every single animal on the planet with a pure and enduring passion, Phyllis regarded the interloper with disgust. She hopped down to the rug and, flicking her tail, sauntered upstairs.

"Farewell, Your Majesty," smiled Maddie, taking no offense. "She smells Hellmutt on me."

"Maybe," granted Lindy, "but she pretty much treats everybody that way."

Scooting out to the kitchen to retrieve the snacks she'd made, Lindy hesitated in front of the kettle. "Are you doing tea right now, or—?"

"Coffee, hon," called Maddie. "The richer, the darker, the better. But whatever you've got is probably fine."

Furtively, Lindy reached for the jar of medium roast instant coffee she'd hidden in a kitchen cupboard and dropped a generous amount of the crystals into a small glass pot. While Madelyn nattered on about the antioxidants in coffee being far superior to anything you could get from tea, her hostess plopped a plate of crustless cucumber sandwiches and a platter of water crackers and cashew nut cheese on to the low table in front of her. Then, as her friend made princess noises about how "you shouldn't have gone to so much bother, hon," Lindy hustled back into the kitchen to fill her tea pot and 'brew' the coffee.

At last everything was ready. Madelyn nibbled the delicate sandwiches and sampled the cheese that Lindy had bought at the small Bank Street grocer with a serious vegan air and went into raptures over the coffee's strength and flavour—until Lindy could no longer stand it.

"So—" she ventured, "what did you think of my little project?"

"Glorious," pronounced Madelyn through a mouthful of cucumber.

Lindy wasn't sure if her friend meant her Fimbria show or the sandwiches, so she tried again. "So—do you think you'd like to help out?"

"Of course, hon!" cried Madelyn, her mouth now clear after a delicate sip of coffee. "I wouldn't dream of being left out."

"Oh good," sighed Lindy. "I was really hoping you'd say that."

"Now, first of all," Madelyn settled back on the sofa with what she probably thought of as her business face, "how much was in that little pot of money? Because, you know, if—"

The doorbell rang.

Madelyn regarded her hostess suspiciously. "Were you expecting someone else?"

"Um," muttered Lindy, casting a guilty eye at the door.

Again the doorbell rang.

Lindy arose and fled to the front vestibule, opening her door to Malcolm who was just about to mash the button one more time.

"Ah, Lindy—" he said with a breaking smile on his weathered but still handsome white Celtic-Canadian face.

"Oh, um, Malcolm. Hi! Come on in."

Lindy slid nervously around her tall, greying ex-husband's lean and fit jogger's body and shut the door behind him and then, reaching for a carefree nonchalant tone, added, "Maddie's here—"

Malcolm's face soured. Wordlessly, he hung up his backpack and outdoor gear and followed Lindy into the living room. There, Madelyn, neglected phone in hand, appeared to be in a profound study of the faded university graduation portraits of Greg and Lindy that hung disconsolately on the opposite wall.

"Madelyn," Malcolm greeted her drily. "Long time, no see."

"Oh, hello Malcolm," replied Madelyn graciously, as if she hadn't noticed his arrival until just now. "Nice to see you again too."

With a slight grimace, Malcolm nodded and lowered himself into the straight back armchair.

"How's Elke?" enquired Madelyn, ever so sweetly.

Malcolm shot her a look of disbelief. "Fine, I guess."

"Oh, hon," returned Madelyn, feigning concern, "don't you know? We all supposed that the lovely Elke would soon be Mrs. Malcolm the Fourth—"

"'The lovely Elke'—as I'm damn sure you've heard—left for Halifax six weeks ago—"

One might think that Malcolm would have drowned in the bitter dregs of failed relationships by now, thought Lindy. But she knew that he genuinely liked and respected the female sex. He was always emotionally honest with his lovers about his predisposition for infidelity and conscientiously avoided unwanted pregnancies and otherwise did no physical harm. In fact, the major vibe from every woman Malcolm had ever romanced and strayed from over the years seemed to be one of amiable nostalgia for their lost intimacy and a vague regret that he'd moved on so quickly. As far as Lindy knew, even his two other ex-wives, Roz and Melanie, were still on cordial speaking terms with their erstwhile man.

But Malcolm and Madelyn were an entirely different kettle of fish.

Dear God, winced Lindy, they've always been oil and water. Malcolm had set Maddie's teeth on edge from the day they met, and Maddie was one of the few attractive women Malcolm had never even considered hitting on. So—since she was determined to wrangle them both into helping her with her Fimbria show—she'd better get used to a little friction.

"Tea, Malcolm?" she hastily interjected, "Or coffee? Maddie's having coffee."

A craft beer and beef burger kind of guy, Malcolm looked unimpressed with the vegan dainties on the table. "No thanks, Lindy. I had a late lunch."

"Okay." Lindy sat down again. "So...I was just asking Maddie about my Fimbria show, and she said—"

"Yeah," interrupted Malcolm, "about that—"

"Yes, well, okay, it's just that, as I wrote you guys, I came into a little money from—"

"—and you're going to blow it all on what—?" Malcolm made air quotation marks, "—'a Fimbria show?'"

"Well," hedged Lindy, "it's not that much—"

"So, how much?"

Lindy looked from Malcolm to Madelyn, both leaning forward with unguarded curiosity, and she suddenly felt shy to level with them about the entire amount. Maybe she might want to buy diamonds or visit Paris someday... you never know...

"Oh, about six thousand dollars and change," she lied.

"Not as much as I'd—" began Madelyn, but Malcolm snorted and broke in, "Lindy, come on! That's too much money to waste. Go to Europe. Get an IKEA kitchen. Use it for something of real solid value. Don't just let Madelyn fritter it away on one of her artsy-fartsy pipe dreams!"

"Oh, you should talk Mister 'Professor Government Grant!' bridled Madelyn. "How much did you get for that pillow lava thingy up north? Talk about pipe dreams!"

"Yeah? Well, at least I haven't spent my life mooching off my friends and lovers to finance my 'art!'"

"Yes, well, at least I have some friends and lovers who've actually stuck around!"

"That's none of your business!"

"None of Elke's either, I guess!"

"Fuck you, Madelyn!"

Having taken an invigorating sip of tea to prepare herself mentally for a tussle, Lindy scooped her greying bob behind her ears and leapt in. "Sorry, guys!" she exclaimed, perhaps too loudly, but it got her squabbling friends' attention. " Maybe I wasn't clear," she continued more softly. "I didn't ask you here to debate whether I should put on a Fimbria show. I asked you here to find out whether you are going to give me your support when I do."

Taken aback by their mild friend's sudden self-assertion, Madelyn and Malcolm stared blankly at her.

"Either way, it's not Madelyn's show—it's mine, and I'm going to write it and direct it and produce it, too."

"You are?" chorused her friends, united in their shock.

"But, hon," protested Madelyn, "you haven't got a clue about theatre!"

"And, Lindy," frowned Malcolm, "you've haven't written anything since university."

"Actually, I do and I have," Lindy replied evenly. "I was in a high school musical—remember, Maddie? And I read a bunch of plays in university English classes—" she overrode Malcolm's retort, "—and I often wrote summaries for the English officers at Defence when they didn't have time to read library articles for themselves. They were always complimenting me on how clearly I wrote and how I made complex ideas easy for them to understand—"

"Oh, okay," granted Malcolm unwillingly. "But you've still never written a proper script or directed a bunch of freaking actors." Then, aware that Madelyn was opening her mouth to jump to Lindy's defence, he continued vigorously without a pause, "For Christ's sake, Lindy, where's my sensible girl? Buy yourself a new sofa."

To his amazement, Malcolm saw his meek ex-wife's hackles rise.

"Back off, Malcolm Macoun!" Lindy spat. "I haven't been 'your girl' since 1976, and I don't deserve that condescending tone! I'm an intelligent woman of means, and I'll spend my bequest any way that I want!"

"Oh my gawd!" squealed Madelyn, slapping her hands together. "Lindy, stand up and turn around!"

Bewildered, Lindy scrambled up and flung herself about.

"Look, Malcolm," crowed Maddie, "she's grown a backbone!"

"Ha-ha, very fun—aaahh!" cried Malcolm, fending off Phyllis, who, sensing there was a person in the house who wasn't a cat fan, had sprung up on the back of his chair to rub herself against his neck. "Lindy! Can't you control your damn cat?"

After sweeping Phyllis off to the back porch where she kept her extra litter box, Lindy returned to find Madelyn preening herself with self-satisfaction, and Malcolm, clearly abashed.

"Sorry about that 'my girl' thing, Lindy. Patronising and all that..."

"Sure, Malcolm," Lindy sighed and tucked her greying bob behind her ears once more. "It's just that...listen, you guys, I realize that I'm not a veteran theatre person, but I'm pretty certain that I have at least one show in me. And if I don't—well, I'll fail trying. Maybe I'll get in over my head, maybe I'll get flamed in the reviews, maybe I'm just tossing away my bequest," she shrugged. "But that's not the worst thing that can happen to a sixty-two-year-old woman. And that's why I wanted you two on board."

Now for the serious pitch, Lindy thought.

"Maddie," she caught Madelyn's eyes in a frank gaze, "with your contacts in the arts, you can be my creative muse and help me get my show on its feet. And Malcolm," she levelled her gaze his way, "with your critical eye, you can be my conscience. You know, act as my financial guide and help me keep my budget in line." Ignoring Malcolm's skeptical look, she finished up strong. "So, what do you say, guys? I'm going to forge ahead anyways. Are you in or are you out?"

"Definitely in, hon," pledged Madelyn who, Lindy could see, was nearly moved to tears by her old friend's confidence in her artistry.

Malcolm, however, wasn't so ready to commit. "Well... what are you going to write?" he wanted to know.

"The easiest thing is an anthology, hon" quickly suggested Madelyn. "You just think up a topic, and then the actors workshop it and do all the work for you."

"No," smiled Lindy at her earnest friend, "I want to write the script myself. A serious drama, I think. A story about a weak woman who stays married to a hateful man for almost sixty years and uses her children to shield herself against his abuse."

"Ugh, what a downer," groaned Madelyn, "and it's been done to death."

"I have to agree there," grimaced Malcolm.

Striving to project an image of the highly adult woman she aspired to be, Lindy tried not to let her friends notice her disappointment at their quick dismissal of her pet idea. "It's just that..." She gave herself a mental shake. "Oh, okay, what should I write then?"

"Something light, something funny. You know, something sexy," purred Madelyn. "Oh, I know! How about writing about a bisexual pixie who lives in a jazz club because she was born into an ordinary mortal family but doesn't fit in. I can see that appealing to everyone—artists, hipsters, jazz musicians—anyone who's ever been ostracized."

Malcolm rolled his eyes skyward.

"That doesn't sound like something I'd know much about," demurred Lindy, "and they do say that you should start writing from your own personal experience."

"Write about cats, then," shrugged Madelyn.

"Write about dogs," smiled Malcolm.

"Oh, ha-ha-ha," deadpanned Lindy. But, on the other hand, she thought, that might not be such a bad idea—I would certainly have lots to say…

"Of course," continued Madelyn, scooping up the last of the cashew cheese, "you don't have to have anything written yet to apply."

"Really?" asked Malcolm doubtfully. "She doesn't even need a first draft?"

"Nope," agreed Lindy. "The website just says a company name, a producer—that's me—and twenty-five bucks for the application fee. Oh, and you have to also include the registration fee for when you get in. It's, like, six-and-a-half, seven hundred dollars."

"What kind of lame excuse for a theatre festival is this? If you don't have to show them your script, how do they know that you've got a quality show that they'll want to put on?"

"No, at the Fimbria they don't worry about any of that trivia," explained Madelyn, impatiently. "If you win the lottery, you can bring whatever show you're working on."

"Lottery?!" Malcolm was beginning to look really unsettled.

"Um-hm," nodded Madelyn. "They just put all the applications in a hat and draw out enough to fill their venues. There are Fimbria festivals all over the place with basically the same rules, and fantastic artists that spend their whole lives travelling from Fimbria to Fimbria."

"And you can make a living doing that?"

Madelyn let out a tinkly silver laugh. "Not what a stuffy Geography professor might call 'a living,' Malcolm, but, yes, there are plenty of artists who keep themselves afloat that way."

"If you're a hit, you can make a little money," suggested Lindy cautiously.

"Well, really, it's not about the money," said Madelyn archly. "Anyhow," she continued, turning her full attention on Lindy, "have you got a name for us, hon?"

"A name for—? Oh, right, you mean for the group." Lindy looked solemn. "Well, I thought we could be 'The Three Friends Theatre Company."

Malcolm scowled. "That's dumb, Lindy."

Seeing her friend's face fall, Madelyn quickly added, "I think what Malcolm means is that it's not very...original?"

"Exactly," agreed Malcolm. "If I'm going to be associated with this catastrophe, I want it to have a cool name. Like 'The Friends of the Titanic'—go away!"

Malcolm swept the surreptitiously returning silver-grey cat off his lap. Undeterred, Phyllis circled back and began to play with his shoe lace.

"Lindy!" he pleaded, pushing the cat towards her owner.

"Com'ere, silly beastie," wheedled Madelyn, who Phyllis totally ignored.

"She's selectively friendly," chuckled Lindy. "If you really want her to leave you alone, Malcolm, you need to pretend that you like her. Be a friend of Phyllis, and she'll never give you the time of day."

"I'm not that good at acting," grumbled Malcolm, but Madelyn was aglow with inspiration. "I've got it!" she exclaimed. "Be a friend of Phyllis? Okay! We'll be 'The Friends of Phyllis Theatre Company!'"

"That's—" began Malcolm tartly, but then he saw Lindy's dawning smile and pivoted one-eighty, "—that's a great idea, Maddie."

"Yes, I know," granted The Empress. "But I'm not 'Maddie' to you, Malcolm—I'm 'Madelyn'. Only Lindy gets to call me 'Maddie', and that's only because we've been best friends since first grade. *Capisce?*"

Bowing in mock defeat, Malcolm now asked to see the Fimbria website. So Lindy pulled out her laptop and, with steady in-put from her newly minted theatre Company, she filled out the on-line application.

"In for a penny, in for a pound," she quoted her mother as she submitted the fees on PayPal and heeded Maddie's encouragement to hit 'send.'

Rocked with disbelief at the uncharted world she had just entered, Lindy unsealed Dad's last bottle of imported whiskey, and the three retirees indulged in a celebratory toast to The Friends of Phyllis Theatre Company. Lindy sipped cautiously, her throat afire, while the other two downed the golden liquid with practiced abandon. Then, gathering their belongings, Madelyn and Malcolm left to do what Maddie and Malcolm did with their lives whenever Lindy wasn't around.

Lindy tidied up the living room and fed Phyllis half a tin of her gourmet cat food. Then, deciding that, instead of slapping together a peanut butter sandwich, she should prolong the festivities, she pampered herself by preparing a hot meal. She put a scrubbed potato in the microwave, dumped a pot of undiluted can of cream of cheddar soup in a pot and put it on a burner to warm. About five minutes later, when the potato was cooked, she put it in a bowl, split it open and poured the soup over it. To fancy things up, she sprinkled the soup with some pre-grated parmesan cheese and little dried parsley.

Then she carried the bowl and a glass of apple juice into the dining room where she sat down to feast in the same wooden chair at the same place at her grandparent's heavy wooden table where she'd always eaten her meals.

Soon finished her solitary supper, Lindy plunked the dishes in the dishwasher with the rest of this week's dirty plates and cups and went into the living room to sit on the sofa with Phyllis. She was about to flick on the television to catch the end of the six o'clock news when she noticed her laptop on the coffee table and stopped to think.

For a couple of hours, she sat and thought.

She thought about the plots in the Shakespeare and the Shaw plays that she'd studied in university...

About the characters in the plays that she'd read in high school...

About the Greek myths and fairy tales and ghost stories that she'd absorbed as a child...

About her own family's history and lore...

She thought about her Grandma Styre's oft-repeated tale about her feckless second cousin whose occult experiences in the spiritualist haven of Lily Dale had proven to the family that "poor Gertrude had a screw loose somewhere..."

Then she thought about her own mental challenges...

Picking up her laptop, Lindy carried it to the spot at her folk's dining room table where she'd always sat to eat and began to write.

CHAPTER THREE

Much Ado About Nothing

"Nobody ever wins these things."

Flatly cynical, the disembodied comment drifted through the Crazy Quilt Coffee Shop and Bar, sparking laughter, denials or—in Lindy's case—alarm.

"I told you we were in for a let-down," grouched Malcolm, suspiciously eyeing the pint of apricot ale Lindy had bought for him.

The cafe, dimly lit by stained glass fixtures, was jam-packed. Antique tufted sofas and velveteen armchairs overflowed with early arrivals, and every vintage wooden table was crowded with Fimbria hopefuls who perched on mismatched painted wooden chairs, chatting or consulting their smartphones.

At the rustic bar, customers jostled politely to buy caffeine, cider or beer. Tables of patrons shared jugs of draught and heaps of chili wings or deep fried mushrooms, while singles indulged in servings of vegan poutine or raspberry cheesecake.

Where built-in bookcases ended, exposed brick and carnelian walls were thickly overhung with artisanal quilts and local art for sale. Heavy curtains were pulled back to reveal a plainer overflow room where varnished trestle tables and communal benches also thronged with people.

Lindy had expected to feel like a complete interloper.

She had spent the last month dreading that she and her sixty-ish friends—well, maybe not Madelyn (predictably late) who never looked out of place in any artsy crowd, but certainly she and Malcolm—would stick out among the young artistes like spectres at the feast. But, from what she could see from their front room table, shared with a charming French college girl and her anxious Papa, the Fimbria lottery crowd was pretty miscellaneous.

Across from them sat a tableful of the expected hipsters, but seated next to the trendies were what looked like a suburban soccer Mom and her perfect-lawn-freak husband. And, close beside the table where Fimbria staff had placed the lottery drum, a pair of greying males perched on a window loveseat. They seemed to be card-carrying members of Lindy's own early retired set—an impression which was confirmed when Madelyn finally cruised in and paused to greet them with air kisses and effusive cries.

"Pierre! Darrick! And little Leo—hello, lovey..."

With a cold start, Lindy realized that Maddie was fawning over a tiny dog. The bulbous-eyed chihuahua, a teensy doggington arf, was wearing a green canvas vest and shook with fright as his owner lifted him up for the strange woman to pet.

Lindy shivered in turn and tried not to notice.

Eventually, bestowing royal waves upon other dear friends and acquaintances in the room, Madelyn swanned over to Lindy and Malcolm. Inevitably, she caused a flutter of concern as she canvassed the nearby tables for an unoccupied chair. Chairs were scarce, but, once he'd abandoned his phone screen long enough to notice what was happening around him, one of the bearded hipsters gallantly offered his seat to Maddie and went to lean fetchingly against the bar.

Just as Madelyn nestled into the violet ladderback, the cafe shushed and, standing by the lottery drum with a staff member ready to record the picks, Suzanne the Fimbria Festival Director began her spiel.

After a few words of welcome, she outlined the rules behind the draw.

"We've got a hundred and seventy-seven applicants," Suzanne revealed, "but only sixty-four company spaces are up for grabs. Twenty per cent have been filled by international companies, and another thirty per cent have already gone to Canadians from somewhere else—sorry guys—but thirty-two spots are reserved for you locals. Out of those, we've got two spots each for youth companies and specially mentored artists. Okay? Now, all of your applications have been entered into our lovely lottery drum, and—as you all know—Festival participation is determined simply by the luck of the draw. When the slots in each category are filled, that's our play bill—and then everyone else will end up, in order of selection, on three separate wait lists. Good enough? Okay, let's roll!"

Stepping up, the staff member spun the drum. The Fimbria Festival Director stopped the spin, opened the hatch and drew the first company.

"And our first winner is...The Precious Pumpkin Pokers—!"

The hipsters' table exploded in cheers, and the lottery was officially on.

Lindy tried to watch and listen carefully as one after another company name was added to the Festival listings. But with an unleashed dog hovering at the edge of her field of vision, she found it impossible to concentrate.

Was the little peril aware of her too?

As the chihuahua seemed to struggle against his owner's loose grip, Lindy tensed...and then battled to relax when he settled back down onto his owner's lap.

Why did some people just assume that their dogs were welcome everywhere? she fretted. Why did they just smuggle them in? Weren't cafes and restaurants supposed to be off-limits to dogs?

Dear God, wasn't anywhere safe at all?

"...Strangled Voices in the Night...Barney and the Bastards Theatre Co-op...Actually Moving On Productions...Cordelia's Uncle's Players..."

Maddie generously applauded the success of well-chuffed Darrick and Pierre who'd leapt up to honour Suzanne with courtly bows.

Depending on whether representatives of the local companies were absent or present in the rooms, rumbling murmurs or whoops of joy greeted the Director's picks. But as the lottery went on—and it was becoming increasingly apparent that the chances of being drawn were getting pretty scarce—the atmosphere of anticipation which had electrified the cafe was becoming diluted by the growing anxiety wafting from the tables of still unselected artists.

"So, finally," read Festival Director Suzanne, "our last lucky duckies—Les Gars de Lochmine—"

With glad cries of relief, the French college student and her Papa had bounced into each others' arms.

"—and that's all, folks! Next, for you guys on our wait lists..." the Director spun and dipped into the drum again, "...and it's...Yellow/Amarillo/Jaune...Tell It To Trudy Tinder Productions...The Friends of Phyllis Theatre Company... Not Another Soap Opera..."

While the wait-list selections continued, much quicker than the previous draws, neighbouring artists buzzed in conversation or on the ubiquitous phones, firming up contacts and making plans. A few Fimbria hopefuls already stood, energized or disappointed, pulling on coats and hats against the early December sleet, to leave the cafe.

As the French college student and her Papa eagerly plied their phones to give Maman and various *amis* the wonderful news, Lindy, Malcolm and Madelyn sat stunned. Their Company name had come up—but not in time.

So they weren't in the Fimbria Festival.

It was unfathomable...

Not that they'd taken for granted that they would be among the chosen, they assured each other in low voices, but, then again, despite Malcolm's outspoken pessimism, even he hadn't really supposed that they'd number among the also-rans.

"Of course, we're somewhere near the top of the wait-list," said Madelyn, rallying her optimism so that she'd sound like a pragmatic member of the theatre community, "and I've heard that, for all kinds of reasons—we're talking about artistic temperaments, of course—literally tons of companies drop out before the Festival. Plus, if we don't get a spot that way, we can always apply as a

Bring-Your-Own-Venue. I think the website starts up in sometime in January. Lindy, didn't you check that out last week, hon?"

Lindy had pulled up the relevant pages on the previous Tuesday, but just out of idle curiosity. At the time, she'd felt absolutely sure that The Friends of Phyllis were bound to be chosen in the lottery. It had simply seemed...inevitable.

But she'd been wrong.

And she'd worked damned hard! Lindy complained in her head to the unfeeling Fimbria gods. Since the evening of their first Company meeting, she'd pushed her imagination into perilous territory and then forcibly tamed the higgledy-piggledy results into a presentable script. The one-act play—named in a flash of inspiration by the bakery showcase at the grocery store—was called *Small Comforts*.

Now she looked closely at her friends. "So you'd still be interested in marching ahead with me even if we haven't got a real venue? Even if it's got to be a BYOV?"

"Absolutely, hon!" nodded Madelyn eagerly, and Malcolm grimaced his agreement as he downed the last of his warmed beer.

So that was all good, at least...

Lindy wasn't a fast writer, and she'd had to spend a tedious afternoon comparing playscripts at the neighbourhood public library to get her format right. But, as the leafy month of October had chilled into a dark November, her word count had mounted, and now, in the first week of what promised to be a bleak December, she was honing in on her second draft.

Set in the pre-home-computer, pre-cellphone nineteen-seventies, *Small Comforts* was a story about a candy store owner, Mary Yerst, who consults a pair of unscrupulous psychics in hopes that they can cure her of her morbid fear of dogs.

Which—despite what Dad and Greg would probably say—was okay, because Malcolm had suggested that Lindy write about dogs. And besides—other than Mary's neurosis—her story was quite different from Lindy's.

Orphaned early in life—like most of the characters in Lindy's favourite children's books—and a true loner with few acquaintances and no close friends, Mary had pulled herself up the economic ladder on her own merits. Now, at thirty-two years old, she was a successful—if isolated—entrepreneur with a well patronized Bank Street confectionery.

But, according to Lindy, Mary's severe anxiety had made the further expansion of her business into a better location in the ByWard Market very difficult. And, despairing of ever getting the assistance she needed from the medical establishment, the candy store owner had taken her employee's advice to seek out help from the shadowy Peevers.

As she wrote—in a nod to Grandma Styre's gullible second cousin, Gertrude—Lindy had made the characters of spiritual medium Margaret Peever and her occultist husband Bradley Peever more and more plausible to Mary, but—based on Grandma's outspoken disapproval—less and less sympathetic to the audience. And she was making it very clear that the couple's shameless 'shock therapy' and all of its clairvoyant claptrap had done Mary's psyche no good—all the while greatly swelling the Peevers' bank account and vastly depleting hers.

Then, finally, in a searing denouement—which Lindy had fought to write as honestly as possible—she'd shown Mary rejecting the Peevers and their deceitful treatments but, tragically, remaining a hostage to her own disabling fears.

In the earliest version, Lindy had jealously hoarded every word she wrote, but over time she'd sadly come to realize that what she often thought of as her best ideas and choicest lines sometimes had to be culled. She'd even brutally cut out an entire character—the well-meaning employee who'd tipped Mary about the Peevers—when, no matter how she tried, his personality just wouldn't fit into a faithful portrayal of her heroine's developmental arc. She'd felt like an axe murderer when she'd finished tracking down his dialogue and hit that final delete, but, for the benefit of the whole work, he'd had to go.

Unfortunately, when Lindy offered snippets of her work to her fellow Friends of Phyllis to read, neither Maddie nor Malcolm had liked her plot or theme very much, and none of scenes she'd come up with so far had met with their complete approval.

"It's too pedestrian," Madelyn had criticized. "You need to add more whimsy..."

"It's too weird," Malcolm had disagreed. "You need to be more grounded..."

But they'd both seemed extremely pleased—or, in Maddie's case, astounded—to discover that Lindy's script displayed an unsuspected talent for dependable characterization and authentic dialogue. Both had independently confided to her that they now believed that she was capable of writing a viable show, so that—somewhat insulated by their tempered praise—she was doing an adequate job of keeping the nasty voice at bay.

Therefore, despite tonight's setback, Lindy was still determined to put on *Small Comforts* at the Fimbria next June in a Bring-Your-Own-Venue, and she was profoundly grateful for her friends' loyal support.

Which was what Lindy was about to tell them, when she suddenly felt a shudder of apprehension and, turning her head, came nose to snout with Leo, the green-garbed chihuahua.

Suffice to say, neither she nor the dog responded well.

Afterwards Malcolm observed that he had never witnessed a woman and a dog so mutually terrified. Chairs were knocked over, beer glasses went flying, and the entire cafe, including the lottery draw, was brought to an instant standstill by the unearthly sound of an unholy shrieking yelp. Or yelping shriek. It was impossible to discern which sound had its source in which panic-stricken throat.

Leo was swiftly removed to be consoled by his indignant owner. Malcolm helped Lindy lurch up from the floor onto her rubbery legs, and Madelyn, the soul of solicitude, half led and half carried her through the glare of the curious to the ungendered washroom so that Lindy could lean weakly against the sink and splash cold water on her livid cheeks.

"You know, hon," gently chided Maddie when Lindy came up for air, "Leo is really a very friendly little guy. He's Darrick's emotional support dog and comes with Darrick every single place he goes."

Lindy gazed blearily at her friend and tried to frame a reply. Finding no words, she slumped against the wall and quietly sobbed while Maddie made sympathetic noises and dabbed ineffectually at Lindy's face with a scented handkerchief that she'd fished out of her bodice.

At last repeated loud knocking on the washroom door forced Lindy to gather what dignity she could muster in order to skulk through the rapidly thinning Fimbria crowd. With Madelyn following like a muzzy sheep dog, they made their way to Malcolm, waiting with their coats and purses by the cafe's outer door.

"Another group wanted the table," he explained briefly, as the two women donned their outerwear and shouldered their bags. "And Darrick got over his snit and came back to apologize for startling you. But, really Lindy," he added as they trudged en masse through the needling sleet to his ancient Volvo, "you've got to get a grip on yourself."

Completely drained, Lindy merely nodded and muttered something noncommittal.

It had been a rough night all around, and she wondered how she was going to find the strength in her lonely bedroom to fend off the hateful nasty voice when all the lights were out.

CHAPTER FOUR

The Comedy of Errors

After a long pause, Madelyn ordered a latte.

The milk for the latte had to be soy based, of course, and the coffee beans sustainably sourced. And no sugar, no artificial flavour shots, no nonsense.

Grateful for any decision, the server nodded, smiling, and walked away.

In Lindy's opinion, waiting for Maddie to order anything at a restaurant or cafe was truly annoying. She brought such gravity to every decision about food, no matter how mundane. As if, on a per-second universal scale, it actually mattered what morsel or sip passed her lips.

Except that it was all a load of baloney, thought Lindy. The latte was just a hot drink, one of thousands Madelyn would consume in her lifetime. She'd drink it today and completely forget it tomorrow. Why make such a big deal?

Of course, Lindy had never seen the point of getting stretched out of shape about food. Dad had preferred plain Anglo-Canadian 'meat, potato, and two veg' and Lindy had grown up purchasing, cooking and eating whatever was on sale at the grocery store. But Maddie, the middle child of a world-weary immigrant Czech divorcee, had always been so very particular, 'mindful' she said, about what she ate and drank. And Lindy cared enough about her childhood friend to cater to her eccentricities at home and never call her on her foodie tendencies in public.

Besides, there were much more important things to discuss.

Auditions. Rehearsal scheduling. Sound and music tech. Sets, props, costumes.

Budgeting.

At least their roles were well defined. Lindy was the Scriptwriter, the Producer, and the Director. Madelyn, the Designer, the Assistant Producer and the Assistant Director. And Malcolm, who'd phoned to say that he was stuck in traffic but would soon join them, final script consultant, budget coach and Stage Manager.

As it was now written, *Small Comforts* required three actors, one female protagonist and a pair of villains. In her mind's eye, Lindy saw the antagonists as a married couple, but there wasn't any reason, she supposed, to limit them to the male-female paradigm. Weren't actresses or, rather, women actors—as, she suspected, would be closer to the correct terminology nowadays—easier to hire than male actors? Weren't they thicker on the ground? And lesbian marriages were old hat in Canada these days. It might be a good way to ensure that filling roles wasn't a problem. Maybe she should put her script through a third revision and make all the roles clearly female?

This is why I need Madelyn, thought Lindy soberly. Maddie will know these insider theatrical things and give me good advice.

"Hello, ladies." Malcolm had approached while she was busy thinking and was shedding his winter jacket and hat. "It's still snowing out there. What a lousy December it's shaping up to be. Does this place do table service?"

His question was answered by the reappearance of the server with Lindy's English breakfast tea and Madelyn's latte. Despite Lindy's reluctance, they'd come back to the Crazy Quilt—the scene of her latest shameful melt down—for their Company meeting because Madelyn had assured her that they made the best vegan desserts in town. However, Lindy suspected Maddie actually had some sneaky psycho-babble reason for insisting that she brave the place again.

My friends are always trying to improve me, Lindy groused to herself.

Whatever.

Doctors, therapists, co-workers—they'd all had a thwack at Lindy too.

Nothing much had helped, although 'calm pills' had seemed like a feasible option at one time. Dad had been disgusted when he found out, though—there'd be no dope fiends in his family!—and she'd never even finished her trial prescription. As far as he and Greg had been concerned, all Lindy lacked was self-discipline. And Dad hadn't understood how a man of his superb constraint could have sired such a wimpy daughter—Crack!

Lindy decided she'd indulge in a chocolate brownie, and Madelyn, a gluten-free vegan bread pudding—no sauce.

Malcolm crisply ordered the smoked duck pasta special and a local draught, and the server hustled off.

"Duck—!" Madelyn blurted out, shocked into brevity.

"Yeah, I got a taste for it when I was honeymooning in San Francisco with Melanie. I had to rope her into going for dinner in Chinatown a lot." Pulling his packsack onto his lap, Malcolm shrugged. "It was either that or eat at some damn fish place every night. Anyhow," he continued, coming up with a paper from the depths of a side pocket, "I brought the form to book the studio for our auditions. The Theatre Department secretary didn't turn a hair when I asked. I guess it's a pretty standard request." He handed Lindy the form. "Also, Milda suggested that, as a retired Geography Professor in good standing, I should be able to get a substantial discount. She said she'd talk to her Department Head about that."

Lindy scanned the paper. As a former library clerk, she'd seen her share of these documents and knew the tricks to fill them out so that they'd pass muster with the powers-that-be—namely, the secretaries, clerks and custodians who actually run the world.

"Good. And how about the venue? Did she have any leads there?"

"Milda mentioned that some of the local churches will rent you space. Also bars or galleries or coffee places. She said I should also chat with the Geography guys about finding a classroom that might work—but I didn't think that sounded very...well, you know..."

"Practical?" suggested Lindy.

"Dramatic," corrected Madelyn decisively.

"Yeah, and it would be hard to put up lights and curtains and stuff," continued Malcolm, "so I thought I wouldn't do that."

The server dropped off their food, and the trio tucked into it silently for a moment. Then Lindy, stirring more milk into her tea, said noncommittally, "I imagine all this renting costs quite a bit of money, so I could up the budget a bit if we had to..."

"Oh, that would be—" began Madelyn in a gush, but Malcolm overrode her through a chewy mouthful of duck, "—No!—," he swallowed, cleared his throat and continued, "You're already putting too much money into this crap fair, Lindy. If I'm supposed to be your 'conscience,' then your conscience is telling you to stick to the budget we talked about in the first place. Six thousand bucks is more than enough. In fact, I think that we should drop it to maybe five thousand and leave a thousand for emergencies. Okay?"

"Okay," nodded Lindy, feeling rather relieved, while Madelyn took a dainty forkful of her dry bread pudding and pouted, "Our mutual artistic endeavours are not a 'crap fair,' Malcolm. One never has to be rude to make one's point."

"Yeah, well, one is here to make sure that you two don't toss money around like a couple of drunken princesses, and one is damn well going to do one's job!"

"Drunken princesses!" Madelyn set down her latte with a clunk. "How dare—"

"And we're very grateful to you," hastily interjected Lindy, worried that her friends' bickering would sideline their meeting. "Aren't we, Maddie? You and I are far too immersed in the creative process to be concerned about dull, boring budgeting, and we know Malcolm has tons of other important stuff he could be doing."

Malcolm looked mollified, and Maddie unruffled, so Lindy adopted a business-like tone. "Now—auditioning spaces. Right. According to the form, we can have the studio only on off-hours when the building is still open, so that restricts our potential auditioning hours, and we need to submit our request at least a full month before we intend to use the space. Which takes us to January—" she consulted the calendar from her purse, "—okay, around January tenth or thereabouts, and when would be best? We probably can't get the studio on a regular week night—they'll want it themselves for classes—so should we try the weekend? Or do actors all have shows on Fridays and Saturdays?"

This was, presumably, Madelyn area of expertise, so Lindy and Malcolm looked expectantly at her.

But Maddie had found something interesting on her phone while Lindy was "droning on" and had to be brought up to date before she could put her five cents into the conversation that, yes, most actors would have jobs on the weekend, hon, but any who were 'reading scripts' would, naturally, be available. When Malcolm testily demanded what she meant by that, Lindy jumped in to say that she supposed any actor interested in getting a role would be motivated to move their job schedule around to get to an audition.

Which wasn't a big help, but poured balm on the easily roiled waters of Maddie's and Malcolm's relationship.

"Okay," said, Lindy, consulting her calendar in a business-like manner again, "how about we try a Friday night? So—" writing in the information, "—Friday the sixteenth of January...Auditions...no, Possible Auditions. You guys need to make a note of that too. Now—" she put her calendar down and reached for a brief case that sat under the table at her feet, "—our budget."

Lindy removed a handful of papers from the case and handed out copies to her friends.

"I made a preliminary overview of foreseeable expenses. But, if we're adjusting the budget so we have some money in reserve, you'll have to mentally lower all of the projections."

Madelyn and Malcolm pushed away their empty plates and gave the numbers their full attention.

"Lindy, hon," objected Madelyn, "I really don't think this is going to be enough to make a splash. Don't you want our audiences to be just phenomenally blown away by our show?"

"Would you rather Lindy's retirement funds got blown away?" asked Malcolm, sharply. "Like I said, she's risking more than enough already."

"Is that why Elke left you? Because you were so cheap?"

"Elke left me because her new lover's cock was bigger than mine—"

Lindy was already tired of refereeing.

"Shut up, the both of you!" she snapped, pushing her hair behind her ears with savage flip. "We're not in high school! So, if it's too much to ask that you be civil to one another for five minutes in a row, you can both be damned, and I'll do the show on my own!"

Startled by another sharp outburst from their normally tepid friend, Madelyn and Malcolm halted mid-mudsling and glanced uncomfortably at Lindy who, still riled by their bad behaviour, glared back. Then—muttering muted apologies—both returned to discussing the budget.

"The hard amounts, you know, lottery fee, registration fee, seem correct, which leaves us with $4,315.00 left to spend," calculated Malcolm. "But I see you've designated two-thousand-five-hundred bucks for salaries, honorariums, or stipends which would pretty quickly bring it down to less than half. Where'd you get those figures?"

Composed once more, Lindy shrugged. "I multiplied two hundred fifty by ten. There's you, me, and Maddie. Three actors. Someone to do the costumes. Someone to do the set and props. And a sound person. Oh, and a music person. See what I mean? Ten."

"But you don't pay the people who work with you on a Fimbria show," laughed Madelyn. "They just do it for love," she waved grandly, "and then they get a little share from whatever you take in at the door."

"No," said Lindy, frowning, "that can't be right. Talented people aren't just going to hop on our wagon for free."

"Yeah," agreed Malcolm, making notes on his paper, "that does sound a bit sketchy. But see here, ladies, do we really have to have salaries for ourselves? None of us need them." The women nodded consent. "And couldn't we look for people who could do, say, both costumes and sets and props, or both sound and music? That would easily bring our total pay-outs down to five and halve our expenses. And then we've got more than three thousand left to spend on the other categories."

"You don't need to budget anything for talent," murmured Madelyn, rolling her eyes to the ceiling, "but don't listen to me..."

Ignoring her, Malcolm plunged on. "Audition and rehearsal space. Well, I'll see what I can work out with Milda at the Theatre Department. But let's say you're correct, Lindy, and it's going to cost another cool thousand. Which allows us two-thousand-sixty-five to cover our Bring-Your-Own-Venue, sets and props, costumes and make-up, sound equipment and music fees, and posters and programs."

"The Fimbria puts out a program, so we don't have to," chimed in Madelyn, flatly bored with her own extensive knowledge of the Fest.

"Oh good," nodded Malcolm. "So there's an expense we can cut." He struck the line off with relish. "Anything else?"

"And there's all the money you make from tickets when audiences come see your show."

"Right. So how much will that be?"

"It's there on the bottom of the page," offered Lindy. "See? Twelve bucks per ticket with six shows—and maybe twenty paying customers per show—equals fourteen hundred and forty. If we get forty per show, we make twice that amount."

"But, at that rate, to cover the entire five thousand bucks, we'd need to sell—" Malcolm scribbled, as Madelyn commented in a superior tone, "It's called 'making our nut'..."

"—my god, almost seventy tickets per show!"

"There are also discount admissions from the five and ten show ticket packs," added Madelyn helpfully, "and Fimbria artists and volunteers get in free."

"Lindy," Malcolm leveled a serious look at his ex-wife as she tried to look blasé, "this whole disaster is impossible.

Don't be crazy. You're going to lose your shirt. And for what—?"

"For the joy of theatre!" exclaimed Madelyn airily.

Lindy favoured her arty friend with a fond smile and turned to her pragmatic one.

"That's right, Malcolm. For the plain, crazy, idiotic joy of putting on a Fimbria show. Not everything in life is measured in dollars, you know—"

"Your bank account is."

"—and this is simply what I want to do. So, like I asked in the beginning, are you in or are you out?"

Malcolm took a big lungful of air and let loose a long sigh. "In, I guess, but, Lindy—"

Madelyn smiled haughtily. "Oh, Malcolm. It's the Fimbria. We can't go wrong. I'm having another latte. Anyone else?"

* * * * *

"I suppose that's why they call it a deadline." Madelyn was clearly shaken.

Wordlessly, Lindy topped up her friend's whiskey glass.

"Pierre wasn't very old." Maddie took a wobbly sip. "Only just sixty-three. Like you, Lindy. And, although I hadn't known him for long, he'd become one of my dearest friends."

"When did you two meet?" Expecting to be sitting for quite a while to hear out Madelyn's tale of bereavement, Lindy adjusted the pillow behind her back.

"Last June. At the Fimbria. He and Darrick Kinnow had a show in the Arts Court. He was a marvelous artist."

She took a more solid swig. "Talented. Generous with his vision."

"Did we see their show?" asked Lindy, now more curious about the late lamented Pierre.

"Why, yes. Of course." Madelyn dabbed tears from her eyes with an embroidered linen hankie. "The play about a family arguing over who their grandmother should put in her will? You remember…"

Lindy did. It had been a truly clumsy play—histrionic and overlong for its tenuous plot—but she'd enjoyed it anyway. Especially the actor who'd played the ninety-year-old mother. Until the final bow, when he removed his curly white wig, it had never occurred to her that the role had been filled by a young man.

"…it was such a hit…"

Lindy clearly remembered sitting in an audience of about nine patrons, including herself, Maddie and a young woman who got up and left a third of the way through.

Madelyn must have noticed the skeptical look on her friend's face, because she hurriedly amended her assessment to "…a hit for those who appreciate Orwellian dystopias, that is. Darrick wrote it, you know, and his writing has always been flavoured by his unfortunate experiences among the money-grubbing Toronto elite. If you didn't know that, you wouldn't have appreciated the nuances of his script. He grew up in a mansion in Rosedale, of course, and that's why he needs Leo for emotional support."

Lindy, who also clearly remembered Leo, snapped her mental elastic band—Crack!—and abruptly changed the subject. "Are you going to the funeral?"

"Oh, no, hon. I never go to funerals," replied Maddie, her answer coloured with gentle reproach. "I'm far too sensitive for that. The families are always so affected by the depths of my sorrow, that I'm unable to provide them any solace at all."

So that was why Maddie hadn't been around much when Mom and Dad passed away, thought Lindy. So that I wouldn't be 'affected by the depths of her sorrow.'

Right.

How caring...

Noticing something amiss on Lindy's face, it was Madelyn's turn to abruptly change the subject. "Speaking of your folks—"

Were we? wondered Lindy, but Maddie was looking critically at her tatty artificial Christmas tree decorated with the hard plastic baubles that Phyllis couldn't break.

"I know that last Yule you were still too busy with wills and lawyers and all that to pay much attention to your decor, so I didn't say anything, hon," said Madelyn. "But it's been a while since your Dad died, and you did decide to rebuff Greg and Nan's offer to host you over the holidays. Now, please don't mistake me, I relished attending 'The Nutcracker' and wassailing at that quaint resto-pub afterwards with you—it was a genuinely festive salute to the season. But—for gawd's sake, Lindy!—couldn't you have put in the effort to buy a real fir this year? They sold stacks of them over at the Tennis Club, and they'd even deliver and set them up too. You wouldn't have had to purchase a big one—a table top tree would have been charming—but then the air would be perfumed with the scent of pine, and one would really feel that authentic 'Winter Solstice Spirit' throughout your home." With a smile of encouragement Madelyn paused to finish her whiskey.

"I'm allergic to real trees."

Lindy wasn't. It was her mother, or, at least, Mom had always maintained that she had an allergy. In all probability, it was so that she'd have an excuse not to have to listen to Dad whining about wrenching his shoulder when he brought the tree into the house or ranting about the mess its needles made on the carpets. Dad had always called the real blue spruces that Nan decorated with her delicate glass ornaments a 'fire hazard' and—as long as Lindy could recall—the tree that had sprung up in the corner of her living room from Christmas Eve to New Years Day had always been this same artificial one.

"Oh, I'm so sorry," and Madelyn did look authentically sympathetic, "I didn't know."

Uncomfortable with her memories of Mom and particularly Dad—who would have been furious that the Christmas tree was still cluttering up his living room in the second week of January—Lindy snapped her mental elastic once more—Crack!—and turned the conversation again.

"How long had Pierre and Darrick been together?"

"About two years, I think."

"So they weren't married, or whatever, very long."

Madelyn responded with her tinkly silver laugh. "Oh, Lindy, you try. You do try. But you've really never moved into this century. Married, yes. But not to each other, hon. They were partners in a theatre company. Pierre had a lovely accomplished wife who directs one of the big church choirs downtown. And Darrick was married to a woman for a while in his youth, but now he's just as apt to date men. He flits from flower to flower—like Malcolm, really, but bi. Can't keep his pants zipped. Incidentally, did Malcolm tell you that he's been dating Milda, the Theatre Department secretary?"

"Really?" Now, this was interesting news. "Was he able to get us a good deal on the rental charge for the studio?"

"I didn't ask him about that, hon. All I know is that he's moved on from Elke pretty damn quick. Which is too bad because she would have done make-up for us for free."

"I don't think we're going to need a lot of make-up for this play."

"Again, Lindy, you are so innocent," chuckled Madelyn. "Natural stage make-up is so much harder to apply than melodrama or monster paint. We—"

Lindy's cellphone rang. "Excuse me, Maddie." She reached to answer it.

The voice on the other end of the line asked for Lindy in her producer capacity and then identified herself as the Fimbria Festival Director, Suzanne.

"How ya doin' today?" asked Suzanne, and Lindy said she was fine.

"You're going to be finer, I'll bet," said Suzanne, "because I'm phoning to tell you that your company—'The Friends of Phyllis' if I'm correct—yep, that's it—have moved off the wait-list and are now officially in the Festival."

Lindy could hardly breathe.

"That's amazing!" she squeaked.

"Glad to hear it," continued Suzanne, "'cause we're cashing your registration fee. Check the website for the Producer's Handbook, and we'll send all the relevant information to the e-mail address on your application. Enjoy!"

And, with that, Lindy and her show were officially in the Fimbria.

"Good," responded Malcolm with great satisfaction when he found out, "we can take the cost of the Bring-Your-Own-Venue off the budget. And I've managed to get the Theatre Department studio booked for six o'clock on Thursday the fifteenth of January for a nice low rental fee..."

CHAPTER FIVE

Love's Labour's Lost

"Oh, fuck."

Leaning on the railing to get her breath back, Lindy looked down over the edge to see who had spoken. On the landing below, a trim mid-thirty-ish white woman with cropped blue hair and a heavy packsack looked up at her and grinned.

"Is that the top of the staircase?" she called up.

"Just two more half flights and you're done," Lindy called down.

"Thank you, ma'am, and your tiny dog too!"

"My what—?"

But the woman had disappeared into the stairwell again. After a five second pause, she reappeared trudging up the steps leading to Lindy's landing.

"Whew!" she laughed as she finally stepped up beside Lindy. "That was a bitch of a climb!" Despite her comment, the crisply attractive woman didn't seem to be particularly out of breath. "Are you here to audition too?"

"Um, no," admitted Lindy, suddenly shy. "I'm the, um, playwright."

"Wow! *C'est cool!*" exclaimed the blue-haired woman. "It's amazing to be able to write a whole play," she added as Lindy opened the Theatre Department door and led her down the hall to the studio. "How many have you put on? I'm Rochelle Gagnon, by the way."

"Lindy Styre," she smiled tightly, opening the studio door to usher Rochelle inside, "and this is my first show."

"Well, you've gotta start somewhere," grinned Rochelle and loped over to where three other hopefuls were divesting themselves of their winter gear. "Hi! I'm Rochelle—"

Lindy went over to greet Malcolm who had pushed a long table into position and was retrieving chairs hidden behind the black curtain draped wall. She threw her coat and hat onto a bench beside Malcolm's, slung her briefcase onto the table and sat down in the straight back chair that he shoved toward her.

Across the studio, the door swung open and the four waiting actors, fussing with their smartphones while they chatted in a desultory way, were joined by a couple of young university kids. The girl was tall and voluptuous and sported a nose ring. The boy was short and heavy and clothed in all black.

It certainly was an assorted bunch that Madelyn's artsy contacts and Malcolm's Theatre Department posters had yielded, thought Lindy.

Besides the eager blue-haired woman and the two youngsters, there were a pudgy grey-haired bespectacled man, a severely coifed spare middle-aged woman and a plushly dressed woman of uncertain age who reminded Lindy of someone she'd once seen playing a Shakespearean lady-in-waiting.

In Lindy's opinion, however, nobody present resembled any of the characters that she'd painstakingly created for her play. But, when no one else appeared in the next five minutes, it dawned on her that the people in the current motley group were going to be the only actors from which she would be able to chose.

Malcolm walked over to the group to hand out questionnaires.

"Oh, not for me," smiled the plushy woman. "I'm only here for Jenn." She indicated the spare woman, who took a form, put on her reading glasses and began to fill it in.

"Not for us either," said the university students, shaking their heads.

"We're just here to practice auditioning," lisped the girl.

"Our professor said it would be a useful experience for when we were actually interested in getting cast," explained the boy.

Blue-haired Rochelle took a questionnaire, however, as did the pudgy bespectacled man.

"I told you we should name our company after the Titanic," mouthed Malcolm, with his back to the actors, as he returned to where Lindy sat worrying. Wondering when Madelyn was going to grace them with her presence, she was just about to phone the third Friend of Phyllis when the door was flung open and Maddie floundered in.

"Malcolm!" Madelyn gasped. "Did you realize when you booked this gawd-awful place that it was on the fifth floor of a building with NO elevator?"

"Good to see you made it," was Malcolm's even reply, as he marched over to collect the completed questionnaires, "because we're just about to start," he gestured toward the group of auditioners, "and you volunteered to do a warm-up."

Realizing that they had an audience, Madelyn quickly simmered down and turned to acknowledge them. "Bernie! Jenn! How marvelous of you to come out! And Terence! What a treat!" She scanned the other unknowns. "And thank you, everyone, for braving those stairs! I'll be with you all momentarily."

Her dignity now fully restorcd, Madelyn sashayed over to the table, nodded to Lindy, and tossed her scarves, coat and purse on a chair.

"Now," she resumed, gesturing with open arms that the actors should join her in the centre of the studio, "let's open up our breathing and free up our minds…"

Obediently, all six of them formed a circle and awaited further instructions.

Lindy wasn't sure what Madelyn was about to do, but her friend had assured her that she remembered every vocal warm-up and theatre game she'd learned in high school drama classes in minute detail.

"Hands at your sides," Maddie told the actors, "shoulders up and back. Stay relaxed. Raise your arms to shoulder height and push back, like an eagle soaring in flight. Now—open your mouth wide and express your joy!"

The studio was suffused with vocal gymnastics.

"Aaaaaaaa!…Eeeeee!…Iiiiiii!…Ooooo!…Uuuuuu!… Cha, cha…cha, cha,cha… Zooooom… Zooooom… Zooooommmmm…" chanted Madelyn and her willing chorus.

Malcolm buried his face in his hands and rubbed his temples.

"Now, hands float down to your sides," continued Madelyn, "and notice that the floor has grown very, very hot. How do we walk?" The actors began to hop about on tiptoes. "And now it's terribly sticky..." The actors tried and failed to lift their feet from the gluey floor.

Madelyn then had them break into twosomes to pretend to be a mirror and its reflection. And then she had them whirl like twin snowflakes. And then toss and catch invisible balls.

"Now," she glowed, "are we all warmed up?"

"Yes, thank you!" they all chorused, and so Madelyn retired to her seat at the table and grandly turned the rest of the audition over to "Lindy, Our Playwright and The Director of *Small Comforts*."

After stumbling through a short summary of her plot, Lindy—who had never auditioned anyone before—had nothing to give the actors but a couple of copied excerpts from the script, but they all seemed satisfied and took the lines to various corners of the room to study them until individually called.

Figuring she might as well give the three actual auditioners the most time to prepare, Lindy asked the university students to read, first the boy and then the girl. They seemed somewhat skilled, wringing a bit of emotion from the printed words, but Lindy couldn't see either filling the available roles.

Madelyn's Bernie declined to read. So up next was Terence Harrier—a visiting Engineering professor with a dreadful flat nasal accent acquired somewhere in the northern United States—who kept flailing his unoccupied hand about like a landed fish.

And then spare Jenn Lundehund, a federal civil servant who actually did a very decent, if pedestrian, job on the main character's speech.

So there was hope.

Hope that flourished when blue-haired Rochelle stepped up to read the female villain's part in a marvelous voice tinged with true malevolence.

"Okay," breathed Lindy, relieved, "thank you all for your excellent auditions. We'll let you know about our casting decisions as soon as possible. Have we got everyone's contact information?"

Yes, they had, the serious auditioners assured them and, having thanked Madelyn again for the splendid warm-up and gathered their belongings, all the actors quickly departed.

Left alone, Lindy, Madelyn, and Malcolm began to examine their questionnaires.

Unfortunately, there were only three, and only two that held much appeal. The two women, Rochelle and Jenn, had, at the very least, read well. However, as Madelyn remarked, "Beggars can't be choosers, and Terence is a very dear friend of mine..."

"I need a beer," growled Malcolm.

The women shrugged and nodded agreement, so the three Friends of Phyllis wearily picked themselves up to trudge down four long flights and out the door to the icy sidewalk.

On the way over to Malcolm's favourite campus pub—an old converted house set between a modern student residence and a vintage apartment block—Lindy was safely sandwiched between the others. So she quailed inside but didn't dissolve into a messy corpse on the sidewalk when an enormous husky jogged past with its owner, who puffed "Hi, Mal..." to her retired professor friend.

"Luke..." pleasantly returned Malcolm, steering Lindy firmly past.

Finally, after they'd been seated at a solid old wooden table and their cheeky server had delivered two hoppy pints and Madelyn's chamomile tea, Lindy dared to ask the unspoken questions. She hated to offend her friends, but—

"Maddie, what happened to all the great buzz you talked about?" she began, eyes trained stubbornly on the foam atop her pint of ale. "How come nobody much turned up? I thought you said actors were desperate for roles?" Then fixing her gaze onto an Irish lager sign hanging over the bar, "Do you think we should have advertised differently, Malcolm? How many posters did you actually put up?"

Madelyn sighed as she stirred honey into her tea. "I called, I texted, I sent out e-mails. So many people told me they'd be there." She counted on her slender fingers. "Bill, Angelo, Kathleen, Dawna. Oh, and Barb said she'd be auditioning...and Pascale...and Gary definitely said he was very interested, hon." She sighed again and shook her head in wonder. "I guess, they all had somewhere else to be..."

"Well, I put up posters all over the place," stoutly maintained Malcolm. "Everywhere Milda suggested. At her Theatre Department, in the Student Union, at this pub..." He indicated a corkboard by the doorway, crowded with posters and notices. "Maybe this auditioning crap is just harder than we expected..."

Glumly, the friends silently sipped on their drinks for a while.

"Okay," said Lindy, pushing her greying bob behind her ears as the alcohol gave her courage a boost, "I know what we'll do. We're going to cast Jenn as the heroine and Rochelle as the villain—which, I'm sure you'll agree, will work fine—and put Terence—even though he's not particularly great—into the secondary villain role."

Madelyn and Malcolm nodded wisely.

"I'll let them know tomorrow—"

"Tonight," suggested Madelyn. "It's not late and they'll want to know."

"Okay," said Lindy, shyly, "but maybe you..."

"Of course, hon," agreed Madelyn graciously. "As the Assistant Producer, it's my job to notify the cast."

Malcolm came up with phone numbers from the questionnaires, and Maddie pulled out her phone and made two very successful calls to two happy women. But, from her veiled responses, Lindy could tell that her conversation with Terence did not go quite so well.

Her face fallen into a picture of melancholy, Madelyn bid good-bye and reported, "Terence says that he appreciated the opportunity but doesn't feel that our project would be suitable for his talents. He says his forte is 'pure comedy.' So he's turning us down."

"His talents?" gasped Lindy. "What talents?"

"I thought he was shitty," said Malcolm flatly.

"And he positively murdered Mr. Peever," sniffed Madelyn. "He had absolutely no feel for the character at all."

"Yeah. Not good," said Lindy sadly. "Still—as of tonight, he was our only choice, and I don't know who else we can get."

"There's got to be someone better out there," shrugged Malcolm.

"Anyone at all would be better," stated Madelyn. "This mug of chamomile tea could have given a more competent reading."

Alarmed to find that she was tearing up and afraid that the others would notice, Lindy ducked her head to nod.

Malcolm and Maddie exchanged a concerned glance.

"Buck up, Lindy. It'll all come out in the wash," soothed Malcolm.

"Yes," agreed Maddie gently, "casting is often fraught with impediments. But, Friends of Phyllis," she added darkly, "I can assure you of one thing: that man is no longer welcome in my social circle."

Blowing a quiet raspberry, Malcolm caught the server's eye and ordered another round.

* * * * *

A doggington ruff. A doggington arf. A doggington growl...

Sometimes, when anxiety made sleep a far off goal, chanting helped Lindy keep the nasty voice—and bitter memories of life with Dad and Greg—away.

A doggington woof. A doggington yelp. A doggington snarl...

When she was a little girl, she would sometimes sing 'Bye Baby Bunting'—her mother's go-to lullaby—over and over with different consonants.

"Dye Daby Dunting...Rye Raby Runting...Nye Naby Nunting..."

Or reiterate a word aloud until it lost all meaning and became a verbal soother.

"Soap. Soap. Soap. Soap. Soap. Soap. Soap. Soap. Soap. Soap..."

Or make a low beeping noise at intervals until her mind had no room to concentrate on anything else.

"Beep." Pause. "Beep." Pause. "Beep." Pause. "Beep..."

But nothing ever worked so well for Lindy as the doggington chant.

A doggington bark. A doggington ruff. A doggington howl...

Lindy couldn't remember when she came upon it, but the doggington chant seemed to concentrate and acknowledge her worries as it simultaneously assuaged her fears, and, sing-songed on repeat to herself, could often suppress the nasty voice enough to comfort her into slumber.

But, this Saturday night, it wasn't working.

The nasty voice lurked just below the doggington chant and refused to be ignored.

Before it got any louder, Lindy had to throw off her bedding and sneak down to the kitchen to silently make some milky tea and peanut butter crackers. Then, turning the volume incredibly low—so low that sleeping Dad and Greg wouldn't been disturbed had they still been there to complain—she curled up with her snack in front of the television on the front room sofa. Intently, she watched a midnight sales pitch for a miraculous smoothie maker that would turn her life around in twenty days by saving her piles of money while making her fifty pounds thinner.

Or something like that.

The point wasn't to listen closely to the toothy hawker and his sycophantic sidekick. The point was to drown out the scathing words in the back of her mind. Which— eventually—it did. Or, at least, quieted the nasty voice enough to allow Lindy to fall asleep, because, around three in the morning when her landline phone on the corner desk began to buzz insistently, she startled awake on the sofa.

Groggily, she stumbled across the room to answer it. "Hello—?"

"Lindy? Is that you?" enquired the caller brightly. "Gawd, hon, you sound awful!"

"Madelyn?" Lindy tried to clear the wool from her brain. "Is something wrong?"

"Why would something be wrong?"

"It's so late…I just thought—"

Madelyn's voice rippled with tinkly silver laughter. "Late? Oh, hon, you're getting to be such a stodge! Of course, nothing's wrong. In fact, everything's right!"

Lindy stifled a yawn. "And why is that, Maddie?"

Madelyn's voice was charged with joy. "I've found our third actor!"

Now she had all of Lindy's attention. "Really? How did you do that?"

"Remember Terence?"

"Ye-es…" Lindy wasn't sure where Maddie was going and she wasn't sure if she wanted to know.

"Well," Madelyn continued, "I invited my dear friends Debra and Mark for dinner at my place tonight and James and Susan, you know, to fill out the table. And then I thought, my gawd, if I'm going to go to all the trouble of paying Maria extra to really tidy up and then spend hours booking the caterer—I went with The Purple Yam—I might as well make it a real celebration, so I invited Cynthia and Ricardo too. But they had a previous engagement."

"Maddie—"

"Hush, now, I'm getting there. Okay, let's see, I had Debra and Mark and James and Susan, and then Nancy and Gary jumped at the chance—you know that Gary loves that I always make sure that my menu is nut-free, and, of course, egg-free for Nancy, and gluten- and lactose-free for Debra, 'cause, as you know, hon, I always make the greatest efforts to make my guests supremely comfortable. So we started with The Yam's lovely curried coconut carrot soup, followed by their fabulous couscous—they make it with the yummiest caramelized pineapple—as well as their truly special soba noodle salad, and then their scrumptious vegan and gluten-free chocolate cupcakes with coconut icing—well, it probably would be too much coconut for you, Lindy, I know it's not your favourite, but all of my guests just loved my menu choices—"

"Maddie." Lindy's exhaustion was making her woozy. "Is there a point that you're trying to make?" She sank into the antique padded desk chair her mother had taken pains to have reupholstered in an entirely inaccurate orange velveteen.

"Well, of course, hon." Maddie sounded a little put out. "Don't be so impatient. Let me see, where was I? Carrot soup. Chocolate cupcakes. You don't like coconut—oh, right, okay, so then I needed a single guest to balance the group—so I thought of Terence!"

"But isn't he 'out of your social circle?'"

"Oh, Lindy—you are such an intolerant little lady! I've always had a much simpler heart." As she anticipated her friend's grateful reaction to her triumph, Madelyn was quickly regaining her good humour. "Besides, Terence has been one of my dearest friends for ages—" Lindy had never heard Maddie mention him before the auditions last week, "—and of course I immediately thought 'why not?—'"

"Okay," sighed Lindy.

"—and we were talking about the play over post-prandial brandy—James brought a bottle of De Valcourt Napoleon—so divine! Of course, Debra had brought a couple of bottles of a rather modest Chilean Brut Sparkling white, and Nancy had turned up with her usual contribution of boring Australian Chardonnays—so we were ready for a treat—"

"Maddie—"

"—and I was telling them how amazing your script is and how we still haven't found the absolutely perfect cast, and Terence confided that he 'sadly regretted'—those were the very words he used!—'sadly regretted' that he had turned us down!"

"Oh, Maddie," breathed Lindy. "What have you done?"

"Just completed the casting of our play, is all!" crowed Madelyn.

"No," sighed Lindy.

"Yes!" squealed her fellow Friend of Phyllis, "yes, I've done it! I've cast Terence as our second villain, Bradley Peever, and now we can get on with setting up our rehearsal schedule and sourcing our costumer and hiring our set and prop people and all those other delightful activities. It's such a relief, don't you agree?"

"Fantastic," allowed Lindy, drained of all hope.

"Oh, hon, you sound so tired. Maybe I should let you go. And I'm not going to phone Malcolm until morning. You know how grouchy he gets when he doesn't get his beauty rest. What an old fogey he's getting to be! Well, ta-ta, hon!" Maddie ended the call as cheerfully as she had begun.

Lindy was grateful that Madelyn had volunteered to inform the third member of their Company. She could imagine Malcolm's reaction to hearing that, without any consultation with either of them, squiddy talentless Terence had been given the nod.

Yes, she could imagine the disbelief, the criticism, the wrath, the shouting, the injured feelings, the resignations— Oh Dear God—the destruction of her Company, the death of her Fimbria show—

Praying that Malcolm would check his e-mails before Madelyn could throw off her Egyptian cotton sheets, Lindy picked up her laptop to send a carefully worded warning salvo to her unsuspecting ex.

CHAPTER SIX

Misalliance

It had been a busy time since the show had been cast. After the irritating process of trying to match each person's availability with everyone else's, Lindy had come to the conclusion that they were only going to be able to rehearse twice a week. So she'd been forced to extend the rehearsal schedule a whole month more than she'd expected.

With her actors' strengths and weaknesses in mind, she'd also tweaked her script, buffering Mrs. Peever's role and slimming down Mr. Peever's considerably.

Meanwhile, Madelyn had dreamed up elaborate plans for their nineteen-seventies sets and costumes. With reference to their budgetary constraints, Malcolm had nixed those and Lindy had asked for simpler designs. Maddie had reluctantly agreed but insisted that, if her vision for the play were to be diminished, she needed to incorporate higher quality materials, by which the others understood her to mean 'more expensive.'

Immediately after that, Madelyn had disappeared to Florida for two weeks with her new 'dear friend,' Jasper Lowchen, so only Lindy and Malcolm had attended an affable Fimbria information night in a wood-paneled meeting room at the Arts Court.

Much of the meeting had concentrated on expanding and underlining the policies and procedures in the on-line Producer's Handbook. But the two Friends of Phyllis had found it quite useful to hear, first hand, details about their upcoming experience.

It also had been interesting, and quite reassuring, to discover they hadn't been the only company in the room tackling the Festival for the first time. The suburban soccer Mom and her perfect-lawn-freak husband hadn't been there—Lindy wasn't sure if they'd even made it past the lottery—but the hipsters and the French college student and her Papa were, as well as many others she vaguely recognized from that mortifying night at the Crazy Quilt.

Hoping that no one would recognize her, Lindy had sunk low in her chair. When he'd noticed, Malcolm had elbowed her sharply and whispered, "Sit up, Lindy. All these people are egoistical 'artists' like Madelyn. Nobody gives a damn."

She hadn't completely believed him but, since no one had given her more than a polite glance when Malcolm introduced their Company around the table, she'd eventually decided that what he'd said was at least partially true and had given herself permission to unfold from her crouch.

Suzanne, the Festival Director, had been genial and frank.

She'd pointed out dates and deadlines—which Lindy had already practically memorized.

She'd emphasized that most companies wouldn't need to submit taxes, because most wouldn't make much money. Some of the new people around the table had seemed surprised, but the Friends of Phyllis had already been sadly aware of that...

She'd talked about getting liability insurance for your company, and obtaining rights and permissions for playscripts and music. Lindy and Malcolm hadn't been sure about buying insurance—in fact, they'd decided that they wouldn't bother—and they'd been glad to note that their written material, at least, was going to be entirely original so there'd be no royalties to pay.

Basic technical limitations at the venues had been discussed. Out of her depth, Lindy had just let that part swim past. City and university postering and flyering restrictions had been stressed. Remembering what Milda, the Theatre Department secretary, had told him about their audition notices, Malcolm had nodded wisely. Ticket and pass processes had been reviewed. The Friends of Phyllis had taken plenty of notes. Then Suzanne had talked about how producers were supposed to access their company's earnings—and Malcolm had been particularly interested in that.

Half-price shows. Volunteer Appreciation shows. Best of Fest shows. Distributing complimentary tickets and choosing a secret password to admit other Fimbria artists in for free to your show. Suzanne had covered it all.

Lindy had mentally checked off the information she'd gleaned from the Handbook and had paid careful attention to the facts that she hadn't. By the time she'd been placing her coffee cup into the dirty dishes bin, she'd started to see herself as an authentic theatre person. As Malcolm had reassured her, nobody present had fingered her as the halfwit from the Crazy Quilt and, while they bid adieu to their fellow Fimbrians, she'd felt like a true member of the artistic elite.

That feeling had persisted for exactly three days. Then she'd opened a Fimbria e-mail specifying their venue—and realized that she didn't have a clue.

Following the link in the Producer's Handbook to her Company's selected show space, Lindy had been taken aback to see that it was really nothing more than a large rectangular room with two entrance doors, one backstage for the performers and one on the side for everyone else. The stage area, measuring about seventeen by thirteen feet, had only been a foot wider and two feet shorter than Lindy's own front room and ran on the same level as the first two rows of audience chairs. At the opposite end from the seating area, behind a curtain indicated by a wiggly line—which constituted the 'back wall' of the stage, she guessed—had been a simple narrow passage labeled both as a 'crossover space' and as the storage area for the venue.

It certainly hadn't looked anything like the generously proportioned high school stage and backstage area Lindy thought she remembered from *Brigadoon*.

And what was Lindy supposed to make of the super-imposed lighting plot? Along heavily drawn lines, there'd been numbered geometric shapes keyed to an inset box at the top of the sheet.

Fresnel? Boom? Parnel?

What the hell were those?

Different sorts of theatre lights, she'd guessed, and—while she could consult Wikipedia to find out what they were—how was she supposed to know which one she needed to do what type of lighting with?

And there must be a sound system too. Where the hell was that on the diagram—?

Panicking, she'd phoned Malcolm to breathlessly bemoan her appalling theatrical ignorance. Why did the venue—which she'd actually sat in to watch that racy Polish sex comedy—why did it looked so totally different on the house plot than it had from her seat eight rows up in the audience last June?

Malcolm had listened patiently as Lindy had poured out her lament. Eventually he'd managed to calm her, however, with the observation that, although they needed to submit their technical questionnaire quite soon, the document she'd forwarded seemed pretty basic to him. And, besides—if all else failed—there was a Fimbria technical workshop scheduled for some time in March.

"Plus," Malcolm had added, the soul of reason, "some kind of techie geek is supposed to come with the venue, so—" over the phone, Lindy had heard him shrug, "—I don't think we need to worry. Did you see the people who turned up at that info session? There had to be half a dozen newbies. If they think they can do it, why not us? Really, Lindy, how hard can it be?"

Lindy, less confident in their ability to conquer a whole new area of expertise in the next few months, hadn't totally bought Malcolm's sangfroid attitude but, then again, what else had there been to do? Having come this far, was she going to let Dad's and Greg's low expectations of her win the day...?

Right.

In for a penny, in for a pound.

Stay with the tour, Lindy.

And tonight the first official rehearsal had finally arrived.

As the Company awaited Madelyn who was—surprise, surprise—running late, breezy Rochelle was amusing everyone else by relating how she got lost while she was trying to get to Lindy's house. Apparently, she'd left her bus at the correct stop near the Dunbar Bridge and, crossing Bronson Avenue, had trekked along the snowy path across Brewer Park. But, instead of veering toward Lindy's Avenue, she'd continued up a street that teemed with dogwalkers going to and from their river run.

How bold, thought Lindy, repressing a shiver. I'd never walk up that street.

According to Rochelle, she'd almost made it to Bank Street before she'd stopped to check her smartphone for Lindy's directions. She'd then walked too many streets north before belatedly heading west and missing Lindy's Avenue again. Only by calling up a map of the area had she eventually been able to find her way to the right address.

"So you're lucky I got here at all!" laughed Rochelle, her hair now dyed a vibrant red "for winter warmth," she'd grinned.

Her fellow actors, pudgy bespectacled Terence, resplendent in a natty hunter green vest, and severely coifed Jenn, sitting ramrod stiff on the sofa, laughed and nodded back. Malcolm winked encouragement as he helped Lindy arrange chairs in the dining room, and once Madelyn had kerfuffled in to lead an abbreviated vocal warm up, it was time for the initial read-through of *Small Comforts*.

The Company sitting around Lindy's heavy wooden dining table with its centered trayful of glasses and water jugs looked expectantly at their Playwright and Director. Lindy took a deep breath and passed around the latest version of her script. After everyone had had a moment to flip through it, she deliberately tucked her hair behind her ears and began her long considered opening remarks.

"Welcome, everyone," she said too softly and had to repeat herself in a louder voice. "What you have in your hands is the final version of my play *Small Comforts*." She cleared her tetchy throat and continued on more strongly. "So, what I'd like you to do tonight is very simple: deliver a clean and unadorned first read-through of the script. To that end, please read your lines as written, but please put as little emotion or characterization into them as possible. That way, we can start your roles from a level playing field and develop your characters as we rehearse. It will also help me do some last-minute changes in the script. Is everyone on board with that?"

All three actors solemnly nodded.

Madelyn gave her an encouraging smile.

Malcolm settled more comfortably into his chair and looked as if he was preparing himself to be bored out of his mind.

Pleased, Lindy continued. "As per our casting, Jenn, you are our heroine, Mary Yerst. Rochelle, you are Mrs. Margaret Peever. Terence, you are Mr. Bradley Peever. All good? Okay, let's begin. Scene One opens as Mary arrives for her first visit to the Peevers' lair…"

Later, after the actors had left, Madelyn moaned over a restorative glass of sherry, "My gawd, that was awful!"

And it was.

Not every bit of it, of course.

Just the bits that Terence took part in.

Which, unluckily, was way too much of it.

Rochelle and Jenn were, thankfully, rather good. They usually remembered to read their parts without trying to impose much character or broadly emote and gave Lindy a very useful sense of where she needed to add to, clarify or cut their lines in the script.

Terence, on the other hand, insisted on embroidering. He'd flip his lines over so they'd read backwards or assume the other characters' words. He'd freely modify verbs or add random adjectives that just weren't appropriate. Eventually, he began using odd accents, suggesting that the character could be Irish, or, if Lindy didn't like that, how about "Jamaican, mon?"

After mildly—but repeatedly—correcting her exasperating actor, Lindy had finally had enough and snapped that he needed to rein his 'creativity' in.

Terence was defensive. "I'm just trying to infuse a little life—a little bit of humour—" he stressed, "—into what, you've got to admit, is a pretty dull script."

Offended, Lindy coolly thanked him for his efforts but doubled down strongly on her direction that he do as the other actors were doing and quietly read only what was printed on the page.

At this point, Terence decided to show his disapproval for her criticism of his improvements by reading his part in a flat robotic voice. Which actually did manage to add some unintentional humour to the proceedings, but also effectively sabotaged the read-through by making all of his dialogue sound ridiculous and putting both of the other actors off their game.

Yet, somehow or other, they got through it, with at least two of the actors appearing to be quite satisfied with the script. In fact, as they packed up and left, rehearsal schedules in hand, all three—even Terence—made a lot of noise about appreciating the chance to be in a Fimbria play. So Lindy was left with the impression that their experience had been mostly positive.

But still...

"What a shame we had to cast Terence," sighed Madelyn, reaching for the sherry bottle again.

Whereupon Lindy gave Malcolm such a fierce scowl of 'Don't you dare-!' that he contented himself with simply rolling his eyes and topping off his glass too.

* * * * *

"Don't be silly," chided Maddie with her tinkly silver laugh. "It's only a play. Ta-ta." Then glancing up from her phone, she tossed her coat over a hook in the front vestibule and smiled sweetly at Lindy to report, "Malcolm's going to be a little tardy. His car battery died."

But Lindy was standing just inside the living room doorway, wide-eyed and very still.

Madelyn had brought Hellmutt.

The giant Alsatian's gaze was fixed on his terrified host. Alarmed by her pulsing fear, he flattened his ears. His lips curled back to show his teeth and a low rumble began in his throat.

"Naughty, naughty," trilled Madelyn, picking up the dog's leash—which she'd looped loosely over a door knob—and stroking his head. "Auntie Lindy doesn't like it when you make that snarly-warly noise. I'll just stick him by the laundry, shall I, hon?"

She tugged Hellmutt, still grumbling, out to the kitchen and down the basement stairs.

Lindy stumbled back with a faint cry as the doggington growl stalked by, then sank onto the sofa beside flame-haired Rochelle and starched Jenn who, busily inserting new pages of edits into her script, hadn't noticed Lindy's fright.

Roly-poly Terence, featuring a pair of deep blue corded pants today, who had observed Lindy shrink, winked at her and grinned. "Nikt a fan avf dem Joyrmans?" he enquired in his best evil Nazi accent.

Not able to find her voice as yet, Lindy merely responded with a tremulous smile.

Quickly Madelyn returned, full of pride that, in order to make practical arrangements for her pet, for once she'd arrived at a scheduled time. "I filled Hellmutt's bowl with water and brought his favourite chew toys," she reported, "so he should be good down there for a while. But, seriously Lindy, he could have just relaxed in the living room. You know he's a very friendly dog."

Rochelle looked up, grinning. "I have a dog too. A shih tzu. Gérard is also *très amicale*. Shall I bring him next time?"

Lindy gulped back a scream of "No!" and gasped, rather forcefully, instead, "Uh-uh! Our rehearsals are going to be at the university from now on, so—sorry, no, that won't be an option."

Unquenchable as usual, Rochelle chuckled and let it pass.

Rehearsal was planned as a second table work day so, after Madelyn led a short but vigorous vocal warm up, everyone took a seat in the dining room and another read-through began. Now more conversant with their parts, the actors were directed to explore initial emotional characterization through the words.

Lindy had been looking forward to hearing how her amended script sounded as the actors worked on developing their roles, but, instead, found it impossible to concentrate.

Terence had taken her direction to add more emotional flavour as an invitation to get up to his old tricks, so she felt compelled to frequently stop the reading to discourage him with mild rebukes.

Rochelle was blithely questioning some of the new lines which she had to fit into her vision of her character, so discussion around that caused some disruption.

And, every time Hellmutt's enquiring bark sent Madelyn scurrying down to "make sure he's comfy," the reading was further delayed.

Meanwhile, Lindy's intense anxiety that her friend would return with the dog set her heart pounding in her chest and made the others' comments on her playscript difficult to follow until Madelyn returned, dog-free, once more.

Yet the most distracting factor came from an entirely unexpected source. Despite Lindy's unflagging gentle encouragement, Jenn still said every one of her lines without a hint of character or emotion.

"Try to have some fun with it," Lindy softly prodded Jenn at last. "Try experimenting with your emphasis, perhaps?"

Obediently, Jenn tried out each word as the main accent in her current line. "I'VE never thought of it that way. I've NEVER thought of it that way. I've never THOUGHT of it that way. I've never thought of IT that way. I've never thought of it THAT way. I've never thought of it that WAY." She looked up at Lindy hopefully. "Did any of those work for you?"

God take me now, thought Lindy in despair. With Hellmutt in my basement and Terence and Jenn in my play, I've never been so ready to meet You...

Jenn read the expression on Lindy's face.

"Yes, I know," she said humbly. "I'm not a natural talent like Rochelle or Terence. It doesn't come to me so easily. I mean, Rochelle just breathes Mrs. Peevers," Jenn spoke as if Rochelle had a natural affinity for evil, "and Terence is so—so—expressive," Jenn sighed. "But, Lindy, I promise you," she continued earnestly, showing more emotion than she had all evening, "I will do everything I can to show you how much I appreciate this opportunity, and—somehow—I will make Mary come alive."

"Oh, hon," jumped in deeply-moved Madelyn before Lindy could reply, "we all know that you are giving your absolute all to our show! Please don't worry about that!"

Rochelle and Terence nodded agreement.

"All you need is a little more loosening up." Maddie's face flushed with inspiration. "I'll tell you what! Let's all follow Lindy's direction and have some fun with the script! How about you all speak your next lines as your favourite farm animal?"

Oh Dear God, thought Lindy, but out loud she lightly encouraged the actors to give Madelyn's ideas a try, so the next scene got sillier and sillier as the actors brayed and mooed and oinked their lines.

Next Madelyn suggested that everyone should try a foreign accent—Terence was thrilled—and then that everyone should "translate the lines to gibberish and just convey the meaning, not the actual words..."

From the basement came a lonely howl. As the actors began to garble incoherently, Madelyn ran down to comfort her beloved pet and, just as Lindy had dreaded, reappeared a few minutes later with Hellmutt himself. Tying his leash to the leg of a heavy armchair in the living room, Madelyn returned to the rehearsal table.

"You all sound marvelous!" she gushed. "Now let's continue playing by using our most dramatic voice..." and the script instantly became a Victorian melodrama.

Lindy hated the direction in which the rehearsal was going but, with Hellmutt lurking only ten feet away, she was too preoccupied and unnerved to stop it.

"Fabulous, Rochelle!" purred Madelyn. "Wonderful, Jenn! You see, you just needed to unwind and let the play take you where you were destined to go."

Jenn turned pink and Rochelle grinned, reaching over to pat Jenn's boney hand.

Obviously, however, Terence felt that the women were getting far too much of Madelyn's attention. He proposed that, next, his character's lines and Rochelle's character's lines should be switched.

Madelyn frowned and looked at Lindy. "No, Terence, I don't think that would work. Right, Lindy?"

"Um, right," agreed Lindy, attempting to pull herself together and take back some control of the rehearsal. "In fact," she said in as business-like a tone as she could muster, "let's all just go back to reading the script as written and exploring for actual characters."

"Yes," said Madelyn, in a voice dripping with support, "I think that now we should."

The two women immediately acquiesced, but Terence seemed annoyed. As the scene resumed and they came to his next line, he stared at the ceiling for a while and then made a low tooting noise. When the rest of the cast looked at him in surprise, he explained, "I think maybe instead of saying this line, Peever should just fart. Like a lazzy in comedy dellarty, you know?"

The door bell rang, and the front door opened. "Hi there—"

To Lindy's joy, Malcolm, who'd finally got a battery boost, had popped in to see what was happening, and she had an excuse to completely ignore Terence's latest suggestion.

"In here, Malcolm!" she called, not daring to go through Hellmutt-land to meet him in the front vestibule.

With little fuss, Malcolm joined the group in the dining room.

"Don't let me interrupt," he said, deliberately choosing a seat that blocked Lindy's line of sight with Hellmutt.

And, for a short while, the second read-through actually went fairly well. Rochelle seemed inspired by all of Madelyn's foolishness and was beginning to discover a genuine character in Mrs. Peever. Jenn was struggling but also seemed enlivened. And even Terence was simmering down and making some progress.

But then it all went sideways.

It was Terence's fault, of course.

After stating that, if the Peevers were supposed to be married, they ought to display some physical affection, he made an ungainly seated shuffle to his left where Rochelle was. Then, without so much as a how'd-ye-do, he reached over to paw Rochelle's breast and wedged his other hand beneath her buttock. A split second later he was gasping and flailing as Rochelle tightened her squeeze on his crotch.

"Only guys I give permission to are allowed to touch me," the flame-haired woman said, smiling wickedly. "Did I give you permission to touch me, Terence?"

"Nooo!" squeaked Terence writhing about in his chair. "Let go! Let go!!"

"Okay, Terence" acceded Rochelle, relinquishing her grip. "We can be friends again for now," she beamed, "but don't you ever do anything like that again."

The rehearsal subsided into shocked silence.

Terence slumped in his chair, his hands cradling his balls. His eyes were hot with anger.

Malcolm grimly shook his head.

Nervously, Lindy tried to find a neutral place to look.

Jenn was staring straight ahead with her mouth open. Madelyn stubbornly surveyed her manicure. Alerted by the passing violence, Hellmutt perked his ears and watched closely from the living room.

Rochelle placidly studied her script.

With, at the very least, his pride bruised, Terence looked up to glare at Lindy, obviously ready to throw the blame for his predicament on her.

"Hey, you—Director Lady!" he grated. "You're the one who cast that crazy bitch! What're you going to do about this?"

Fruitlessly, Lindy tried to come up with something useful to say. "I, um...gee..."

Lindy's lack of response seemed to further enrage Terence. "Com'on, Lindy! You're supposed to be The Director!" Scrambling to his feet and puffing out his chest, he bullied his way towards her, shaking his fist. "I demand that you—"

Lindy shrank back in her chair. Despite the tubby little man's lack of height, the shadow of her father loomed over her. Again, she was that helpless child...

"Na-ah!" Malcolm sprang up and stepped between the furious actor and his quarry.

Across the table, Madelyn rose to her feet as well. "Don't be so rude, Terence!" she scolded. "That was entirely your fault."

"Yeah, you don't get to demand anything," announced Malcolm coldly.

Terence turned on the taller man, sputtering, "B-but Lindy's got to—!"

"Be quiet, Terence!" insisted Madelyn, rapping the table for emphasis. "We all saw you. It was your fault."

A shiver of deeper fear froze Lindy as, in the living room, Hellmutt whined in excitement.

Meanwhile, ignoring Maddie's rear-guard attack, Terence concentrated his rage on Malcolm. "I—she—that bitch—!"

Supremely calm, Malcolm folded his arms. "You know very well that you never touch a woman without her say-so."

"She—!"

"You crossed the line, Bub."

"If that bitch stays in the play, then I quit!" snarled Terence, thrusting a damning finger at Rochelle, still idly reviewing her role.

"Fine," sniffed Maddie. "Go."

"You'll never get another actor like me—!" Terence glared wildly about.

"That's okay," said Malcolm evenly.

"I'm the best thing you've got—" Terence looked for reinforcement from Jenn but she wouldn't meet his eyes, "—and, if I don't get an apology PRONTO, I'm going to quit!"

"So quit." Regally dismissing Terence's importance to the play—and to the world in general—Empress Madelyn sank gracefully back into her chair and resumed a careful assessment of her manicure. His owner's crisis evidently past, Hellmutt settled quietly back down onto the living room rug.

Rallying behind Fortress Malcolm, Lindy held her breath. Were they really going to get rid of Terence so easily?

Yes, they were.

Cursing the lot of them—and scrupulously avoiding Hellmutt—Terence hastily grabbed his belongings and slammed out the door.

No one said a word in his defence.

For the rest of the rehearsal, Malcolm read Bradley Peever's part. He wasn't particularly good in the role, but there seemed be an unspoken agreement around the table that he was definitely better than Terence.

CHAPTER SEVEN

She Stoops to Conquer

"Why don't you scream in my ear and see what I do?" offered Madelyn, striving to inject some pizzazz into Lindy's lacklustre directing.

"No, Maddie," sighed Lindy, "I'm not going to do that."

It was Lindy's first blocking rehearsal—'blocking' being Maddie's theatrical term for telling the actors when to move and where.

With Terence gone and the play recast, Ms. and Ms. Peever now were lesbians. Which was fine—except that Lindy was finding it ridiculously awkward to direct her two actors to move naturally through the positions and attitudes she'd so vividly seen in her mind's eye when she originally wrote the Peevers as a two-sex couple in her script.

Maybe Madelyn was right.

Maybe—despite being, in Dad's and Greg's opinions, a flaming leftist—her mentality was hopelessly mired in the mid-twentieth century.

The world had moved on, but Lindy, who'd never owned a smartphone, streamed a movie or browsed a dating site, had not. If she was going to take her rightful place among the heterogeneous Fimbria artists this June, she figured, she'd just have to root out and burn any remaining dinosaur sexual attitudes she'd accrued as a child of the nineteen-fifties.

Easy to say, hard to do.

Although, perhaps, Lindy wasn't entirely the old-fashioned prude Maddie always characterized her to be.

Back on the morning after Terence quit, Lindy had awoken to the familiar sound of Malcolm softly snoring on the pillow next to hers. Knowing that Lindy had had a rough rehearsal, he'd stayed to comfort her. After making careful love around midnight, they'd slept fondly together in her double bed.

Nothing new there.

Since they'd met on that first day of registration at the University of Ottawa—when he wasn't encamped somewhere in Northern Ontario doing field research—Malcolm had often turned up in between girlfriends, lovers and wives.

While Lindy's parents were alive, they'd mainly met afternoons at the Sandy Hill pied-à-terre he'd quietly rented for the last forty years. But sometimes he'd come to her house while Dad and Mom were away on their annual Florida vacation or, later, when Dad spent those three months in the retirement residence. Then, in the month after Dad, weak from cirrhosis of the liver and grieving the loss of his family castle, had unexpectedly succumbed in his suite to a mild case of the flu, Malcolm had practically lived at her house, generously giving her all of his warm hearted support.

Malcolm was the reason she'd moved into the big bedroom, of course.

Complaining that her childhood bedroom was too squishy for two, he'd insisted she buy a new IKEA mattress for her grandparents' old oak double bed and helped her move in her stuff. Left to her own devices, Lindy was pretty sure it would have taken her many more years to usurp her parents' realm.

If, that is, she'd ever gotten up the guts to do it at all...

And, oddly enough—since he didn't like cats—Malcolm was also the reason why Lindy owned Phyllis. Suggesting that she would enjoy having something alive in the house after he was gone, he'd driven her over to the SPCA shelter to pick out a long-coveted kitten, her second major purchase since Dad had died.

That was before Elke had come and gone—just another brief feminine paragraph in Malcolm's life story—and, as she'd made coffee and fed Phyllis her kibble, Lindy had idly wondered how Malcolm's flirtation with Milda, the Theatre Department secretary, was progressing—but then quickly decided that that wasn't any of her business. Despite Malcolm's innate inability to be faithful to any one sexual partner, genuine ties of affection had persisted between Lindy and her ex-husband—ties that she never wanted jealousy or possessiveness on her part to disturb.

"Coffee?" she'd offered when he came downstairs, as tidy as possible in yesterday's clothes.

Malcolm had accepted a well-sugared cup, scrounged in a cupboard for the cereal that Lindy always kept around for him, grabbed a carton from the fridge and sat down in the dining room with his bowl.

"That was quite a rehearsal," he'd remarked through a mouthful of milky flakes.

"No kidding," Lindy had sighed, popping a frozen waffle into the toaster. "I hope I never get put on Rochelle's hit list."

Malcolm had chuckled. "She's a terror, all right. I like her a lot."

Lindy had raised her eyebrows. "Really?"

"No, Lindy, not like that. I'm old enough to have some sense of self-preservation."

The pair had eaten and drunk their coffee companionably for a while, then Lindy had tentatively begun, "I don't suppose you'd—?"

"No."

"You don't even know what I was going to ask."

"Yeah, I do, and, no, I'm not interested."

"You were pretty good."

Malcolm had picked up his bowl and drunk off the excess milk. "I can read, yes," he'd conceded. "I've spent most of my life lecturing and giving papers, after all. But I don't think I'm the guy you want on stage forgetting his lines and knocking over the scenery. Besides, I just found out that Sarah and Jamie are flying in on Wednesday to help her step-sister with her new baby, so I won't be coming to rehearsals for a couple of weeks."

Brilliant Sarah, a doctoral student in Chemistry at the University of Calgary, was Malcolm's beloved only child from his marriage to Roz. And Jamie, a rambunctious five-year-old, was his treasured only grandchild. Whenever they could make time to be with him, everything else in Malcolm's life was inevitably put on hold. They'd be staying with his ex-wife's family, of course, but he would want to be available to see them on a moment's notice for the duration of their visit. The loyalty and faithfulness he couldn't summon for any of his women occurred quite naturally in his close relationship with his daughter and grandson.

Understanding completely, Lindy had smiled. "So, what would you suggest? Ask Maddie to buttonhole another one of her 'dear friends?'"

"I have no idea..." Malcolm had shrugged.

Then Phyllis had brought up a hairball on the kitchen floor.

"Damn cat," was Malcolm's tranquil comment, as Lindy had hustled over to clean up the mess.

Her conversation later that day with Madelyn had gone quite differently.

"Lindy," Madelyn had said over the phone, her voice oozing with practicality, "the answer to our casting problems is right in front of you."

"Oh?" Lindy had wondered uneasily who her friend was about to propose.

"Yes, Lindy, you dumb bunny! We don't need another outsider. We can cast me!"

"Oh," Lindy had repeated, blankly.

"Yes!" Maddie'd enthused. "I would be perfect!"

"And who would you play?" Lindy had asked, her heart sinking.

"Well, Bradley Peever, of course."

"But—he's a man—?" Lindy had faintly objected.

"Not as a man, silly-billy!" Maddie had scoffed. "As— oh, I don't know—Bridget Peever."

"Bridget? Oh, you mean, as a woman?"

"Yes," Madelyn had continued cheerfully, "as a lesbian."

"So," Lindy had said, trying to sound liberal and up-to-date, "the Peevers would have a same sex marriage."

"Yes, of course, you antiquated girl," Maddie had responded with her tinkly silver laugh. "All you have to do is tweak the role a little—and we're golden!"

Lindy hadn't been able to come up with any alternative, so she'd spent a nerve wracking few days rewriting the Peevers as entirely feminine. And tonight the actors were trying to cope with the script changes as they learned their blocking—safe from all doggington interruptions—in an uninspiring Geography Department classroom at the university.

As usual, Rochelle, now sporting a unicorn pink and blue pixie cut, took the modification to the casting and the script with great composure, and starchy Jenn, whose role was largely unaltered, was managing okay.

But Madelyn, unfortunately, was quite critical. "Do you think that's something Bridget would actually say?" she began with her first line, and, as the evening went on, her nitpicking continued apace.

Finally Lindy testily demanded that she "just go with it, dammit!" and Madelyn, startled once again by her old friend's new intensity, shut up about the script for a while.

However, that didn't mean that Maddie was going to stop trying to assistant direct by constantly stepping outside of her role to make creative suggestions.

Which is why she was offering to let Lindy scream in her ear.

"No," sighed Lindy, "I'm not going to do that. In fact, Maddie, I want you to stay very still right now. Upstage, you know, over there." She indicated the furthest left of the area she'd cleared of desks and chairs before the actors arrived.

"Up right, you mean," sniffed Madelyn, flouncing into place.

"Yes, up right, or whatever. Okay, Jenn, er, Mary, please make that entrance again. From, um, down left. And try to be a little more…fluid? Remember, at this point Mary is slowly gaining confidence as she interacts with the Peevers…"

The initial blocking rehearsal eventually lurched to a close.

"I really like what you've done with the script," laughed Rochelle as she wrapped a chunky hand knitted scarf around her neck.

"Yes, I can't imagine having the talent to just alter it like that," smiled Jenn, deliberately buttoning up her long black woolen coat.

"It's not so bad, I guess," yawned Madelyn over a glass of red wine a half hour later at Lindy's house. "Considering that it had to be kind of a rush job…"

And whose fault was that? groused Lindy to herself. But Maddie had made something of a concession, so aloud she said, "Yes, the show seems to be coming together okay. I'm sure we're on the right track."

Although deep within her antediluvian mind, Lindy harboured unsettling fears that they weren't.

* * * * *

Sometimes Lindy typed any noun into her browser and then added 'porn' to see what images would come up. At first, she was shocked to discover the breadth and width of human lust. What a marshmallow existence she had lived up until now, she thought.

'Normal' was Dad's yardstick for proper social ties. But, as Lindy was finding, 'normal' simply meant that people had gotten used to seeing themselves as feeling and acting in a certain predictable way and expected others to follow suit. But nobody actually felt and acted 'normal.' The internet gave plenty of proof of that.

Who was 'normal' anyway? And who was qualified to judge?

So why get hung up on defining relationships by gender? Lindy wondered. And why am I feeling so awkward about all of this? Here she was the author of a lesbian play—or a play with lesbians, at any rate—and she was finding that writing and directing a same sex relationship was relentlessly uncovering the limited sexual and social assumptions her conservative upbringing had unconsciously instilled.

For example, she pondered, did same sex couples natter and spar the same way double sex couples did? Or were they more likely to see matters from the same side and agree? Lindy hadn't the foggiest notion and, in her mind's ear, she could hear her preconceptions crack and groan as they split open to make room for new ideas.

So, although the nasty voice continued to haunt her, her broadening worldview was handing her some ammunition against its accusations of impropriety and its damning curse of shame and guilt.

Get your fusty opinions out of my head, old man! Lindy's brain demanded whenever the fresh places her writing took her made her feel particularly brave and free. Take your narrow patriarchy and its rotting assumptions and stick'em where the sun don't shine!

* * * * *

March was passing through with warming winds and unexpected snow dumps, and rehearsals were grinding on.

As per Rochelle's advice, Lindy had begun taping rectangles on the Geography room floor to mimic the set that she had finally decided on. Sarah and Jamie had returned home to Calgary, so Malcolm was back in the picture with his budget sheets. Scatterbrained Madelyn had remained unmurdered—but only just—and Lindy was now grappling with her Fimbria program blurb.

The blurb was due tomorrow, and, following the guidelines she'd been given in the Producer's Handbook, she was trying to make it unique and intriguing and sexy and short.

All at once.

Come see *Small Comforts*, she wished she could write, because we've really worked hard, we'd really appreciate having a big audience, and you'll really like it!

But that wasn't how blurbs were composed.

Blurbs were clever and punchy, teasing the Fimbria public with promises of poignant thrills, audacious titillations, or belly-busting guffaws. Ideally, when patrons were undecided about which Fimbria show to bless with their hard currency, a well written blurb in the Fimbria program could convince them to put their lovely twelve bucks in your coffers.

Or not to.

So it was super-important that Lindy get her show's blurb right.

Lindy took another swig of her cooling English Breakfast tea.

Okay, she said to herself, I'll start again. What is appealing about my show? What will audiences enjoy about it? What do I want them to be talking about as they leave?

My show is honest. My show is interesting—no, engrossing. My show is gripping.

My show will have great word of mouth—or, as Maddie says, wom.

Maddie.

Oh Dear God.

Maddie was a problem. She had largely given up criticizing the script, which was a huge relief. But, no matter how Lindy much coached, prodded or cajoled her, Madelyn seemed incapable of following her blocking or memorizing a single line.

Nope, don't think about that, Lindy cautioned herself. Don't. That way lies madness. Keep your mind on your blurb.

"An honest portrayal of clinical anxiety," ventured Lindy aloud. "An alarming tale of fearsome dread." Okay, she thought, typing her ideas out, that's not too bad. But on the laptop page, the first sentence looked lame, and the second, melodramatic.

"Gaah!" exclaimed Lindy, springing up to brew fresh tea.

The doorbell rang, so she detoured to the front vestibule to answer it.

Madelyn fell through the door.

"I am drained to my dregs!" she cried. "I can no longer cope! You have forced me to assume way too many personae! I CAN'T be The Assistant Producer and The Assistant Director and The Actor! I CAN'T source talent and materials and lead rehearsals and memorize endless dialogue! It is ALL too exhausting! I MUST have some respite!"

"I see," soothed Lindy, hanging up Madelyn's faux leather coat. "Well, come in and we'll have a glass of sherry and a chat, and maybe we can arrive at some sort of resolution."

Warmed by the promise of a drink, Madelyn calmed down momentarily and allowed herself to be led to a seat on the dumpy old sofa. Lindy left her with the sherry bottle and a couple of glasses while she ransacked the refrigerator for something vegan to serve her choosy guest. Then, armed with a platter of baby carrots and hummus dip, she returned to face Madelyn's litany of complaints.

"Come here, Phyllis, darling," her friend was cooing. "Come have a pat..."

Unimpressed, the silver-grey cat slicked back her ears and trotted upstairs.

Madelyn turned sourly on her friend. "Your cat doesn't like me," she charged.

I suppose that that's my fault too, thought Lindy, but said instead, "I'm so sorry. She's usually very friendly."

"Not to me, she isn't," sniffed Madelyn. Not yet ready to be mollified, she took a delicate sip of sherry. "But why I should expect kindness in this house is beyond me."

She loaded up a carrot with hummus and sadly bit into it.

Lindy took a gulp of sherry and counted to ten. That wasn't enough, so she counted to twenty-five. "You know what, Maddie?" she started. "I—"

Madelyn didn't let her finish. "Yes, you!" she snapped through another mouthful of hummus. "It's always about you. You and your show. You and your cat. You and your selfish fear of dogs!" She held her glass out for another pour. "What about the rest of us, Lindy? What about me? Have you ever for one moment thought about me?" Lindy tried to break in but Madelyn tore along. "I'm a person too! I have feelings and hopes and dreams—and a life!" She downed her second glass. "A life, Lindy! I have things to do, a lover to see, a dog to care for. I don't have time to worry about your show every minute of the day!"

While Madelyn stopped to load up another carrot, Lindy finally managed to get a word in edgewise. Fortunately, Maddie's list of complaints had given her time to think of an appropriately nonhostile response. "I know that, Madelyn," she said as sympathetically as she could, "and I'm sorry that you've been overburdened." Which was the truth. Lindy had never wanted flighty Madelyn to become so deeply involved in her show. "With your highly artistic and sensitive personality, I should have realized that you would be more suited to an advisory position. I have asked for far too much. Perhaps it would be best for you, as well as for our friendship, if you were to resign from the most taxing of your responsibilities."

A martyr's mantel pleased Empress Madelyn. It was a role that she could actually play. With a gracious nod of her head, she accepted Lindy's offering.

"I'm sorry, too," she sighed. "I fear that I shall have to relinquish the part of Bridget Peever. I know that will be difficult for you and the other actors," she granted, "but, as you say, I am not constitutionally equipped to suffer the fate of a Grecian pack mule." Maddie sighed and adjusted her bangles. "Now, hon, do you think we could have our coffee?" she asked, indulgently polite in the face of her friend's neglect. "Anything dark roasted would be fine..."

Relieved at the positive shift in Madelyn's mood, Lindy headed back to the kitchen to put on the kettle, retrieve the jar of medium roast instant coffee and regretfully plate the last of the Oreo cookies, reliably vegan, that she'd been saving to sweeten her next bout of midnight terrors. Then, coffee and cookies in hand, she slid back into the living room in time to catch Maddie in the midst of a soft-spoken phone call.

"Yes, hon, you would be doing us the most gargantuan favour," murmured Madelyn. "Yes, we can certainly accommodate him...No, she won't—I'll make sure of it... Yes, but she'll have me there in an advisory capacity...Yes, well, Rochelle, at least, exhibits some talent, and, under my tutelage, Jenn has been improving...No, the money aspect has all been taken care of. We wouldn't expect you to contribute...Oh, an honorarium, at the very least...Yes, we can do that...Well, that is marvelous!" Maddie's voice brightened and took on a confident volume. "Thank you, hon! I'll email the schedule to you right away. Ta-ta!" Madelyn signed off and greeted Lindy with a radiant smile. "You'll never guess how clever I've been!"

"Again?"

Carefully—so as not to be tempted to throw them—Lindy placed the cookies and Madelyn's cup of coffee on the table.

"Who else can you rely on for fantastic ideas?"

Attempting to hide her alarm, Lindy simply shook her head, outmatched by her impulsive friend once more.

"I've got another actor for our show," sang Madelyn, hugging herself with delight. "A great actor. An accomplished actor, and a very dear friend. Actually, when I told Rochelle that I was thinking of vacating my role, she did mention that he was free—but, of course, I was already leaning toward casting him anyway—"

"Who?" asked Lindy, readying herself to hear the worst. But when Madelyn revealed his name, it was worse than the worst.

It was Darrick from the Crazy Quilt.

And where Darrick was, so too would be Leo, his green-canvas-vest-wearing emotional support chihuahua.

His doggington yelp.

Supremely frustrated, unnerved and angry, Lindy fled back to the kitchen for her tea, only returning after a moment to make a point of downing every one of the damn vegan Oreos left on the damn plate right in front of damn traitor Maddie's damn dopey face.

Gaaaah!!!

What was done, was done.

But Lindy knew she'd never forgive Madelyn.

Not ever.

Not in a trillion years...

CHAPTER EIGHT

The Misanthrope

There's so much I don't understand any more, grumbled Lindy. Perhaps Malcolm's on top of all this technical stuff? Covertly, she searched his grave face. Nope, she couldn't tell.

They were sitting around a table with representatives from about ten other companies in the same wood panelled Arts Court meeting room where they'd met for the introductory session. This time, however, the Fimbria workshop was being led by Sadie-Jim, the festival's amiable non-binary Technical Director.

Sadie-Jim moved further and further into the technical woods, speaking quietly about loading in and striking sets and props and getting maximum usage from lighting plots and sound systems. Other participants were asking intelligent-sounding questions about motion graphics or gobos or frequency spectrums. They nodded knowledgeably at their answers and made detailed notes.

Meanwhile, Lindy was getting completely lost in the techno trees and not a single breadcrumb was appearing to lead her home. She felt rebuffed by Malcolm, who may have been as bewildered as she, but sat stolidly, not saying a word. Looking at the deeply engaged faces around the table, Lindy realized that she, alone in the room, was confused. Panic began to rise in her chest. Deliberately, she snapped her mental elastic band—Crack!—and forced it down.

A doggington arf. A doggington ruff. A doggington growl...

At long last the workshop was over. People smiled and chatted companionably, siblings of the theatre, as they placed their coffee cups in the plastic bin, donned their coats and went their separate ways. Malcolm finally made contact with the Technical Director, but it was just to compliment Sadie-Jim on their presentation.

"Beer?" enquired Malcolm as the elevator door closed.

"Something stronger, I think," sighed Lindy.

Malcolm laughed.

Walking towards the pub, they encountered the jogging husky and his owner, Luke. But they were on the opposite sidewalk, and while he and Malcolm exchanged greetings, Lindy, heart pumping, was able to deke behind a parked car. Unfortunately, that put her directly in the path of an on-coming beagle, but Malcolm grabbed her arm and, getting in between her and the doggington ruff, muscled her past before she could melt down.

A couple of minutes later, she was sitting rigidly in the pub with both a shot of rye and a pint of draught coming her way from the bar. Malcolm let her swallow the shot and taste the beer before he spoke.

"Lindy," he frowned, "if you're going to get this show up and running, you have got to try to get your shit together."

"Malcolm, I'm really lost with this technic—"

"No, Lindy!" he sternly cut in. "You spent that entire workshop worrying about Darrick's dog. Don't try to deny it. I saw you." He took a pull of beer. "Look, Lindy. You need a good actor like Darrick in your play—you saw how quickly he was picking up the role—and you managed to survive last night's rehearsal in one piece. You have to deep six all those doggie fears. I know it's not easy for you, but Leo's only a chihuahua, after all."

Her cheeks burning with shame, Lindy struggled to keep tears from springing to her eyes. "I'm so sorry, Malcolm..." she mumbled.

But he wasn't going to settle for a half-assed apology. "No, Lindy, 'sorry' isn't going to cut it. If you want to get this turkey on the runway, you've got to buck up and take it on the chin. There was a lot of info tonight, and we both needed to be on top of it. But you were hardly even listening. You've got to shut off that scaredy-cat sound track in your head so you can concentrate—"

"Don't you think I know that?" Lindy finally snapped. "Don't you think that that's what I've told myself a ba-jillion times? Get off my case, Malcolm Macoun! I've been dealing with this idiotic terror of dogs my whole life, and nothing you say is news to me!" Lindy stopped abruptly mid-rant. Why the hell was she beating up on her best friend?

But Malcolm grinned. "That's the spirit, Lindy. Get mad. Get even! So what if Madelyn stuck you in an awkward place with Darrick and his moronic 'emotional support dog?' You're stronger than any fucking chihuahua! Remember how you fought with me to get this ludicrous project on the rails? Take that energy and run with it. I'll be there, and I've got your back, so all you need to do is look like you're brave and you'll manage great."

"Whistle past the graveyard, you mean?"

"Exactly."

Easier said than done, of course.

The day after she'd dropped a cluster bomb on Lindy's life, Madelyn had said that she "required a mental health break" and beetled off to Merry Olde Englande for a week's vacation in London with her 'very dearest friend,' Jasper Lowchen.

Thanks a bunch, Maddie, Lindy had bristled to herself. But—I know, I know—you never go to funerals...

Darrick had phoned to confirm that he was in the play—"We'll let bygones be bygones, shall we, my dear?" he'd said heartily—and, after a stern talk with herself, Lindy had resigned herself to morphing the Peevers back into a two-sex couple.

When alerted to this re-edit, Rochelle had been predictably cheerful and, as long as it didn't affect her lines, Jenn hadn't cared. The script had been revised, the next scheduled rehearsal had arrived and, her pulse racing from the moment she'd stepped outside her door, Lindy had revved up Dad's seldom used Ford to motor over to the university.

Luckily, Malcolm had met her in the parking garage, so they'd walked over to the Geography room together. Luckily, because, along with Rochelle and Jenn, Darrick and his doggington arf had already made it to the rehearsal space before them.

When she sensed the dog, Lindy's heart rate had sky-rocketed. Her palms had gone sweaty. Her brain had screamed to her that she had to—absolutely had to!—run, run, run away...!

But she hadn't.

Instead, she'd walked blindly into the room, mouthing a general "Hi, gang." She'd stripped off her coat, opened her case and transferred a script to Malcolm to hand to Darrick. She'd refused to look directly at her new actor, cradling his miniature devil-hound in the crook of his arm.

Since Madelyn was AWOL, she'd led her players in a very basic warm-up. "Stand up. Shoulders back, chest out, feel your breathing. Aaaa—eeee—iiii—oooo—uuuu. March in place, swing your arms, touch your toes. Waddle like a duck. Moo like a cow. Okay, positions, please, for scene twelve."

She'd directed.

The actors had done their thing.

Malcolm had watched from the side without comment.

Eventually, she'd had to meet Darrick's gaze, but she'd never looked at Leo, the green-canvas-vest-wearing emotional support chihuahua, carried snug in his owner's grip, even once.

She'd looked around Leo. Over Leo. Past Leo.

She'd tried to pretend that Leo wasn't actually there.

But her senses had known, her body had known, every fiber of her nervous system had known. And, after the three hour rehearsal had finished—after the actors, buzzed by the renewed dynamism that Darrick had brought to the role of Bradley Peever, had left the room—she'd sat and cried for five minutes straight in Malcolm's arms.

They would have still been there, she thought—as a large rowdy group of students seated themselves beside them in the pub—if that janitor hadn't turned up and asked if he could turn off the lights on the floor. Malcolm had walked her back to her car and then had saved her from the nasty voice by following her home and staying the night.

As Malcolm just said, she had survived.

But it hadn't been pretty, and she knew it wasn't going to get prettier any time soon.

* * * * *

"For example, I built this Greek mask out of cardboard."

It was impressive. If the doe-eyed twenty-year-old girl hadn't handed it to Lindy to examine, she would have sworn that the mask was made of bronze. From the front, only its weight gave it away. From the back, however, you could clearly see that it had been constructed out of a cereal box.

Carefully, Lindy passed the mask back to its artisan. "I'm blown away," she admitted.

Platinum tressed Andrea Spitzer, the props builder who Madelyn had sourced from her London companion's recommendation, tucked the beautiful object into her portfolio case and smiled. "So I'm hired?"

"Oh, absolutely!" gushed Madelyn. "We can't wait for you to perform your magic for our show!"

"Right," nodded Andrea, satisfied. "So—hand me the first check, give me your props list, and I'll get started as soon as possible."

"The first check?" queried Malcolm, who had insisted on driving with Lindy to the Crazy Quilt as a foil to Madelyn's impulses.

"Yeah," smiled Andrea, "as Madelyn and I agreed. Five hundred now, for talent and materials—"

"To buy cereal boxes?" squinted Malcolm.

"—and the balance on delivery of the props. That's a thousand for the job."

"A thousand—!" Malcolm gasped.

Lindy gulped back her own astounded cry.

"Yeah," said Andrea levelly, "you pay for the materials and I get a thousand clear for my time and talent. That's what Madelyn said. Why? Aren't those the terms you were expecting?"

"If we want superior talent," said Madelyn archly, "—and I know for certain that I, myself, do—we must be prepared to pay the going rate."

"But aren't you a third-year theatre student?" asked Lindy, trying to get her head around Madelyn's extraordinary generosity.

"At the end of term, I will be. Right now I'm in second, but classes end next week and then I'll be studying for spring exams. I'm very experienced though," Andrea offered complacently, examining her purple polished fingernails with satisfaction. "I've done props for all sorts of high school and university shows."

"But have you ever made props professionally?"

"Well, I did some for a musical at the Little Theatre."

"But aren't they an amateur company too?" Lindy was beginning to become rather disenchanted with Maddie's pick.

Andrea wrinkled her delicate nose. "I guess..."

"And how much did they pay you?"

Andrea rolled her perfectly lined eyes. "I was an apprentice. You don't get paid to be an apprentice. Duh."

"So, why are we paying you like a professional?" Malcolm was using his professor voice now. "You know, young lady, your thousand-dollar fee would be a fifth of our budget—and that's not counting the money you're planning to spend on cereal boxes."

Andrea's glossy lips set in a practiced moue. She leaned down to pick up her portfolio case. "Okay, you know what? If you're not going to treat me with respect, I don't need this job. I was only doing it as a favour to my Uncle Jasper, anyhow—"

And, with that parting shot, Andrea was gone in a puff of expensive scent.

Madelyn glowered accusingly at Malcom. "For gawd's sake, you idiot, look what you've just done!"

"I've saved us a thousand bucks!"

"You've sabotaged Lindy's show!" Madelyn shook her finger at Malcolm. "We should have known you'd be a traitor! You've never really approved of our creative aspirations from the first!"

"Well, at least I—"

"Shut up, the both of you," Lindy interrupted flatly, "and let me think."

"Did anyone here want anything else?" the stealthy server who'd appeared at Lindy's elbow asked blandly.

"Yes," Lindy decided for all of them, "bring us a jug of apricot ale. And a large poutine. With three forks. Thanks."

"I don't drink apricot—" started the other two Friends of Phyllis, but a fierce glare from Lindy cut them both off mid-complaint.

"I do," stated Lindy conclusively. "Now both of you shut up while I figure this out."

Ignoring the others' sulky faces, Lindy dived into a deep study. She only resurfaced several minutes later when the server glided over with their beer and poutine.

"Okay," she began, sharing the ale into glasses, "we are now all going to agree on something. By which I mean," she said, overriding an interjection from Madelyn as she grabbed her fork, "you two are going to do as I say. Whenever there is a Company decision to make, Maddie, we are going to do it as a Company. No more hiring people without talking to the rest of us. Right?"

Madelyn pouted doubtfully at the foam atop her glass of ale and shrugged.

"And Malcolm? No more dismissing Madelyn and my artistic decisions with snotty comments before we even get a chance to explain ourselves. Okay?"

Malcolm scowled but shrugged his acceptance as well.

"Now, Maddie, obviously, as Malcolm has pointed out, we cannot hire that girl to put together our props—"

"Build our props—" corrected Madelyn faintly.

Lindy decided to forgive her. "Whatever." She sampled a healthy forkful of the poutine and forged on with her mouth full. "We can't afford her services. So, what are we going to do? Any ideas that won't sink our budget as low as the Edmund Fitzgerald?"

Neither friend was willing to jump.

"Okay then, Maddie," continued Lindy, "let me ask you this. Is a thousand bucks per show really the going rate for a props person?"

Nibbling on a naked french fry, Madelyn shrugged again. "That's what Andrea told me—"

"No kidding," muttered Malcolm to the cheese curd on his fork.

"—but I don't actually know. I just assumed—"

"That's okay," nodded Lindy, cutting in again, "because, the fact is, none of us know. How much is talent worth? To us, not much—because we don't have much. So, how would it be if we became our own prop mak—builders?" Could it be possible for Madelyn and Malcolm to look more skeptical, she wondered, but soldiered on. "Look, guys, the whole production of this Fimbria show is kind of a baptism of fire. We don't actually know how to do any of this theatrical stuff—no, Maddie, not even you—so we can't protest that we don't know how to make—yes, okay, Maddie—build props."

"Can you build a metal mask from a cereal box?" Madelyn was tired of pouting and ready to be 'the reasonable one' again.

"No," admitted Lindy. "But we don't know how to sew costumes or put a set together, and props have to be easier than doing either of those. So why not give our budget a break and build them ourselves?"

Malcolm ran his finger around a water ring on the table. "I'm for anything that saves money. And, on the topic of budgeting, I have something not so great to report." He poured himself the rest of the contents of the jug. "The Geography Department says that, with exams in the offing, they need the room we're currently using for the student study group program they've decided to implement this year. So, as of the end of next week, we have to find somewhere else to rehearse."

"And, I'm guessing from your tone of voice," said Lindy, hoping she was wrong, "you haven't been able to find us anything."

"Oh no, it's not quite as bad as that. I can find places—theatre studios, rooms in community centres, church halls—but they all cost a bundle to rent. From what I can see, the cheapest space is at St. Martin's past St. Laurent on Montreal Road—"

Lindy wondered if the actors would want to travel so far from their previous rehearsals. "How about near the university in Sandy Hill?"

Malcolm shook his head. "All pretty much booked. Or way too expensive. But there is St. Jude's in the Glebe. They've got a space that's only pricey-ish to rent."

"The actors were all happy to come to your place, Lindy," offered Madelyn, "and that's not too far away from that church. And Bank Street's on several major bus routes."

"How much—" Lindy wished that life could be simpler, "—oh, never mind. If you think that it's our best option, Malcolm, just book it, and we'll let the actors know. They'll just have to bounce with the breaks. But, for the sake of our bottom line, I think that this move makes it absolutely necessary that we do the props ourselves."

"Well, we can take small comfort in that," opined Malcolm slyly.

While Lindy groaned, Madelyn looked from one to the other, puzzled. "I think you're both nuts," she sighed.

CHAPTER NINE

Waiting for Godot

"Do not, I repeat, do not bring me just any glass."

"No, Darrick, sorry to interrupt again, but no." Lindy was rehearsing the beginning of the séance scene 'off-book'—as Maddie informed her that rehearsing without scripts in hand was called—at St. Jude's church hall. "The reason for that line is so that Bradley can get Mary used to following his suggestions without question. So it needs to be spoken with an air of pure authority. Do you see?"

"Do not, I repeat, do not bring me just any glass!"

"Great! Okay, let's try again from where Mary stands up."

After a number of rehearsals with Leo tucked quietly in the crook of Darrick's arm, Lindy no longer even saw the tiny dog. Darrick and Leo were a single unit who moved as one and Lindy, although always shaken with anticipatory fright as she approached the rehearsal hall, found herself—most of the time—calmly directing her actors or chatting freely during the ten-minute break without a single chill from Leo's doggington arf presence at all.

Most of the time.

There had been that one Sunday afternoon when, leaning in to point out a particular line in the script to Darrick, she'd suddenly become aware of a small wet nose touching her hand, and startling back with a cry, had seen Leo, his enormous eyes glistening with alarm, startling back from her as well.

"I've told you—he's a very friendly dog," Darrick had said, exasperated to have to remind Lindy once more of this self-evident fact while he pacified his emotional support animal with comforting pats, "as most domestic canines are."

Lindy was definitely not sure about that, but it was true that Leo seemed to be a pretty meek member of his species.

As Malcolm laughed, "If Leo was named after a lion, it was certainly a cowardly one."

Uneasily, Lindy wondered how she was going to break it to Darrick that, eventually, he would have to leave Leo backstage. She prayed that he wouldn't want to quit the show when he found out.

Lindy's actors were all successfully moving off-book and remembering their blocking as well. Rochelle was the best, but Darrick was swiftly catching up, and even Jenn was losing some of her stiff awkwardness as she read more meaning into Mary's lines. Lindy felt that all of them had a long way to go to make their characters authentically alive, but she wasn't exactly sure how to help them accomplish that. Madelyn, with her self-proclaimed wealth of theatrical knowledge, had contracted a bad case of 'la gripe' and wasn't available for rehearsals right now.

Lindy's Fimbria program blurb had somehow got itself written. It wasn't perfect, but she'd run out of time and had to submit whatever she'd penned. She hoped that her rather torrid description of *Small Comforts* would have a positive effect on what Maddie referred to as their 'house numbers' or, more colloquially, 'bums in seats.'

Glue gun and thrift store membership cards in hand, Lindy—and Madelyn when she occasionally felt up to providing her friend with her artistic insight—were nibbling away at their now severely edited list of props and costumes. She'd scoured the internet to find plans for a foamboard typewriter and a papier mache dog and found a lovely crackled glass lampshade at the Sally Ann to use upside down as a crystal ball.

Meanwhile, with apocalyptic budgetary warnings from Malcolm, Madelyn's elaborate stage set had been whittled down to just a few basics—a table, three chairs and a séance cabinet.

That séance cabinet was the bane of Malcolm's existence. In his uncompromising opinion, it "sucked dead bears..."

As specified in Lindy's stage directions, the cabinet had to be a six-foot-high black curtained box. It was where 'psychic' Margaret Peever sat, her hands 'securely' tied, to concentrate her spiritual energies into the trances that produced the ghostly messengers who frightened and advised Mary. A complicated set piece, the cabinet had to be solid enough to withstand various scripted séance tricks—but also needed to be dismantled for transport and storage between performances.

Malcolm, who had never built anything for the stage before, was unacquainted with the use of fabric-draped pipes or lightweight canvas flats. So he'd simply gone to the nearest big box hardware outlet to buy a likely looking wooden storage shed and cobbled it together with added hooks and eyes in Lindy's basement. Then, because he'd left the doors off to leave a space for the curtains, he'd discovered that the assembled cabinet had a tendency to list, so he'd affixed heavy wooden bracing to the sides and back. He'd then attached a curtain rod above the door opening and painted the whole contraption black.

Which was clearly a mistake.

For, when they'd decided to wrest it out of Lindy's basement into a borrowed truck to practice its reconstruction in St. Jude's rehearsal hall, they'd found that the goddammed hooks had gotten paint-glued into the freakin' eyes, and it had taken more than half an hour of concentrated swearing to get the monstrosity apart. In fact, it had required determined muscle from all five of The Friends of Phyllis Theatre Company there—Maddie'd had a hair appointment that day—to get the lumpish thing standing and then to pry it apart again after rehearsal. So, once Malcolm had hefted the slabs of spirit cabinet back down Lindy's stairs that night, he'd told his ex-wife in extremely frank terms that the pieces were going to remain stacked against her basement wall until absolutely necessary.

For now, he'd snarled, the actors would just have to pretend.

Lindy wanted a large rolling blackboard as well but, after his misadventure with the spirit cabinet, Malcolm had become mule-ish about keeping their purchases down to the minimum. Still, Lindy was determined to acquire one somehow—she felt it would make all the difference in her secret final scene.

And then there were the preparations for their first unofficial public performance.

Last week during the mid-rehearsal recess, over a glass of the sparkling cranberry juice that Lindy had brought, Darrick had broached the subject of that daunting undertaking. It was a project that neither of the original Friends of Phyllis present in the church rehearsal hall had even considered, and Lindy and Malcolm were absolutely blindsided when he'd remarked, "I hate to be a nudge, my dears, but I fear that you've left all of the details regarding our Preview off of our schedules. Where and when is it to be, exactly?"

"And what sort of audience will there be?" Jenn had asked, her eyes wide with queasy excitement.

Blithely munching on a ginger snap cookie Lindy had also provided, Rochelle had signaled her curiosity too.

Realizing that, as a theatrical world newbie, she'd completely dropped the ball, Lindy had hastily lied to the actors that she and Malcolm were working hard to "finalize their booking." The details, she assured them, would be forthcoming soon.

But, in reality, a formal Preview hadn't even been on her radar.

Madelyn, who might have warned Lindy that, along with a full-dress rehearsal, a well-attended Preview— complete with whatever technical elements they could throw together—ought to be on their timetable, had been dismissive when consulted over the phone. "I just assumed you knew..."

Malcolm, sharing Lindy's dismay, had rushed her over to the pub that night, where they had hurriedly reviewed their schedule and determined that Malcolm had better book somewhere pronto.

Somewhere, preferably, that came with a built-in stage and a built-in audience.

"Oh Dear God," Lindy had moaned, when Malcolm had announced the location he'd found, "do you think they'll be able to hear us over their respirators?"

"No. But a bunch of them, at least, won't be able to get up and walk out."

Malcolm was hoping, he told her, to book their Preview into the very large activity room at the retirement residence where—in the few months before Lindy's father had taken his last breath in one of its pricey suites—Malcolm had met and briefly dated a still eager-to-be-helpful receptionist.

Time was tight and, even though the audience might be a bit antique—and being in the building might bring back unpleasant memories of Dad's last days—Lindy knew the space, so she'd given Malcolm the thumbs up. Subsequently, Malcolm had taken the compliant receptionist out for a couple of very expensive dinners in the ByWard Market, which had allowed them to update the actors' schedules with a specific Preview place, date and time.

And now as the months ticked down to this year's Fimbria Festival, with Madelyn's continuing absences greatly helping with Lindy's direction, everything with *Small Comforts* was going gangbusters.

Lindy was keeping her fingers crossed.

* * * * *

"He said that he felt like a Clydesdale, all bound up in leather and chains," Rochelle snickered.

During the mid-rehearsal break at the church hall, the three actors were swapping funny costume stories from other shows they'd been involved in.

Lindy listened avidly. Perhaps they would drop a few clues about how real theatre folk dressed their cast for mere pennies an outfit. It was a secret she hadn't yet discovered. The total cost of the few appropriate thrift store finds that she and Madelyn had acquired was mounting at a breakneck speed.

Madelyn's capricious buys, thought Lindy glumly, were a major part of the problem. She was inclined toward the garish and the shiny, defending even the tawdriest of her independent purchases as "evocative of the seventies" or "impressionistic" or "reading well from the house..."

Whatever that meant.

Lindy had gotten tired of trying to explain to Maddie what was wrong with the outfits that she picked. She'd gotten tired of trying to return unsuitable items and then swallowing the price tag when the high end consignment stores that Madelyn frequented stubbornly refused to take them back. And she'd gotten really tired of trying to keep Malcolm from ripping Madelyn into teensy tiny pieces on sight.

Oddly, Leo the Emotional Support Chihuahua seemed like the most infinitesimal of her problems right now.

"I whipped up a steampunk Lady MacBee for that one, and I sewed a—"

Wait a moment, thought Lindy. What did Jenn just say?

"I'm sorry, Jenn" she interjected, "I was daydreaming. You 'whipped up'—?"

"—a steampunk Lady MacBee. For the Scottish play. When my oldest nephew was in high school, I did quite a few costumes for his drama teacher."

"Really?" Now Lindy was very interested. "And are you still, ah, building?"

"Sewing? Oh yes, but mostly for my younger niece and her step-brother. I did a super-fun ketchup bottle for Leila last Halloween. And Jayden wanted to go out trick-or-treating as a zombie pizza delivery guy. It was crazy." Passing the pictures on her phone around to her fellow artists' oohs and aahs, Jenn shook her head indulgently at the insanity of youth.

"Crazy," echoed Rochelle cosily, handing back Jenn's phone. "I love Halloween. Last year I was 'The Destroying Angel.'"

"A mushroom?" grinned Malcolm.

"A succubus." Rochelle ran her ebony polished finger tips through her freshly dyed sable mop.

"Mmm, very sexy." Malcolm raised an eyebrow.

Rochelle laughed again.

Leo emitted a dispirited whimper.

Darrick was instantly concerned. "Do we still have enough time to go walkies, Lindy? Malcolm? Need a little air?"

"Yeah," Lindy nodded, preoccupied with the realization that Jenn might be the answer to her costuming problems.

Exeunt Darrick, carrying Leo, and Malcolm, stage right.

"You have so much confidence, Rochelle," sighed Jenn when the guys had gone, "and I wish I had half your talent."

"*Ben là*, Jenn! You've got talent too. Just remember to have fun. That's all I do."

Exit Rochelle, bubbly as usual, to the ladies room.

As she disappeared, Lindy got ready to pounce, but Jenn beat her to the punch.

"Lindy," she said solemnly, "I have something to tell you, and I didn't want to say it in front of the others..."

Oh no, thought Lindy. Just shoot me now...

However, what Jenn was about to say wasn't quite what Lindy had feared.

"Lindy," she said, taking a deep breath, "I'm pregnant."

"Um—what?" Spare, stiff, starchy Jenn was—?

"Pregnant."

Oh Dear God. "Was...it...someone from the show?"

"Yes." Jenn was fighting back tears now.

"Was it—?"

"Yes, I knew you'd guess..."

"Malcolm," Lindy sighed. Well, he was a very good father to Sarah...

"Who—? Malcolm? Oh, yuck, no!"

Relieved—yet somewhat offended—Lindy guessed again. "Darrick—?"

"Oh, no-no-no..." wailed Jenn, getting more and more upset as Lindy ran out of male candidates.

But who else could she mean? Leo? And then it dawned on Lindy. Oh boy.

"Terence?" Lindy suggested, and when Jenn, lip trembling, bobbed her head in agreement, added as sympathetically as she could manage, "and I suppose he's denying it?"

Forlornly, Jenn pulled out a neatly folded square of tissue and wiped her weepy eyes. "He says it couldn't possibly be him. We were only together that one time."

Lindy couldn't imagine copulating with Terence even once, but, for her distraught actor's sake, she buried her distaste. "It only takes once, Jenn. He should know that."

"I know," wailed Jenn, dissolving into a fastidious storm of despair, "but-but-but...he says that I must have been with another guy around the same time. I wasn't, Lindy! I've only ever slept with three men in my whole life, and both of the other guys are long gone!"

Unnoticed, Rochelle had returned from the ladies room and caught the end of their conversation.

Silently, she swept Jenn into her arms.

"Don't be scared, Jenn," she soothed, stroking her rigid back. "It'll be okay. You're among friends, and we'll help you do whatever you need to do. I can go with you to the abortion clinic—"

Jenn jerked away from Rochelle's embrace. "Oh no, Rochelle! I'd never do that! Babies are precious. You can't just sweep them from your life like...like crumbs off the floor!"

"Then I'll make sure that you get into the prenatal clinic. That's what 'choice' is all about, don't you think?" Rochelle patted Jenn's shoulder kindly. "Do you know when you're due?"

"Around November fifteenth. Give or take. At least that's what the app said. I'll know more after I talk to a doctor, I guess."

"Yes, you will, Jenn. And, when you know more, you can make the rest of your choices." Rochelle cocked an ear. "Now, hustle off and tidy up. The guys will be back in no time."

"Thanks, Rochelle," mumbled Jenn and fled.

Rochelle looked shrewdly at Lindy, who hadn't been a part of that last bit of conversation.

"You ever have a kid, Lindy?"

Lindy shook her head. "No, not even a niece or a nephew, in fact."

"It's not compulsory," chuckled Rochelle. "Between us, Serge the Orthodontist and I have three, and sometimes I think they're the best thing in my life, and sometimes I wish I was on a fast boat to China. I think Jenn's going to find it pretty difficult on her own. It's messy, for one thing, and expensive, for another, and you can't just up and quit. Or, I guess some people do, but you have to be fucking tough to do that."

"Malcolm has a daughter." Lindy didn't know why she was confiding that to Rochelle. She supposed she was trying to demonstrate by association that she wasn't averse to kids, even if she'd never particularly envied women who had them. "And a grandson who he loves very much..."

Rochelle regarded her astutely.

"And he loves you very much too." Then she gave Lindy—blushing to hear an independent confirmation of Malcolm's affection spoken aloud—a broad commedia dell'arte wink. "Don't worry, babe. November's a hell of a long time away and skinny Jenn won't show until at least July. Playing a lead's something she'll probably never get a chance to do again, so I doubt she'll quit if she has a choice."

They could hear the men stomping the slush off their feet outside of the hall door.

"Besides, if Jenn does decide it's all just too much for her, there are plenty of other good actors out there, *n'est-ce pas?* Oh, hi guys!" Rochelle called as Darrick, Leo and Malcolm trundled in. "Is it snowing yet?"

With Rochelle's view of the situation to chew on, Lindy gathered her thoughts. Jenn soon rejoined the group, and the rehearsal carried on unscathed.

* * * * *

March died in a blizzard. April shook off its blanket of snow and arose, warm and wet.

Feeling kind of foolish, Lindy submitted her show for consideration by the Prix Bytown Awards. She signed and returned the official Festival letter of invitation so that the actors would get paid and sent in her on-line listing update. Then it was time to gather at the Arts Court again to hear all about marketing and publicity.

"The trick is to make boatloads of money—all on the cheap!" advised Marie-Paule, the Fimbria Festival's perky Haitian-Canadian marketing guru. A hundred bucks should be enough for photography, posters, and flyers, she declared, although Lindy didn't think the young woman was adding in the cost of accessing the apps on a smartphone or cruising the internet. For young women in their twenties, the price of their social media access was as necessary for life as the cost of food or shelter, and they never counted the toll.

"Scrounge around. Beg, borrow and steal. Get steep discounts, get it for free, get your family and friends to do it. Do it yourself!"

In fact, 'Do It Yourself' was the main theme of the budgeting section. DYI poster distribution, DIY flyering, DYI publicity. Rely on word of mouth—that mythic 'wom'—and use social media extensively. Flog your show to local print and broadcast media. Let everybody know you're in the Festival and be ready to rock and roll.

And do it sooner than now.

Lindy and Malcolm watched the presentation, studied the examples, made lots of notes. But they both knew that, once more, they were innocents in the wild compared to even the least social media savvy twenty- or thirty- or forty-something at the workshop.

Posting on multiple platforms came naturally to those who hadn't yet reached their sixtieth birthday. Their handheld devices held more computing power than Lindy's current laptop and Malcolm's three-year-old desktop combined. They understood what others meant when they texted in acronyms. They knew how to condense their messages into bit-sized chunks of Twitter. They realized innately that people's attention spans were now measured in micro-seconds.

Yes, despite Malcolm's smartphone, he and Lindy were old in years and ancient in terms of modern technology.

Even though they'd made their livings in a library and as a Geography professor, extensively involved with data and information for their whole working lives—and weren't entirely uninformed about computers—they weren't wholly comfortable with them either. Both Lindy and Malcolm still preferred to speak to people face-to-face or to hear a live voice on the other end of the phone. Hopefully, they agreed, the skills they possessed in face-time and live-voice situations would help with the flyering of the Fimbria-going public as potential patrons waited in line for other shows to go in. But they both had to admit that the finer points of Fimbria on-line marketing that Marie-Paule enthusiastically recommended completely eluded them.

"Hi!" barked the whippet-faced thirty-ish guy seated beside Malcolm after the workshop's Q&A session ran down. "I'm Chuckie Calamansi from Actually Moving On Productions. I used to work with a bunch of merry thespians, but this year I'm bringing my one-man *bouffon* clown show, *Ramblin' Jones*, to the Fimbria. Who're you guys and what's your excuse?"

"We're Malcolm Macoun and Lindy Styre, from The Friends of Phyllis Theatre Company," readily replied Malcolm, "and we're producing a melodrama called *Small Comforts*—"

"Strictly speaking, it's a drama," Lindy crisply maintained.

"—and it's going to be an unqualified disaster."

Lindy favoured Malcolm with a sour glare.

"I hear ya, brother," commiserated Chuckie. "I've done multo of these Fests and I should know the ropes. But this single-hander's gonna be the death of me." He mimed tying a noose around his neck, which he then pulled tight, cocking his head and sticking his tongue out.

"Great," grinned Malcolm. "If we see your ghost around the Fimbria, we'll buy it a drink."

Chuckie grinned back. "As the skeleton said to the barman, 'I'll take a beer and a mop.'"

And with that exchange, Lindy supposed, she and Malcolm were officially inducted into the fellowship of Fimbria artists. Or were at least 'in' enough to buy them free drinks.

Which might turn out to be exactly the same thing.

With a quiver of expectancy, Lindy acknowledged that—no matter what snags and pitfalls Dad and Greg would have predicted—she'd soon find out.

CHAPTER TEN

Measure for Measure

"Push the sofa in front of the fireplace—"

"We should have left the rug down. It's going to wreck the hardwood—"

"Never mind. The floor's ninety years old. It'll have to be refinished if I ever sell this hovel anyhow. Now, lift that corner of the sofa up a bit—"

"It's too heavy, Lindy. For Christ's sake, think of my back!"

"Malcolm," sighed Lindy, "it has to be done. Now, come on—bend your knees, lift, and push—!"

The obstinate old brontosaur of a sofa finally slid into place.

"Okay," puffed Lindy, "that looks good." She surveyed her mainly empty living room. "With the sofa smooshed over there, it's about sixteen by twelve, so we've got enough square feet to just about equal the venue's stage area, give or take a few backstage bits."

"The sofa's blocking your bookcase—" sighed Malcolm.

"Whatever. There's no more money for rehearsal space, so it's simply got to work."

It was Madelyn, as usual, who had forced this sorry outcome.

"Lindy," she'd boasted over the phone, "I have just saved us sooo much cash, hon! Mes Antiquités Précieuses—you know?—they've been on Sussex in the Market forever?—well, Archie's going out of business, and everything left in the shop is going for simply a song! He's retiring to Paris and desperate to get rid of his stuff, so I bargained him down and got us the most perfect table and chairs—completely in period—for—wait for it!—seven hundred and fifty dollars! All we have to do now is rent a truck or a van or something to haul them away."

"Seven hundred—" Lindy had breathed, afraid that she might faint.

"—and fifty, hon. Well, that's not including tax. But it's a fantastic deal! On its own, the vintage oak table was originally over a thousand. And the chairs—well, I had to take all four, but they're oak too and sooo beautiful with their pressed backs—they were tagged at two hundred each. I saved us over half! Steal of the century, I'd say..."

Lindy's mouth had gone dry, and it took a lot of throat clearing for her to croak, "Can you cancel the order, Maddie? Can you get your money back?"

"Why would I want to do that?" Madelyn had been totally mystified. "Besides, I only put down two hundred dollars—I knew you'd pay me back—and I promised Archie you'd give him the rest in cash when you picked the furniture up. You've only got until Friday morning, by the way. That's the day Archie's closing for good."

"But Madelyn—"

Yet Lindy had known that protests were useless. Madelyn had probably signed the sales slip in blood. "Okay," she'd sighed. And sighed again. Really loudly. So that nitwit Madelyn would hear. "Maybe Malcolm can call his friend with the truck."

Once he'd finished venting to Lindy, Malcolm had calmed down enough to make some rather unsatisfactory calls and, promptly on Thursday morning, the overpriced 'antiques' arrived via an expensive rental van at Lindy's house.

One of the chairs was wobbly, requiring quite a bit of glue, so, along with most of her living room furniture, Malcolm had helped Lindy put the rickety one in her basement and piled the other three chairs in a corner of her dining room. The scratched up table top, with its unattached legs and two extra leaves, had been leaned against her sideboard, dwarfing that solid piece of Victoriana.

"The table looks so much more massive than it did in the shop," frowned Madelyn, who had arrived at Lindy's door promptly after all the work had been done. Her head tilted judgmentally to one side, she enquired, "Are you sure that Archie gave you the right one?"

Malcolm, who'd wrenched his back wrestling the behemoth into Lindy's house, muttered curses under his breath and stomped into the kitchen. He clutched the edge of the sink hard and stared sullenly out of the window at the new baby squirrels rioting in the maple trees in Lindy's backyard.

Sagely, Lindy decided to give her ex-husband, who looked mere seconds away from apoplexy, an uninterrupted moment of peace. She retrieved a large sketch pad from the top of the glass-doored apothecary case her grandparents had used as a sideboard and opened it out on her dining room table.

"I've got a few ideas for our poster," she said to Madelyn, who was texting like mad on her phone and didn't reply. "Madelyn, our poster? Maddie!"

Her friend looked up, surprised. "Why are you yelling at me, Lindy? I'm right here. What's this on the table?" She drew the pad toward her and smiled indulgently. "Oh, hon, you do try, don't you? But you should leave the art to the artists." Maddie indicated herself with a modest flutter.

"They're just ideas," snapped Lindy, nettled. She'd laboured for hours on those mock-ups, and she figured they were quite...arty, for lack of a better word. "At any rate, you haven't come up with anything better."

Which was generous, since Madelyn hadn't come up with anything at all.

"Okay, don't get your knickers in a twist." Madelyn bent to study what Lindy had drawn. "Actually, hon, this one's not too bad. I like the spectral dog in the cabinet and the tarot cards on the table. But it's too crowded. It lacks drama. And where are we going to put all our information?"

"Here," said Lindy, pointing, "and here."

"Mmm, no. It'll be too...messy. Look, get me your art case and I'll fix it, hon. Or, no, I'll start again but use the primary motifs." Maddie sat down, turned to a fresh page, selected one of the pencils that Lindy had fetched her and began to sketch.

Lindy left Maddie to work her artistic magic and moved the three pressed back chairs into the living room.

Then she went in to the kitchen where Malcolm was rooting through the refrigerator for a bottle of apple juice.

"Are you ready to help me put the table in the living room?"

"Yeah."

Not much of a response, but at least he was still talking to her, thought Lindy.

Malcolm poured a glass of juice, threw it back and followed Lindy into the dining room. As quietly as possible, so as not to disturb Madelyn's artistic inspiration, the pair hoisted the oak table top and half-lifted and half-dragged it into the centre of what was to become the Company's new rehearsal hall. Malcolm transferred the legs in too, and, with the top upside down on the floor, began to attach them with a screw driver.

Lindy measured the available rehearsal space left around the table top with her eyes. She hated to say it but—

"Um, Malcolm. Wait," she urged. "I kind of think we have a problem here."

Malcolm put down his screwdriver, took a look around and regarded her wearily.

"Really."

It wasn't a question. It was a statement. He could see the trouble as plain as day.

The table was going to be too big for the space. If they used the heavy wooden monster, the actors would have no place to act.

"Dammit, Madelyn!" he snarled, rising, "you've fucked us all over again!"

Madelyn looked up, startled. "What? Why?"

"You stupid—!"

Lindy grabbed her sputtering friend by the arm. "Stop, Malcolm!" she urged. "That's not going to help. Maddie's just been...Madelyn. Leave her alone..."

Malcolm turned on Lindy instead. "She's destroyed our budget, wrecked my back—and you're sticking up for her? What the hell, Lindy! I thought you wanted me to be your 'conscience' in this catastrophe—a watch dog for your bequest! And I can't do my job if you're going to excuse her for frittering away all our money every damn time!" Malcolm finally paused for breath, but, before Lindy could reply to his charges, plunged on—although, seeing Lindy's pleading eyes, more quietly this time. "Do you realize where our budget is now? In the La Brea tar pits. That's right—totally sunk and out of air. We've got about a hundred left for the posters and flyers and printing and stuff, but, otherwise, we're done."

Lindy let go of his arm and bit her lip. "What about the thousand in reserve?" she asked. "We can tap into that, can't we?"

"Marvelous idea, hon!" Madelyn chimed in from the dining room.

Malcolm rolled his eyes, completely exasperated with having to deal with two foolish spendthrifts. "That's supposed to be for emergencies," he stressed, as if explaining something unbelievably self-evident about the Canadian Shield to a wide-eyed freshman. "Not for regular expenses. Unless your roof actually falls in, Lindy, I really don't want to go there."

For a split second, Lindy considered telling her friends about the other twenty thousand dollars she was holding back, but then, just as quickly, she rejected the notion.

Granted, Maddie's spending had been ludicrous, but the Company as a whole had to be held responsible for tearing through that first five thousand. Why should she expect that adding money to the pot would make them, as a group, any more frugal?

"Okay," Lindy declared, smoothing her greying bob behind her ears, "we'll have to make do." She gestured about at her front room. "We've gotten rid of our rehearsal space expenses. So that's a huge saving. And we can use whatever costume pieces and material for props we've already bought—and—and use the pressed back chairs."

Stymied for a moment, Lindy gently kicked the hulking tabletop, but then had a brilliant idea. "And we'll take the leaves out of my folk's dining room table and that'll work too."

Pleased to see Malcolm cautiously nod, she continued more confidently. "I'm just about finished the on-line media questionnaire, which doesn't cost a thing, and Madelyn's getting our poster in gear." Then, just when she needed a big finish to really hearten the troops, another promising thought occurred to her. "And maybe Darrick can give us some valuable advice about the posters! He's done Fimbria before. A couple of times, I think. He probably knows what to do and where to go to get them on the cheap. So, perhaps things aren't that bad, guys."

"Ab-solutely!" Madelyn was buoyed by Lindy's words. With renewed enthusiasm, she reapplied herself to pencil and paper.

In agreement, but still viscerally annoyed, Malcolm just grunted and began to unscrew the table leg he'd been fastening. Then he and Lindy manhandled the ugly top and the legs back into the dining room and—after asking oblivious Madelyn to tidy up her job and stand up—removed the leaves from Lindy's dining room table. It shrank to a gratifying round which was easily shifted into the living room.

While Madelyn resettled on the 'set,' Lindy helped Malcolm screw the legs on the oak colossus and hoist it, with many squawks and groans, upright in the midst of the dining room, where it occupied way more space, unleafed, than Lindy's two leafed wooden table had.

"Stop interrupting my muse!" protested Maddie, as they reassigned her and her drawing pad back into the dining room again. "Oh my gawd, the top of this table is sooo bumpy..."

Lindy and Malcolm took a mutual deep breath, did not allow themselves the joy of throttling Maddie and proceeded to move all the furniture into position in the living room.

Then, while Malcolm ran the rental van back to the shop, Lindy whipped up both egg salad and vegan cheese sandwiches and heated canned vegetarian vegetable soup for their lunch, which they all consumed with well-earned appetites when he returned forty-five minutes later.

The actors arrived one at a time about a half hour after that.

Darrick, who had never been to Lindy's house before, came first. Carefully, he placed Leo on the vestibule floor while he hung up his Burberry raincoat and Tilley hat. Phyllis, alerted by the unfamiliar fearful doggie smell, padded over to investigate, throwing the quivering chihuahua into a frenzy of panicky yips. Unimpressed by the tiny doggington arf, the cat regarded with him with undisguised disdain and, queen of her domain, sat to lick a velvet paw.

"Well, hello, lovely pussycat," smiled Darrick.

Realizing that she had an admirer, Phyllis bestowed a baleful glare upon the actor, stood up and, with a flick of her tail, stalked off.

Scooping up his tiny companion, whom he fondly shushed, Darrick accepted Malcolm's invitation to come through to the dining room to await his fellow actors. Lindy, who had been shuffling furniture in the basement and missed Leo's meltdown, joined them as Madelyn offered the actor her poster design to critique.

"Interesting," allowed Darrick, but it was painfully obvious that he wasn't excited by her sketch.

"Ooooohhh..." Madelyn dragged out the monosyllable so it meant, 'Well, that's your opinion, Bub.'

Darrick was undeterred. "I like the spooky dog. But the design is too jampacked. It lacks punch. And where are you going to put all our information?"

Scornfully, The Empress slid her pencils over to her 'dear friend.' "If you can do better, Darrick, be my guest."

"Look," he said, flipping to a new page and beginning to sketch with the hand that wasn't holding Leo, "it needs to be simpler, more defined. How about we take that ghost dog and make it into the central image."

Lindy moved closer to watch as Darrick deftly drew a barking spectral dog's head—remarkably like Leo's—in the centre of the paper. He quickly added *Small Comforts* as a header in deliberately shaky script and indicated with blank lines where the rest of the Festival information would fit.

"That's amazing!" exclaimed Lindy with honest admiration. "It just pops! Can we use it for our poster, Darrick?"

"It's rather naive, I think. But if you like it, Lindy..." Madelyn sniffed and got up to go answer the doorbell.

Malcolm studied Darrick's design. "I like it," he decided, "but do we want a drawing, Darrick? Or would it be more effective if it were a photo? Doctored, you know, to look scary."

Spotting Phyllis glowering wickedly down at him from her lofty perch atop the sideboard, Leo let out a frightened whine.

Darrick laughed and petted his support animal. "Well, my goodness, Leo certainly believes that a photo would be best. What do you think, Rochelle?" he asked the actor whom Madelyn had ushered into the dining room. "A drawing or a photo?"

"Oooh, that's really nice, Darrick," smiled Rochelle, examining his work. "But how about a double-focused photo so there'd be movement—you know, like he's actually shivering with fear?"

"Yes," said Darrick, eagerly adding lines that made the drawn dog tremble with ague, "you're so correct. And I have several of Leo's portraits that will work perfectly."

Rubbing the tiny dog's ear, Rochelle laughed to him, "*Très cool*, Leo!"

Easily picturing the final poster, Lindy enthused, "Wonderful, Darrick!"

Ostensibly fixated on her smartphone's apps, Madelyn remained unmoved.

The doorbell sounded again.

Leaving Malcolm to work out the technical and printing details with Darrick and Rochelle, Lindy went to answer the door.

CHAPTER ELEVEN

As You Like It

Only she was allowed to quit!

It was a new rule she'd just thought up.

Damn it to hell! What was the matter with actors?

Lindy was striding down her street. She got to the corner and kept on going over the cross street and straight toward Bank.

Damn Jenn!

Damn Terence!

Damn—Taffy—?

Taffy, the spoodle.

Lindy came to a skidding halt.

Yes, that was Taffy. Way down on the next block, but, yes, it was that sinister doggington ruff. Who she couldn't see completely clearly because—damn, damn, damn!—she'd fled out of her house so fast, she'd forgotten to put on her protective sunglasses.

And Taffy really hated her guts.

But she seemed to be on a leash, thank God, and was still half a block away on the other side of the next cross street.

Alternative actions flashed through Lindy's brain.

She could turn around and scoot as fast as possible back to the safety of her house.

No, Taffy's long-legged owner would just overtake her stubby ones and, with her back turned to the on-coming danger, she wouldn't be able to see Taffy catching up.

Not safe.

She could cross the street and then beetle back home. But then Taffy would lap her progress from across the street.

Not safe either.

Or, she could cross the street and carefully continue walking toward Bank.

But that presented a similar problem. Her jangled nerves were telling her that passing within Taffy's sniff-zone wasn't safe in any direction.

Plus, she realized, glancing back up her one-way street, there were three cars in a row coming from behind her, so she couldn't immediately bolt across.

Damn, damn, damn!

Taffy had reached the cross street. Maybe the dog would turn right or left...but, no, Taffy was crossing the intersection and heading dead toward her.

To her left, Lindy was aware of a stone walk leading to the stairs up to a sheltered porch. In a split second, she was on the porch, huddled behind a brick post.

Briskly, Taffy and his owner strode by.

Letting out her held breath in a rush, Lindy cautiously stood up, looked about her—and was shocked to discover that tied to a spindle at the other end of the porch, regarding her with mild surprise, was a large golden retriever, a honey-coloured doggington woof.

Lindy froze.

The dog's mouth split into an open friendly smile. Hello, its soft brown eyes said. How nice of you to visit me.

The house door opened and a young mother holding a toddler looked out.

"Hi—?" she began. "Can I help you?" She appraised Lindy's ashen face. "Oh, I know who you are," she continued lightly.

Putting her child down and ordering her dog, "Stay, Goldie," the young mom swiftly slipped past Lindy to glance up and down the block. Seeing Taffy's owner climbing up the front steps to his veranda, she smiled and waved, "Hi, Danny!" and turned to reassure Lindy, "Taffy's going into her house—it's safe to leave now."

Taking the toddler's hand, the young mom then walked over to Goldie and, squatting down to grab her collar, said to Lindy, "Don't worry, I'll hold her 'til you get down the stairs."

Her toddler reached out, giggling, to tug the dog's fluffy ear. Goldie's grin got wider and she yawned.

Taking a chance on trusting the young woman to actually hold on tightly to her dog, Lindy stumbled down to the stone walk and hurried to the roadway. Then, ashamed of her absurd fear, she turned and waved.

"Thanks," she called weakly, and then added more firmly, "I'm Lindy, by the way."

From the end of the porch, where her toddler was now hugging the gentle dog, the young mom smiled and called back pleasantly, "Yes, I thought so. I'm Brittany. Bye now."

"Bye," returned Lindy and darted up the street to the sanctuary of her own front porch. Taking a cleansing deep breath, she opened the door and went inside.

By this time, Jenn had stopped crying and was sitting upright on the sofa that they'd pushed in front of the fireplace tentatively sipping a cup of tea.

"Over your snit?" Malcolm greeted Lindy. He was applying glue to the pressed back of the chair she'd knocked over as she tore out of the room five minutes ago.

Madelyn and Darrick craned around the corner from the dining room looking concerned. Leo cocked an enquiring ear.

Leaning against the doorway to the kitchen, Rochelle glanced up briefly from her phone and gave Lindy a supportive wink.

"I broke the chair?" Lindy felt more of a fool than ever. "I'm so sorry, guys. I just lost it." With relief, she saw Jenn respond with a watery smile.

"Apology accepted, my dear" granted Darrick magnanimously, as he and Leo came into the living room and took a seat on the set. "It's not unusual for artists to be temperamental, and we've certainly all witnessed far worse behaviour from far inferior talents in far less trying circumstances."

"Thanks, Darrick," grimaced Lindy, "but I think I'm maybe taking my play too seriously. I need to step away and look at the bigger picture." She gave Jenn a sympathetic nod. "If Jenn's wiped out by morning sickness all day long, of course she can't carry on. And Madelyn will be fine as Mary Yerst."

"Mary?" exclaimed Maddie, following Darrick's example by alighting in a wooden chair in the living room. "Oh no, hon! If I volunteer to be part of the cast again, I will re-assume the role of Bridget Peever. You wouldn't expect me to learn a whole new set of character's lines this late in the rehearsal period, would you?"

Despite her best efforts, Lindy felt her anger rising again. Since Madelyn hadn't learned any lines in the first place, what possible difference could it make now if she played Mary instead of Ms. Peever? But aloud she asked, "So who would you suggest for Mary?"

Madelyn looked perplexed. "Well, Rochelle, of course."

"Not happening." Rochelle had pocketed her phone and joined the group, settling in beside Jenn on the sofa. "I'm a Peever in this production or I quit too."

Her comment brought a murmur of dissent from the rest of the Company, but Rochelle cut them off with a laugh. "Fortunately, I don't think we have to worry about that. I just phoned my husband—you know, Serge the Orthodontist?—and told him that he's got to do a fabulous deal with an actor that I know. He's union, but permission isn't usually too hard to get. Darrick could handle that for us."

"Yes, it was no trouble to obtain last year," agreed Darrick, helpfully.

"I don't understand." Lindy was beginning to lose hope once more.

"It's simple," said Rochelle, infinitely patient with her newbie director. "Serge has a practice where he fixes a lot of smiles, but he charges a ton of money for it. So, if he offers this certain professional actor some *pro bono* dental work in exchange for his artistic services, I'll bet we can get a topnotch Mary for free. How about it? Will you trust me on this one?"

"And just for extra reassurance, I can ask around as well," Darrick chimed in. "I wonder if Philippe would still be at liberty this late in the game?"

"Um, thanks, Darrick," said Lindy, "but we're looking for the role of Mary, you know, and she's definitely a woman."

Darrick was amused. "Philippe has played many a female, my dear. Last year poor dear Pierre cast him as Grandmother Fitz-Engel in my Fimbria show. All very Shakespearean breeches kind of thing."

"Yes, I remember him," said Lindy, thoughtfully. "He was excellent." She frowned. "But I still think Mary would be best played by an actual woman—"

"So conventional. So very twentieth century," interrupted Madelyn, shaking her head at Darrick while nodding toward Lindy. "If you think you can get Philippe, Darrick, for goodness sake invite him in. He may be all that saves us from total disgrace."

Rochelle and Darrick contented themselves with quizzical glances, but Malcolm sprang up hastily from the floor.

"Oh shut up, Madelyn!" he snapped. "Lindy can do without all your negativity!"

Madelyn's raised her nose in the air. "I'm only saying, Malcolm, that if we fail to find acting talent on par with the rest of the cast, we open ourselves to—"

"You're only saying that Lindy's an old fart and her opinion doesn't count!"

"I said no such thing, Malcolm! And I would thank you not to—"

"Not to what—? Point out that you're—"

"Aaarrrggggghhhhh—!"

The pair went silent and stared at Lindy's crimson face.

"Stop it! Stop it! Stop it! I can't stand this anymore!" she howled at her startled friends. "Now, I'm going upstairs and when I come down, you, Madelyn, and you, Malcolm, had better be gone! I'm finished with your bickering and I want to rehearse my play in peace!"

With that, Lindy stomped upstairs to the bathroom and locked herself in.

Malcolm snorted something that sounded like "Fine!" and, with a general wave, swiftly gathered his gear and headed out the door.

Coming out of her shock, Madelyn pursed her mouth, flounced over to the front vestibule, grabbed her wraps and turned back to pontificate to the remaining Company.

"If you people want to stay after that—that rude outburst, I pity you! I, myself, refuse to be treated in this cavalier way." She assumed a righteous tone. "You may tell Lindy that I have very grave doubts about the artistic direction in which she is taking this play. And I will not be any part of a failing production. It has been a privilege to work with you all. Farewell."

Unfortunately, Madelyn had taken so long to begin leaving, Lindy had caught the last bit of the speech as she rounded the top flight of the staircase.

"Sure, Maddie," she said bitterly, descending to the main floor, "you go ahead and quit too. I'll put on my show without you. And, like you say, the play may fail—but at least I'm in it for the long haul. Now, I'm going to brew myself a cup of tea and we'll get started. Actors, please review your scripts. Jenn, if you're well enough, will you please read Mary one final time? Thank you."

Lindy stalked into the kitchen with Phyllis trailing hopefully behind.

"You should all be jumping out of this bus right now," declared Madelyn spitefully. "It's heading for a precipice, and soon it'll crash and burn!"

"Oh, I doubt that, my dear," replied Darrick, contentedly stroking Leo as he opened his script.

"Well, I don't doubt it at all!" snarled Madelyn. "This show was doomed from day one! And I'm getting off this ride—right NOW!"

Maddie slammed out the front door.

Looking up from checking her phone, Rochelle laughed again. "You never know, Madelyn," she purred toward the empty front vestibule with her wickedest grin. "Lindy's managed to steer us safely up the mountain track so far. And there may be one or two surprises hitchhiking along the side of the road."

"Amen," agreed Darrick, petting Leo with a complacent smile.

* * * * *

The year was moving towards mid-May, the Fimbria Festival website was firing on all cylinders, and tickets were already up for sale.

To Lindy's gratification—and Malcolm's astonishment—a small number of seats for their assorted performances had already been snapped up.

Rochelle and Darrick were less impressed.

They're for family, they explained, and friends and acquaintances and maybe some workmates. People who'd be coming anyway. The trick is to get the general public's bums in your seats—and, with so many Fimbria choices, that might be a lot harder. They advised Lindy and Malcolm not to bother checking their ticket sales again until the Festival was actually on.

Still, The Friends of Phyllis felt pretty chuffed.

Even Madelyn who, after several days of moping about and sending condescending messages to Lindy and superior notes to Malcolm, had decided that the others probably couldn't continue without her valuable artistic contribution. All was forgiven—on her part at least—and she graciously returned to the fold.

Rochelle's new actor had also turned up—a male after all—but precisely the one in that tenuous family drama at last June's Fimbria who'd made Lindy wholeheartedly believe that he was a doddering ninety-year-old grandmother right up to the final bow.

Philippe.

So Darrick's candidate as well.

And sad-eyed Philippe Tangor, the most pliable and charming of actors with his slender body and crooked smile, took the role of Mary Yerst to heights to which Lindy never would have aspired with spare Jenn. For, as soon as Philippe began to read, he didn't merely become a caricature of a woman—he portrayed an actual female. He didn't merely say her dialogue—he spoke as Mary. He didn't merely act like Mary—he became Mary.

And Mary Yerst became genuine, she became vulnerable, she came alive in her world. The lonely, angry, wistful desperation that had driven her to the psychics' lair underlay his every line, every word, every measured pause. And for the first time Lindy truly appreciated what her Elizabethan Literature Professor had meant when she'd gravely praised the extraordinary talent that gender-bending male actors must have possessed to tackle ambitious female roles like caustic Beatrice or clever Rosalind or fractious Kate.

Catalyzed by Mary's new energy, Rochelle's and Darrick's performances seemed to amplify and, by Philippe's second rehearsal, Lindy's *Small Comforts* had begun to breathe on its own. Lindy hoped that her direction had something to do with this state of affairs but humbly had to accept that much of what was improving in the show had obviously developed from Mary's and the Peevers' refreshed relationship.

But now the point was past where Lindy felt that Darrick should have relinquished his grip on Leo. It was all very well, she told herself sternly, to allow Darrick the comfort of holding the cute little guy in rehearsals, but she was determined not to have any doggington arf—even one as docile as Leo—taking attention away from the plot or the other actors at their Preview performance next week or during their run at the Fimbria Festival.

Taking a deep breath to steady herself, Lindy turned to her self-diagnosed social-anxiety-prone actor.

"I know what we're going to do with Leo," she announced in her most no-nonsense tone and continued confidently with the direction, "Darrick, while you're on stage, Leo can lie comfortably backstage in this doggie bed that I bought for him yesterday."

She displayed the bed, a perfect cloud of warm fuzziness.

How could Darrick refuse?

Easily.

And with emphasis.

Guarding Leo from the sight of the homewrecker who wanted to come between their precious friendship, he leapt up and spat, "I quit."

"No," moaned Lindy, as the other members of the Company watched with interest. "Look, Darrick, it's a beautiful bed—so soft and snuggly. Leo will love it and—"

But, without another word, Darrick strode to the front vestibule and, setting Leo down on his trembling little legs, shrugged into his Burberry raincoat.

"Darrick," pleaded Lindy, following him as far as the hall, "please! The play makes no sense if Mary spends all her time at the psychics with a dog. She's supposed to be morbidly terrified of them. If she'd walked into their office and seen Leo, she'd have walked right out again. You must see that?" Darrick, donning his Tilley hat, appeared unmoved, so Lindy decided to change tack. "And you can't quit just before our Preview. Show some loyalty to your fellow actors!"

Without a word, Darrick picked up his chihuahua and hooked his umbrella over his free arm. He put his hand deliberately on the door knob and gave it a twist.

"Okay! Okay!" With no other option, Lindy gave in.

His hand still on the door knob, Darrick regarded her with suspicion. "'Okay,' you'll allow Leo on stage? Or 'okay,' you'll lure us back in, but secretly plan to eventually exclude my emotional support companion from the play?"

With no other foreseeable option, Lindy caved completely. "If the others don't mind, we'll figure out how to do it with Leo on stage," she sighed.

Satisfied, Darrick went into reverse and soon was back in the living room among his fellow Friends of Phyllis.

"So," Lindy said, wearily flopping on to the sofa, "does anyone have any suggestions about how we're going to do this?"

"Perhaps Leo could be portrayed as a cat," gently offered Philippe. "He's smaller than Phyllis."

Rochelle and Madelyn nodded.

Darrick looked pleased. "Of course," he said, "Leo would make a perfect cat."

"But he doesn't look anything like a cat!" protested Lindy.

"Well, there is his name..." Malcolm suggested slyly.

Rochelle snickered, but Lindy thought sourly that her ex had never seemed so unattractive.

"With the magic of costuming—" began Darrick.

"—perhaps a headpiece?" proposed Philippe.

"—and some sort of fake kitty fur over his service coat?" added Rochelle.

For a moment Lindy wondered if she was the dupe in an elaborate prank, but, looking around, realized that everybody speaking was deadly serious. They all honestly thought poor little Leo could pull it off.

She had to say something. "But what if he barks?"

"He's never made a peep during rehearsals," replied Darrick smoothly, "and I don't see why he would start now."

Again, the others nodded.

"But the Fimbria stage will be different. There'll be an audience for one thing. And music and lights and noise and special effects—"

"I'll tell you what, Lindy."

Now Darrick was prepared to be reasonable? Lindy hoped so, but nope.

"Leo will play my cat in the Preview, and, if that goes smoothly, as I believe it will, we will say no more about marooning him backstage. Yes, Madame Director?"

Lindy's head hurt. She had a lot of other nagging problems and this one didn't look like it was going to be solved any time soon. Maybe she ought to simply surrender and live to fight another day.

"Okay," she sighed, "and, Leo," she said, addressing the little dog directly, "I hope you'll be ready for your close-up."

Darrick smiled and, raising one of chihuahua's teensy paws, swore in a little dog voice, "I promise I will," then added in his own, "and, my dear, you'll expect me to take Leo's lovely new doggie bed home with us, of course?"

All through the rehearsal and into the evening, Lindy's head continued to throb with those other nagging problems. Among the most demanding were those related to the technical flourishes that she was pretty sure would spook Leo. Specifically, the sound effects and music.

Nagging problem number one.

She'd trusted Malcolm to find a sound effects tape for the séance scene, and she'd found that her confidence had been sorely misplaced.

Malcolm had bought a CD full of corny Halloween noises at the thrift store. He was trying to co-ordinate them on a master when, reading the small print on the box, he'd discovered that the producer of the tape required permission to use it for professional—that is, for money-making—performances. Therefore, although he suspected that the producer in question would never hear of it, he now was hesitant to employ the CD's chain-rattling and ghostly groans in their show.

When, at Lindy's urging, Malcolm consulted Darrick, to her annoyance, the seasoned Fimbrian supported his reluctance.

"You never know who'll show up in the audience," he cautioned, "and with everyone having a smartphone in their pocket..." He shook his head, foreboding doom.

As an alternative, Darrick suggested that the actors themselves make an original sound tape—as the Peevers undoubtably would have, he assured Lindy—and, along with Rochelle and Philippe, volunteered to produce it. The resulting spectral hubbub, recorded at a hilarious actors-only dinner at Darrick's place, sounded like, as Lindy's Mom would have described it, nothing on God's green earth. Lindy was reluctant to use it, but Malcolm and Madelyn were in favour of employing the tape—it was free, after all—and so they did. But, even with Malcolm modifying the volume and intensity, she winced at the way its unholy racket reverberated in her living room.

Then there was nagging problem number two.

No matter which way you accessed it, music was not free, Madelyn had argued in March. So why not invest in the cachet of a live musician with an original score?

And, Maddie had declared, she had the perfect fit for their show! Her younger sister's eldest son, eighteen-year-old Merrill, was at this very moment studying composition at a prestigious private academy and, for a mere pittance, had agreed to provide their play with both his genius and his presence.

The 'mere pittance' had turned out to be five hundred dollars for the composition and—instead of a share of the ticket sales—a flat two hundred and fifty for the run.

Oh Dear God, no, Lindy had thought.

But "It's such a fabulous deal!" had enthused Madelyn.

And so, Lindy had reluctantly decided, the teenaged boy had to be hired and paid because he was, after all, Madelyn's nephew.

The score, when thickset musician Merrill had appeared in Lindy's living room on another rainy May afternoon, was arranged for oboe—which Merrill played—and viola—which he didn't. Because of this, he'd brought along a viola-playing friend who, unfortunately, would not be available during the Fimbria Festival—but Merrill had promised he'd find someone else to take the gig.

"Not a professional," Lindy had specified, belatedly putting her budgetary foot down. "Just find another student who'd take two or three hundred bucks for the run."

Luckily, by now Malcolm—who'd already surrendered the thousand-dollar reserve for general expenses—had given up shouting, so the extra three hundred dollars— Lindy should never have given Merrill a range of payment possibilities—passed quietly into the Company's bleeding ledgers. The music, which consisted of entrance and exit themes for each character, some mood music and a finale, sounded fine but, as Lindy sighed to herself, it had been awfully expensive for what it was.

For the show's subsequent music and tech runs, the two young musicians who arrived set up in the dining room. There was Merrill on oboe and a delicate Chinese exchange student named Hua who, surprisingly, played flute. Merrill apologized for having to alter the instruments in his arrangement, but said that he couldn't find another viola.

It was okay, though, as Lindy liked the flute music better than the viola, and everyone else seemed pleased that the show now had live musicians. Everyone else, that is, except for poor little Leo who responded to Hua's highest notes with frail whines and whimpers. After much soothing from Darrick, however, and after Merrill asked the flutist to lower her playing a full octave, he eventually settled down into his usual quiet self.

Learning nothing from that experience, at the next music and sound tech Madelyn showed up with Hellmutt— who obviously hated the flute music even more than Leo did. His pained moans and yodeling cries from the basement, Maddie maintained, added piquancy to the macabre mood of the play. Yet, despite Malcolm's cheerful pretense of heartily endorsing the idea, Lindy—her heart stuttering along with Leo's every time the huge Alsatian howled—refused Madelyn's generous offer to record Hellmutt's agonized wails for future use.

So the month of May flowed on.

By just ignoring her mounting self-doubts and soldiering through, Lindy at long last lay down her glue gun and declared that she'd finished building all of the props. Aware that papier mache, fiber board and foam sheets did not constitute the strongest of building materials, she pleaded with the actors to use them gently and not force endless repairs. Then she okayed the working costumes for the show at the retirement residence and submitted the form for including a Volunteer Appreciation night in their Fimbria run.

And, with all that accomplished, Lindy finally summoned the courage to formally invite Greg and Nan to her play. For reasons she couldn't have consciously described, it was tremendously important to her that her older brother see, understand and appreciate what she was doing with Dad's cash bequest.

Initially, Greg was predictably doubtful when she disclosed the creative escapade in which she was now enmeshed.

"A play...?"

"Yes, a play that I wrote," she explained in as bright a tone as she could muster. "I'm directing it now..."

"Oh, I don't know, Lindy," hedged Greg, clearly uncomfortable with his little sister's revelation. "Now that we're retired, that four or five hours to Ottawa's a bit of a hike for us. The highway traffic is a killer and don't gas prices always go up in June? Plus there's that 'Don't leave your dog in a hot car' thing. Nan would be beside herself with worry if we needed to stop. No, we couldn't drive that far with Paulie, so we'd have to pay for a dogsitter until we got home..."

"Well, yes, I guess so," agreed Lindy, relieved to hear Greg's hesitation about bringing their doggington snarl. Then, marshalling her nerves, she jumped in bravely with the counterarguments she'd rehearsed multiple times in her head. "But you know Greg, if you're not bringing Paulie, you and Nan are welcome to stay at my house, so you won't need to pay for a motel. And I'll be glad to cover all your meals while you're here. You could see the nine o'clock show on Friday evening—"

"You mean Friday at nine pee emm—?"

"Well, yes, but we don't get to choose our time slots—they're just assigned—and you'll probably see a better production toward the end of our run when we've had four other performances to get the bugs out. Anyway, it would be great if you could visit for a few days, and you could be on your way whenever you liked. Saturday, Sunday, Monday—whenever you guys felt you wanted to go. I'll be busy at the Festival, but you could use my house as your base and tour Nan around some of the nicer Ottawa tourist sites. Museums, art galleries—you know she'd love those—"

"Well, okay," Greg eventually sighed, "if you really think it would be worth the drive—"

"Yes, I really do."

"Okay. But Nan and I have to have non-allergenic bedding—"

"I'll buy some fresh sheets and pillows tomorrow," promised Lindy, and that was that daunting chore completed too.

The intimidating Preview now loomed large on the near horizon.

Oh, Dear God and all Angels, Lindy prayed nightly—apparently insulated from the nasty voice by her utter exhaustion—please don't let it be a bloodbath...

But God and the Angels never replied.

CHAPTER TWELVE

A Midsummer Night's Dream

"Nothing says 'Fimbria' like a foam typewriter," Philippe sweetly remarked as he carefully tossed the complex prop Lindy had spent three days building to Malcolm, who just as carefully caught it and placed it on the set.

The members of The Friends of Phyllis Theatre Company were loading into what had once been a hotel ballroom, rented out for office Christmas parties and weddings. It had now been repurposed, however, as a spacious activity room at the exclusive retirement residence where Malcolm had booked their Preview.

Dad had died in a suite here, of course, and Lindy had feared that a return to the residence would stir up some rather prickly memories. But she'd found that today, in practice, she was too busy coordinating her Company's set-up to pay much attention to her anxieties.

A raised wooden platform usually used for visiting choirs or olde tymey bands had measured too small. So Rochelle and Madelyn were arranging the brocade covered chairs into three widely spaced rows facing the stage area that Lindy had masking taped on the parquet dance floor.

Brilliantly lit by electric candle wall sconces and ornate hanging chandeliers, the high-ceilinged room didn't seem appropriate for theatre at all. There were no dimmer switches, and it appeared that the only way to lower the light in the room was to entirely turn off either the multiple wall sconces or the large chandeliers.

As she tried clicking off various configurations of the glittering lights, Lindy was approached by a worried young woman who demanded that every single one be turned back on RIGHT NOW. The geriatric residents might not be able to see where their feet were going, she fussed, and they might break a hip if they slipped and fell. So the play would have to be performed in full glare, with no atmospheric lighting at all.

Lindy wondered how the special effects for the séance and the spirit cabinet would work if there couldn't be any level of black out at all—but then decided that she would say 'Preview' very loudly to herself in her head every time she found the ballroom or the play technically lacking. Those kinds of things could be worked out later at the Fimbria venue, she supposed, and she just didn't have the time or energy to dither about them today.

Costumes were another area where worry wasn't going to help.

Thanks largely to Madelyn's hit or miss wardrobe purchases, they had too many different uncomplimentary pieces that didn't fit anyone well, and so they still hadn't come up with final outfits for the actors. Poor nauseous Jenn, who'd said she'd help tailor the costumes whenever she was up to it, hadn't been up to it very often and finally had to return most of the pieces pretty much unaltered. For the Preview, therefore, working costumes had to suffice.

In fact, the only actor who was perfectly togged out was Leo.

Somewhere on the internet, Darrick had found his tiny dog a lion costume hoodie and had skillfully trimmed its faux fur mane and tail. Accustomed to wearing a service coat, Leo seemed comfortable enough and, with the costume's original round ears sharpened to feline pointy ones, if you weren't paying too much attention—and the light wasn't shining directly on him—he did sort of look like a tan-coloured feline nestled in Darrick's arm.

The overlit stage area meant that stage make up was not particularly necessary. So, while the audience slowly trickled in, the actors repaired to a quiet hall adjacent to the ladies' and gentleman's rooms to apply a little powder, lipstick, and mascara, and step into whatever costume pieces they had. Philippe arranged the beautiful short blonde wig he'd selected from his own collection, Darrick combed in hair cream, and Rochelle, having coloured her hair a relatively sedate salt and pepper, gelled it into a short seventies flip.

As Lindy watched their elderly patrons arrive, her heart sank.

About half of the people seemed hale and hearty, chatting brightly as they took their seats. But many limped in clutching canes or walkers, which had to be accommodated nearby, and a number of wheelchair-bound oldsters were pushed into the audience by attendants who unceremoniously shoved the carefully placed chairs aside.

Some carried bags full of knitting. Some had large hearing devices linked to their ears. Some were hooked up to oxygen tanks. Finally, one unfortunate lady, strung about with medical tubes, was trundled in laying on a mobile bed which Lindy helped her attendant park at the far end of the now ragged front row, close to where Merrill and Hua had set up their music stands.

A few minutes after the advertised start time, as the worried young woman had advised, the doors to the ballroom were shut and the show began.

Actually, as it turned out, the audience wasn't too bad. Not everyone followed the plot—one lady loudly asked her friend, "Are these jokers on a boat?"—but most paid, at the very least, courteous, if not quiet, attention.

One group in particular noticed Leo.

"Oh, look, Doris! A pussycat! Isn't she adorable."

"I used to have a ginger one—a fair bit darker than her—with stripes."

"That's a strange looking cat, Rhonda. She looks a little scared."

"Cute, though."

"I didn't say she wasn't cute, just kinda weird."

"Shhhh, Lloyd! You made me miss what the girl just said..."

The audience also commented positively about Mary.

"That's a pretty young lady they chose for the heroine."

"She's got lovely blonde hair."

"And she speaks right up."

But they really didn't like the Peevers.

"A couple of no-good dirty dealers, I'd say, Gladys."

"That's right, Walt. Not to be trusted as far as you can throw'em."

"That nice little girl better watch out..."

The live music was also a hit, with one of the men loudly humming along, and the audience erupted in gratifying chatter whenever the special effects kicked in, lame as they seemed to Lindy due to the shortcomings of the space.

All in all, except for when people disturbed everyone else in their row as they left for or returned from bathroom breaks—and also when the bedridden lady awoke crying "Help! Help!" and had to be wheeled out—the one act show went fairly well.

As the actors and musicians took their bows to polite applause, Lindy wondered what the actors thought. So, while the elderly audience dispersed to their usual middle of the afternoon occupations, she left Malcolm to negotiate load-out with the worried woman and Madelyn to take care of Hua and Merrill, and followed her players backstage to their dressing area to find out.

However, the actors had questions of their own.

"How did we do?" asked Philippe, doffing his wig.

He and his companions regarded Lindy eagerly, and it suddenly occurred to her that they were, of course, expecting directing notes. Guiltily, she acknowledged to herself, she had been so busy fretting about the audience and the technical elements, she hadn't really watched their performances.

"It went okay," she hedged.

Sensing her tentative tone, Philippe's face fell.

"I'm so sorry," he said. "I just got into that dialogue loop and I had trouble finding my way out. The lines are so similar to the ones in scene four..."

"It wasn't too noticeable. You recovered pretty quickly." Lindy flipped her hair behind her ears and hoped against hope that the actors wouldn't notice she was making it up as she went along. "Maybe we should specifically review that passage in our final rehearsals."

"Okay, *c'est bon*." Philippe seemed relieved.

"And what did you think of that new business I threw in with Leo?" Darrick enquired. "Sorry about springing it on you without any warning, my dear."

"Well," said Lindy, glad to be able to speak honestly, "the audience loved it."

"So should I keep it in?"

"Oh, definitely."

"And what about the mix-up with the music?" asked Rochelle. "Sorry, Lindy, but you know I was on my mark. And I hate to throw Merrill and Hua under the bus, but they started in too early, and so I lost my beat, which is why, I think, no one seemed to get my line."

"Next time, you might do better to wait on that, but I'll tell the musicians they've got to pay closer attention to everyone's dialogue. At any rate, the audience really bought into your evil character."

"So I don't need to ramp it up? Was my level okay?"

"Everyone's levels were fine."

Considering how little of the show she remembered, Lindy decided she'd better get away from individual performance assessments somehow.

"Look, guys," she began, attempting to sound reasonable, "we put on a good Preview show for a challenging audience in an impractical space. I think we should just congratulate ourselves for getting past it all in one piece. Everything I saw that needs to be worked on—we'll work on. We've still got some time to iron the wrinkles out." The actors gravely agreed. "So let's give Leo kudos for his sterling performance and motor on out of here."

With perfect timing, Leo gave forth an infrequent, "Arf!"

Everyone laughed, and Lindy escaped back to the ballroom where Malcolm was wrestling alone with the dismantling of the spirit cabinet.

"Sorry about the shit storm," was his cheerful apology as she came over to see if he needed a hand. "I couldn't get the CD player to sync up. That's why most of the sound clues were crap. But you can't fault me for the special effects. Nobody could have got them to work in this freaking blaze."

"You're totally right, Malcolm. This ballroom was not—"

"Lindy," interrupted Madelyn with Merrill and Hua at her heels, "I've got to get the kids downstairs to wait for their bus, but they wanted to speak to you for a moment."

"We just want to say that we're sorry for our problems with volume this afternoon," said Merrill, as Hua, near tears, echoed a mournful, "Sorry..."

"Considering the space, I thought you sounded quite good," said Lindy, racking her brain to try to remember anything at all about their performance.

"Hey, that's nice of you to say. But we forgot to take into account the lousy acoustics in here, and we're both experienced enough to know that that's no excuse."

"Well, right now, I'm more concerned about your timing," replied Lindy, recalling Rochelle's earlier complaint, "and we'll work on that at the next rehearsal."

"Thanks, ma'am. You're pretty chill," replied Merrill.

And so, with Madelyn sheep-dogging, the young musicians, spirits restored, disappeared to the hall.

Now the actors returned and, handing their costumes to Lindy, began to help box up the props and clear out the set. A couple of the hooks on the spirit cabinet were still giving trouble, so Darrick carefully placed Leo, dressed once more in his green canvas vest, on to the floor so that the actor could help brace the cabinet wall with both arms.

For a minute or so, then, Leo was toodling around, sniffing freely about the room. But Lindy was so inured to the wee canine by now, she hardly noticed as she folded costumes into several tote bags she'd placed on chairs in the first row.

Through the open door came a social worker with her tiny Yorkie therapy dog in tow to check out the activity in the ballroom. She approached Malcolm and Darrick to ask what was happening.

Hearing the woman's voice, Lindy looked up. The second dog was another doggington arf, she saw, which made her nerves tense, but it was firmly leashed and on the other side of the stage area. Therefore, she swallowed hard, snapped her mental elastic band—Crack!—and continued her packing.

The spirit cabinet swayed precariously. Darrick asked the social worker if she'd mind holding a corner. She dropped her dog's leash and leant in.

The pint-sized therapy dog stood, untethered.

Leo emerged from where he'd been snuffling under the chair next to Lindy and wandered onto the Yorkie's radar.

Both dogs froze.

Then, trailing its leash, the Yorkie began to move forward, offering a friendly, "Ruff?"

Leo tucked in his tail and scuttled behind Lindy.

The Yorkie sidled nearer, but when Leo gave a whimper of fear, he stopped mid-dance-floor and flattened his ears. A teensy growl arose in his throat.

Leo emitted a terrified squeak.

For a split second, Lindy was the living centre of a miniature dog-off.

Fight? her panicking nerves demanded. Or flight?

Never able to stand her ground when threatened by a vicious canine, Lindy turned to flee. Snatching up her actor by his green vest, she clambered onto the nearest empty chair.

"Go away!" Lindy shrieked from the heights at the startled Yorkie.

Everyone else in the room came to a dead halt and stared at Lindy perched atop the chair cradling Leo's quivering body under her arm, his bulbous eyes glittering with dread.

"Go away!" she yelled again at the tiny perplexed therapy dog. "Leave Leo and me alone!"

Now Darrick and the social worker were both galvanized into action, abandoning their holds on the spirit cabinet to come to the aid of their respective little friends. While the social worker recovered her dog's leash and bent to pick him up, Darrick raced to where Lindy held his emotional support dog aloft in a solid grip.

"Thank you, Lindy!" he cried, as she leant over to deposit the chihuahua safe and sound into his arms. "I should have been watching out for Leo's welfare myself." He offered shaken Lindy a gallant hand down off her roost.

"Well, you didn't have to make such a flap about Rex," laughed the social worker to Lindy, as she stroked her pet. "He's really a very friendly little guy."

"Yes," allowed Darrick, turning sharply to address the woman, "and, as you can observe, so is Leo. But strange dogs and territorial instincts can equal an explosive mix— am I correct?"

"Oh, yeah," agreed the social worker, "new smells, new temperaments, who can tell? It's best to be cautious, I guess. Are you okay, dearie?"

Lindy, now seated on the chair with Rochelle gently massaging her shoulders from behind, nodded and said sheepishly, "Yes, I'm fine." Filled with her customary shame, she added, "And I'm sorry that I yelled at Rex. It's not your doggie's fault."

"Are you people going to be here much longer?" The worried woman was back. "We need to set up for the Big Band dance tonight."

"We'll get a wiggle on," promised Malcolm, climbing out from under the spirit cabinet. "Well, at least that shook the hooks and eyes loose."

The social worker and Rex pattered away, the Company's stuff was all gathered and conveyed to the waiting rental and, after plunging herself into the busy-ness, Lindy hopped into the van beside Malcolm who was driving it all to her house. Maddie said she'd meet them there and, more usefully, so did Rochelle, Darrick, and Philippe.

While everything was transferred back into her living room, Lindy called a local pizza place who did vegan and gluten-free as well as pepperoni and Hawaiian, and, shortly, the adult members of The Friends of Phyllis Theatre Company were happily discussing its eventful Preview over four kinds of gooey pies and a vat of merlot.

"Wow, Lindy," chuckled Rochelle, setting down her wine glass, "talk about having our backs. I've never seen a director physically rescue an actor from danger before!"

Lindy blushed crimson to her ears. "I must have looked like an idiot."

"Not at all, my dear," protested Darrick. Leo was snuggled asleep in his arms, exhausted from the day's excitement. "Poor Leo! That foul cur who menaced him should have his therapy licence rescinded."

"You were our heroine today," nodded Philippe with his dulcet lopsided smile.

"Oh, I don't know about that," muttered Lindy, while her actors toasted, "To our Playwright and Director—may she always spring to our defence!"

Preview rehashed, pizza consumed, wine drunk to the last drop, the actors and Madelyn bid Lindy farewell and only Malcolm remained to help tidy up.

"You actually were very brave today, Lindy," he remarked, hanging up a dish cloth.

"No, I wasn't," retorted Lindy. "You saw me panic over that itty-bitty dog."

"But you were, Lindy," grinned Malcolm, pulling her near for a hug.

"How?" she asked, relaxing into his familiar nice-smelling body.

"Don't you know?" laughed Malcolm. He drew her face up to look into her skeptical brown eyes. "That was the first time in my life I have ever seen you willingly touch a dog."

Lindy screwed up her face and shook her head. "I didn't touch that dog."

Malcolm laughed again, a nice rumbling sound. "Leo's a dog."

That's true, thought Lindy in surprise. Leo is a dog. And I actually held him. Voluntarily. That's...that's kind of amazing...

But to Malcolm she said, drily, "Leo's an actor. Not really a dog. He only plays a dog in Darrick's life."

Malcolm laughed again. "Have it your way," he smiled, kissing her lightly on the lips. "So—shall I stay the night?"

"Sure," said Lindy. "Should I make up the sofa?"

"Not a chance," he said, and so she didn't and, for that night at least, the nasty badgering voice was drowned out by Malcolm's unimpeachable love.

CHAPTER THIRTEEN

The Bald Soprano

"'You look positively Japanese.' Who said that?" Maddie regarded Rochelle with an approving eye. "Some grand dame of the forties, I believe. 'You look positively Japanese...'"

Rochelle was amused. "I do? Is that okay?" Grinning, she tucked her hands together inside the blouse's droopy sleeves and shuffled forward like a Gilbert and Sullivan little maid from school.

"No, it isn't. But it doesn't matter, Rochelle," sighed Lindy, "because you don't look Japanese, but you don't look right either."

"Would she wear more of a muumuu kind of thing?" suggested Malcolm helpfully.

"No, she would not!" snapped Lindy, finally losing all patience with both of her old friends. "She's not supposed to look like a bloody clown!"

Malcolm threw up his hands and ceremoniously bowed to her opinion.

Lindy felt stupid.

"Sorry," she said, in a more conciliatory tone, "and I appreciate your input, guys, but at heart Mrs. Peever is a businesswoman. She's supposed to be a medium, yes, so she's got to be kind of occult-ish-y, but she also has to look like she could convince wealthy dupes to take her pitch seriously. So—like I keep telling you, Maddie—she needs to wear more on the side of tailored and less on the side of eccentric."

"How about this one?" Darrick proffered another blouse from the pile on the table. "It's still rather glossy, but simpler in design and plain blue."

With a seasoned actor's unpretentiousness, Rochelle doffed the flamboyant blouse and donned the blue one.

"Okay, that fits her better," sighed Lindy in relief, "and it'll go with the jacket in the first scenes."

"I feel like it's more Margaret Peever too," agreed Rochelle, buttoning the cuffs while she considered her reflection in the full length mirror Lindy had asked Malcolm to bring downstairs from her bedroom for the costume parade. She picked up the navy velveteen jacket and, shrugging it on, did a slow pirouette for her audience.

"And she could wear this paisley silk around her neck." Darrick draped the scarf artistically under Rochelle's collar. "And then she'll use it on her head for the séance scene."

He loosed the silk square, and Rochelle quickly wrapped it around her hair.

"Excellent," said Lindy, gratified. "Well, that's it. Those flared dress pants are correct and I like the platform shoes, so now everybody's great."

She swept a glance over her four costumed actors.

Standing beside Rochelle, Darrick was trim in a slightly shiny grey three piece sharkskin business suit from his own closet and a purple ascot tie. Little Leo was enduring his cat-hoodie with his accustomed good grace. And Philippe wore the short blonde wig, a casual Laura Ashley print cotton blouse, an 'above-the-knee-but-not-a-mini'—as Lindy had directed—light blue denim skirt, and a pair of vintage cork-soled wedges, all also from his own extensive wardrobe.

"Perfect," said Lindy, brushing her greying bob behind her ears. "I think we're ready to roll. Maddie, what time did you tell Merrill and Hua to get here?"

Madelyn frowned at her phone. "Um, oh, about a half hour from now..."

"Great. Okay," said Lindy, who had one more piece of business for her actors that she hadn't wanted to propose until final rehearsal, "while Malcolm gets the tech figured out, I've got something I want to try before you put your make-up on."

Lindy pointed to an easel with a wood-framed blackboard placed on it that she'd deposited earlier beside the sofa in the living room. She'd figured that Malcolm wouldn't approve of the late expenditure—and she also thought he might pooh-pooh her unorthodox idea—so she'd just driven up to the Glebe art emporium last week and purchased it on her own. She told herself that it wasn't a frivolous buy, since, if the actors weren't willing to use it or, at any rate, once the show was over, she planned to present it to Madelyn as a belated birthday gift. Money well spent, either way.

"You know how, after the applause and bows," began Lindy, flipping her hair behind her ears, "but before the house lights are turned on—"

"'Come up,'" corrected Madelyn.

"What?"

"Before the house lights come up," emphasized Maddie.

"—before the house lights come up," continued Lindy, annoyed but not having time to count to a hundred and seventy-two, "how the performers usually thank the audience and then give them good tips about which show to see next?"

Her actors, well versed in the Fimbria Festival's ways, all nodded.

"Well—I want you to add one more thing. Take your places on the set in front of the table. Okay. Applause, bows, applause, applause. Now—if Philippe would quickly go pick up the easel and blackboard—thanks Philippe— while the others come forward a bit to start their spiel—"

Rochelle stopped bowing and stood forth obediently.

"Thanks for coming out to see our show...yada, yada, yada..."

"Great. Now, while she's doing that, Philippe, you come up behind her with the easel. That's good." Lindy took a deep breath. "So, then, while Philippe steps away—but not too far, because there'll be more applause, hopefully— Darrick and Rochelle move to one side of the easel. And, as they recommend shows, they begin to interpret the grid I chalked as nearby streets and point out the crosses which I meant to be the dogs that people have to pass on their way to their next venues. Okay? Like, um—"

"Like we're weathercasters on the news, right?" said Rochelle. "Pointing out dangerous storm patterns."

"Yes, exactly!" Linda was delighted that Rochelle was so quick to understand. "But do it as yourselves, not as your characters, if you see what I mean."

"Genius," approved Rochelle, nodding.

"Brilliant," added Darrick. "Just give us a few minutes to work out our schtick."

The two actors began to study Lindy's design.

"And what should I do?" asked Philippe. "I assume I'm out of character now too?"

"No," said Rochelle, turning from the blackboard with an impish grin, "no, it would be better if you weren't, Philippe. If it's okay with Lindy," she continued with a respectful nod toward their director, "why doesn't Mary go backstage to get the blackboard while Darrick and Leo and I take our bow during the first applause? Then Philippe stays in character as Mary throughout the 'weather report,' and then, only after Darrick and Leo and I have said our final 'Thanks,' does he pull off his wig and take his bow."

The other two actors both nodded again and looked expectantly at Lindy.

"Um, fine," she said, "that's sounds even better than what I was thinking. Let's try it that way."

Since the actors seemed content to block the business out by themselves, Lindy went into the dining room to see how Malcolm was fairing with the tech.

"That ending thingy that you've got them doing seems kind of weird to me," Malcolm said, doubtfully. "Do you think the audience will take it seriously?"

"Yes, I think they will," replied Lindy, patiently. "With Philippe staying in character, it will definitely emphasize the gravity of Mary's anxiety and point out that there are no easy fixes for her mental health issues."

Malcolm continued to look dubious, but said no more.

Soon, pleased with their efforts, the actors retired to the bathroom to make up. Merrill and Hua arrived on time toting their instruments, the space was pre-set and, with Madelyn in charge of the dimmer for the living room lights, and Malcolm with his fingers on the CD player, Lindy watched and directed a rather flat but otherwise pretty good final dress rehearsal of *Small Comforts*.

Non-technical bobbles were few. The musicians had to be cautioned not to come in too soon on Rochelle's soliloquy. Darrick had to figure out how to cover for Leo when he stuck his tongue out of his little sharp muzzle and panted in a very un-cat-like manner. And Philippe repeated a couple of Mary's lines in the wrong order.

"I'm sorry," he said, as Lindy gave him his notes, "they always sound better to my ears the other way around—"

Necessarily, the show remained technically unpolished. However, Lindy believed, the rest of its elements could pass muster, particularly now that the theme was so skillfully underlined at the very end by Mary's anxious attention to Darrick's and Rochelle's solemn blackboard demonstration.

The next afternoon, Lindy hopped a bus and, filled with Leo-esque trepidation, reported to the Fimbria Festival's cluttered Arts Court office for her 'Artist Check-in.'

After she waited a little while in line behind a couple of shock-haired and tattooed extravagants, the ever-obliging staff signed her in as The Friends of Phyllis Theatre Company's official Producer and gave her the identification she'd need to collect their festival earnings.

Turning to go, Lindy literally bumped into *bouffon* clown Chuckie Calamansi, who apologized shortly, "Sorry, ma'am," but then recognized her and winked a friendly

"How ya doin', toots?" as he skirted around her to get his own show signed in.

I'm an artist among artists now, Lindy thought happily, as she tripped down the stairs.

On her way home, through the early June birdsong, she encountered Goldie coming toward her on the opposite sidewalk. Through her protective sunglasses, however, she could see that the doggington yawn was leashed securely to the baby stroller its owner was pushing. So when Brittany called "Hello!' Lindy paused directly across the street from them to reply.

"Hi, Brittany. Isn't it a beautiful day?"

"Fantastic, Lindy. We've been for a walk in the sunshine." If her owner was going to stop to chat, the retriever was going to sit, which she did, smiling kindly when the toddler reached over to grab her shoulder fur. "And yourself?"

"I've been downtown at the Arts Court." Lindy hadn't mean to say it, but it just burbled out of her mouth. "I was signing in my show at the Fimbria Festival."

"Really?" Brittany sounded sincerely impressed. "I didn't know that you acted."

"Oh, no, I couldn't do that," Lindy demurred. "I wrote something. A play, you know. With actors and musicians and all that." She waved her hand in humble dismissal. "We've been rehearsing it forever. Maybe—" how bold should she be? "—maybe you'd like to come see it? It's on six times during the Festival..."

"I'd love to come see it," smiled Brittany. "John and I always try to get to the Fimbria for at least one day. Have you got your flyers printed yet?"

"Um, no, we're getting that done tonight. I'll drop one off at your place, shall I?"

"Great." The toddler produced a squawk. "Well, someone's hungry! I'd better get home. See you at the Fimbria, Lindy!"

"Yes, I hope that you can come..."

The toddler's squawking became a squall. Goldie stood, concerned, and stared pointedly at her owner. "What was the name of your show again?"

"*Small Comforts.*"

"*Small Comforts*? Great title. We'll be there!"

And, with that, Lindy had flogged her show to the public for the very first time.

It felt good, she thought as she sped home on the wings of joy but, well, kind of vain.

Now, now, she chided herself, unlocking the side door, for a Fimbria Playwright and Producer to be self-effacing is the kiss of death. The meter of all success is how many bums I can get in my seats. I must learn to promote the fruits of my labours fearlessly.

"Phyllis," she tried bragging to her silver-grey cat, rhythmically grooming herself on the front room sofa, "I have just written and directed a show that's guaranteed to be Best of the Fest!"

Unaffected, Phyllis didn't miss a pink-tongued beat.

"Everyone's a critic," groused Lindy, but nothing, not even the barely discernable nasty voice, could touch her sky-high mood today.

* * * * *

"Please don't confuse me," said Lindy. "I've got plenty of bugs in my hair already."

Which she did, both figuratively, with all this baffling techie talk, and actually, because of the mid-June midges she'd had to swat her way through as they off-loaded their set onto the sidewalk outside of the Arts Court.

It was time for their three-hour technical rehearsal in their assigned venue, and Lindy was already falling behind.

The wonderfully patient and encouraging blonde dredlocked techie guy, Thom Mudi, smiled and began again. "Okay. So I've got a couple of washes I'm going to use to give you an indoor office-y feel, right? And I'm going to dim, you know, lighten or darken them to reflect the different moods you want to show in your play, okay? But now I need to know whether you want your special—that's that one dedicated light I told you about—to be focused on the séance or the—what is it?—the spirit cabinet? I can only give you one special, so you need to decide which one you want to feature. And, remember, I also have a follow spot I can give you that might work for the cabinet in a pinch."

"But I thought you said we'd need to use that for the musicians?" protested Lindy helplessly.

"Yeah, but if they don't need to see their music while the cabinet's in play, the follow spot's going to be at a low enough level to pull it up—"

"No, we don't want to do that, Thom," interjected Malcolm, looking to Darrick, who had helped him prepare their prompt script's lighting and sound cues, for support. Darrick nodded, so Malcolm continued, "We should use the special for the spirit cabinet where most of the spooky crap goes on. Just bring the séance lighting down to a candlelit level, like you said."

"I can do an ice blue gel in the special," suggested Thom. "That'll help with the ghost."

"Good," said Lindy, catching up. Ice blue for the ghost. That she could understand.

"Great," said Thom, "just give me a moment to get the gel in and set my levels. While I do that, why don't you folks practice tearing down and putting up your set one more time? You're only going to have fifteen minutes in and out per show, you know, and I'll bet that cabinet-thingy is gonna be a royal pain in the ass. Oh, and give me that effects tape, Malcolm, and I'll set that up too."

Everyone in the Company—except Madelyn—had gotten to the load in right on time. With the help of a borrowed dolly, Lindy, Malcolm, the three actors and the two musicians had transferred and toted everything up in the elevator to the hallway that served as their venue's lobby. Then Madelyn had finally shown up, just seconds before Thom had arrived to open the main door.

Almost an hour and a half had already gone by, however, and so nobody was surprised when—after the long half hour it took for the set to come down, be put away like a giant puzzle in the close-quartered storage area and then be taken out and put up again—Thom told them that they couldn't do a full run. "You'll have to be satisfied," he said, "with a cue-to-cue."

It was disorienting for Lindy to watch her actors, wearing their basic costumes and make-up, skip through the script, pausing while Thom and Malcolm discussed lighting or sound levels and then moving on to scenes that came several pages later.

And she really couldn't get her head around the séance and spirit cabinet special effects. Without any build-up from the script, the effects seemed rudely abrupt and uncomfortably tawdry. She was pleased with the ice blue spectral lighting, however, and even the unholy racket ghost tape sounded more authentic in the actual venue.

The musicians, wearing their black concert gear, also seemed confused by the disjointed script, sometimes missing cues or jumping in too soon. But Lindy, who had had to prompt Merrill and Hua a little more than she'd liked during rehearsals, thought it might not hurt them to have to concentrate a bit harder on following the story as it lurched by.

Thom found Lindy's applause scene with the blackboard quite intriguing and, with the musicians finished with all but their final bows, he was able to use the follow spot to give it quite a bit more oomph.

Too soon, however, the three hours were threatening to be over, so Thom gave them all the thumbs up and told them to get their set stowed.

Fortunately, all the building and tearing down they'd done that day made the job somewhat smoother. They'd discovered that table could be left up on its legs with the chairs piled on top and props bins shoved underneath. But the bitch of a spirit cabinet still had to be dismantled since there was no room backstage to store anything that big when assembled.

Then they were all back in the hall lobby and Thom was locking the door and wishing them well as the actors padded back to the dressing room across the hall to get into their street clothes. When they reappeared, they handed their costumes to Madelyn for cleaning and repair, and then Lindy and Malcolm walked everyone to a nearby deli to treat them to a well-earned lunch and plan out the next tasks of the day—flyer distribution and poster placement.

Their spectral dog's barking head poster had turned out beautifully.

Using a photo of Leo and a shivery font, Darrick had designed both the poster and a similar haunted doggie handbill on his computer. Then Malcolm had taken downloads of them to a Fimbria-friendly discount printer for lots more copies than Marie-Paule, the Marketing Director, would ever recommend.

So after smoked meat sandwiches, potato latkes, bagels and cream cheese, and a vegan tahini eggplant baguette, The Friends of Phyllis consulted their timetables and divided up the handbills. Each Company member was responsible for flyering the public, particularly the wait lines and areas immediately around the venues, for at least a couple of the days during the week and a half that the Festival ran. But, since the actors needed down time to prepare before and recuperate after their performances, Malcolm acknowledged that he, Lindy and Madelyn were probably going to be doing most of the leg work.

Everybody also got a couple of posters, mostly as souvenirs, and, as the bill was being paid, the Company split up to go their separate ways.

Madelyn had an appointment with her dietician, so only Lindy and Malcolm headed back to the Arts Court to stick up a few posters with magnets on the metal walls of the elevators. Then they wandered about the building tacking or taping up others to the designated message boards inside and outside its walls. A short stroll to the university allowed them to hang posters at the venues there, and Malcolm had obtained permission to stick up some at the Student Centre and the Faculty Club as well.

"Okay, it looks like we've got this thing covered," said Malcolm, apparently satisfied with their modest efforts. "Let's go have a beer."

Lindy didn't want a beer, but she didn't have the will to argue so she walked to the pub with Malcolm. She felt deflated, unsure. What am I doing here? she wondered.

This morning, the abysmal depths of her theatrical ignorance were glaringly apparent to Thom the technician and everyone else in the venue. Rochelle, Darrick, Philippe—they were all theatre geeks. Why had they let her lead them on this journey into failure? Even the teenaged musicians, at home on a stage with their instruments, seemed to understand what was happening so much better than she did.

How could her Company have chatted so cheerfully over lunch? The Producer, Director, and Playwright of their show was obviously a total flake. Didn't they realize that they were being led blindly into the maelstrom on a coffin ship?

"Here we are," declared Malcolm, holding the pub door open for Lindy. "You'll feel better after you've wet your whistle."

Lindy stopped right in the middle of the doorway and stared at him. With a firm nod, Malcolm gave her a tiny shove and she stumbled inside. A few minutes later, they were taking their first sips of a light local spring brew.

"Now you can talk about it," said Malcolm, setting down his glass.

"I don't know what you mean," Lindy lied.

"Yeah, you do," Malcolm sighed. "Look, Lindy, you've put too much time, too much money, too much...heart into this project to give up now. So what if you weren't the brightest kid at the tech? I was just making it up too. And Madelyn always does. It doesn't matter. Everybody was happy—"

"Only because they're all delusional!"

"Well, I'm pretty sure being 'delusional' is a requirement for theatre people," Malcolm took a swig of beer, wiped his mouth and continued, "and, for better or for worse, that's who we are right now."

Silently, Lindy took a few sips of her draft.

"You know," she said, grimly, after a moment, "the last time you said 'for better or for worse' to me, we were getting married. And look how that turned out."

"Yeah, I was a louse," sighed Malcolm, draining his glass and signaling the server for a refill, "and you deserved better. But last time I wasn't so fully committed to your show."

"That's for sure," grumbled Lindy, although she had to laugh too…

CHAPTER FOURTEEN

Rhinoceros

"There's a little light that flashes when it's locked."

Backstage at the Fimbria Festival's Preview Night, another patient techie was explaining to a crowd of Fimbria lottery winners how to use the dressing rooms.

"Now, if everyone who isn't performing in the first half would please go away until after the twelfth show finishes their two minute bit, we'll all be able to breathe. And, if you're not a performer—if you're a director or a producer or a make up artist or somebody's Mommy—please don't come back at all! As you can see, we've got more chaos than we need, and you guys really aren't helping. So shoo, shoo! Go sit in the audience and enjoy!"

Flapping her arms like a gooseherd, the techie dismissed all the hangers on.

Reluctantly, Lindy followed her chattering actors out across the stage to the banked audience rows.

Because this particular venue's roomy lobby with its longstanding bar licence was so critical to the Preview's success, the Preview wasn't being held at the very largest venue at the Festival. Consequently, most of the seats were already filled with buzzing patrons. However, Rochelle,

Philippe and Darrick had said that, in order to sneak out on time, they'd just hover about the back row, and so Malcolm and Maddie had only had to defend a single empty seat between them for their playwriting friend.

"This is so exhilarating, hon!" exclaimed Madelyn, moving her beaded bag so Lindy could sit down. "Did you ever imagine in your whole life that we'd actually make it here?"

"Never a doubt," deadpanned Malcolm.

Lindy grimaced at him. "Liar," she snorted.

The Fimbria Preview was a yearly tradition that Lindy had never heard of until The Friends of Phyllis had moved off the wait list and she'd read about it in the Fimbria Producer's Handbook.

The rules were simple. The night before the official opening of the Festival, companies could present a two minute pitch of their show to an audience overflowing with Fimbria patrons, volunteers, critics and fellow artists. And Darrick had told Lindy that, to beef up their word of mouth, The Friends of Phyllis definitely should.

While most companies performed the catchiest scene they could produce without their major props and set pieces, a few chose to just talk about their productions. As long as the highly-lubricated audience was amused, both types of pitches seemed to be equally well received. In fact, the third pitcher, one of the talk-ers not show-ers, was so funny, she effectively eclipsed the audience's response to the next presentation entirely.

With so many performances in a row, two minutes wasn't long to get your show into people's memories so, as Lindy tried to concentrate on the other lottery winners' shows tumbling by, she prayed that she'd selected the right scene for their brief appearance. The last time she'd turned around to check on her actors, they no longer seemed to be in the rear of the audience, so she assumed they'd made their way backstage.

Oh boy—

What if—

But here was the emcee announcing, "And now, Ladies, Gents, and Everybody Else, I am delighted to present to you—*Small Comforts*—courtesy of The Friends of Phyllis Theatre Company!"

And here were Rochelle, Darrick, and Leo taking their places on stage, and there was Philippe peeking primly out of the wings, ready to make his entrance.

Oh Dear God—

Lindy felt her gorge rise.

Pushing wildly past Madelyn to the open stair, she fled up and out through the lobby bar and across the hall to the ladies room where she vomited everything she'd eaten since last week into a toilet and then rose to lean, eyes closed in exhaustion, against the open door of the stall.

"Sweetie?" enquired a strange but kindly voice. "Are you all right?"

Her cheeks flooding crimson, Lindy began to cry.

"Now, now," commiserated the voice and gentle arms encircled her, bringing her over to the sink. "Splash your face with water and rinse out your mouth, sweetie. You'll feel much better..."

The arms went away, and Lindy heard the toilet flush.

Weakly, Lindy did as the kind voice had directed.

"I'm so sorry..." she quavered, opening her eyes, to accept a proffered tissue and blow her nose.

"Oh, it's okay." The voice belonged to a tanned round middle-aged white woman, resplendent in ropes and ropes of pearls. "Too much excitement can do that to a girl. Do you have friends who—?"

A couple of women nipped into the washroom at a breakneck pace, then, "Lindy—!" Madelyn swept in, "—oh-my-gawd-you-missed-it-all!"

"Were they—were they—any good?" stuttered Lindy, terrified to ask.

"Good? They were fabulous! We brought down the house!" crowed Madelyn. "The whole audience leapt up to applaud!"

"No," protested Lindy, bewildered, "not for my play?"

"Yes!" squealed Maddie. "A Standing-O for our play!"

"The play that I wrote?"

"Yes, the play that you wrote!" Madelyn was getting irritated with Lindy's thickness. "*Small Comforts*—what other play are we doing?"

Maddie hustled into a stall just as a line of impatient women began to form.

Stunned, Lindy lingered by the sinks to wait so she could question her friend more closely.

The kind stranger remained as well. "Ah, you're a playwright, sweetie," she smiled, making it sound like the peak of accomplishment. "I should have guessed."

"Yes, well, sort of," demurred Lindy. "But thank you so much for your help," she added sincerely. "I'm sorry I was so dumb."

"Not at all," said the woman. "We playwrights are delicate blossoms."

"Oh," said Lindy, the light dawning, "do you have a show in the Festival?"

"Not this year," said the woman seriously. "I was approached by Donnella and Kath last fall, so I'm doing the Park in August."

Lindy had no idea who or where the woman was talking about, but "What did you write?" she asked, mainly to be polite.

"An adaptation of '*Dyskolos*.'"

Lindy looked blank.

"By Menander?" The woman chuckled. "Yes, I know, he's pretty obscure. But the play works well with the masks, and The Great God Pan should read nicely among the trees."

"Commedia masks?" guessed Lindy, drawing on her limited knowledge of theatre history.

"Yes, although we did think we'd blend a little more Greek into them this year. We've got a marvelous cast lined up—Tamlin and Arjun and Ronnie and Alison, too. And of course, Ruby's directing, and Glenora's designed the most extraordinary sets. They're all to be articulated so they'll bend and fold and swing about. Such fun! Our rehearsals start this week." The playwright smiled again as she opened the ladies room door. "See you there, sweetie!"

Lindy smiled back and nodded. "Oh, absolutely! Thanks so much, and bye!"

The woman was gone. Lindy was glad because, if she'd stayed to chat, Lindy wouldn't have had the heart to tell her that she hadn't recognized any of the theatre people she'd mentioned so confidently. And that was because, although Ottawa's popular summer outdoor theatre productions often got rave reviews—and she sometimes thought she ought to seek them out—Lindy had never been to any. And never planned to go.

Dogs, of course.

Dogs were always the problem.

Although Madelyn, as far as Lindy knew, had never been to any of the fresh air shows either. But, in her case, it was probably more about not wanting to put up with the bugs.

So the kindly playwright had wasted her pitch.

Lindy felt rotten about that.

She also felt rotten about missing her actors' performance. Theirs had been the second last scene in the first half, and now she could hear the audience being called back to their seats from a brief intermission.

As soon as Maddie had finished primping at the mirrors, drawing on every bit of strength she could muster, Lindy followed her friend back into the theatre to watch the remainder of the two minute previews. Malcolm gave her a concerned glance as she sat down but his attention was immediately grabbed by the emcee urging everyone to turn off their phones again, and he never got a chance to ask after her well-being until after the second half of the Preview was brought to a close.

"You ran out of here like a rocket. Everything okay?" he enquired as they made their way to the lobby. "Now that it's over, can I buy you a drink?"

"No, I—" began Lindy, but whatever she was going to say was smothered by Rochelle who dashed over to give her a huge bear hug. Rochelle's hug was joined by Philippe's, and then, when she finally managed to disentangle herself from them, she was rocked by Darrick's hearty handshake.

"Well done!" cheered Darrick over Leo's head as the others hugged Malcolm and Maddie. "Well done, everyone! Let's repair to the beer tent, and I'll buy the first round!"

Rochelle, however, had noticed that Lindy didn't seem to be quite as pumped as the rest of the Company. "You okay, Lindy?" she enquired, puzzled. "You look kind of pale."

"Oh, I—" Humiliation suffused her face red again, but Lindy figured she'd better confess and get the worst of it over with. "The thing is—I didn't actually see our Preview. I had to run out...to...to throw up."

Lindy wasn't sure where to look.

But Rochelle just grinned. "Hey, guys," she remarked to her fellow actors, "we've got a barfer. Who knew?"

The two men laughed.

"Never mind, my dear," soothed Darrick. "Frayed nerves are a hoary tradition for playwrights."

"They say that Moss Hart had a total mental breakdown before one of his opening nights," nodded Philippe.

"So, com'on out to the beer tent," urged Rochelle. "You're never ever going to get such a good offer from Darrick again..."

"Oh, thanks, guys," sighed Lindy, "but I think I'm done. You go on ahead, and I'll see everyone tomorrow night. No, really," she maintained over their protests, "I'm beat. I'm just going to get my car and drive home."

"I'll walk you over then, Lindy," offered Malcolm, "and meet the rest of the gang at the beer tent."

"Was it really that good?" asked Lindy, as she and Malcolm trudged toward the parking garage, well out of earshot of the other Friends of Phyllis.

"It was great," he shrugged and then considered. "Maybe not exactly what I was expecting from your rehearsals, but really, really entertaining. I liked it. Madelyn loved it. And the audience just ate it up. Yeah, I think you'll probably like what they've done to your show."

Driving timidly home down the darkly lit Rideau Canal parkway, Lindy wondered uncomfortably what Malcolm had meant by that.

In fact, her evening had left her with a lot of questions.

Why had her show been received with such excitement by the crowd? She'd been happy with how her script had finally turned out—but a standing ovation? What had the actors done to her play?

And who was that kindly playwright? Who were all those theatre people whose names she'd dropped? Should Lindy be haled as a fellow artist if she didn't know the first thing about the Ottawa theatre scene?

Still, her idiotic behaviour at the Preview dominated her thoughts, and Lindy was an old hand at beating herself up.

How could she let her Company down like that? Running off to puke out her fear in front of a complete stranger! How could she have disgraced them all like that? Where was her self-discipline? Had she no pride?

And in bed that night, she could not bury the nasty voice.

You're stupid, you're ugly, you're a goddam useless bitch! And, by Jeezus, I'll tan your hide!

Lindy slapped her cheeks. Once...hard...twice...harder...

She pressed her nails into her arm until tears streaked her scarlet cheeks and agony finally muted the evil refrain.

A doggington bark, she whimpered. A doggington bay. A doggington snarl...

Over and over and over, she chanted her mantra.

But sleep was a long time coming.

Merciless Greg and Nan would soon be coming to rejoice in her failure—and milky tea, peanut butter crackers and television could bring her no solace tonight.

* * * * *

You'll eat a peck of dirt before you die.

My mother always used to say that, thought Lindy savagely, as Madelyn babbled on about her visit to her fancy dietician.

"He said I have an undefined food hypersensitivity and will have to go on an exclusion diet. For the next week, I'll be removing all legumes from my diet, including beans, lentils, and also soy. It's going to be tough, but I'm worth it, he said."

"Did you bring the rest of Darrick's suit?" asked Lindy, avoiding the obvious retort. "I can't find his vest or pants." She showed Madelyn the empty clothes bag.

"I know I put them in there," her friend replied. "Are you sure they're not tucked inside the jacket?"

Lindy held up the jacket on its hanger. "See for yourself."

Madelyn took the hanger and fruitlessly searched for the missing pieces. Then her hand flew to her mouth. "Oh, hon," she gasped, "now I remember. I took the vest and the pants off the hanger to check the pockets for tissues and stuff. I wonder if I forgot to put them back?"

Lindy stared at her friend in disbelief. "So where did you leave them?"

"At home, I guess...in my bedroom?"

Lindy and Madelyn—who was on time only because Lindy had told her to come forty minutes earlier than she actually wanted her there—were setting up in the venue dressing room. The actors were due in fifteen minutes. Once they were allowed into the theatre, Lindy and Malcolm had to concentrate on the pre-set, but Madelyn lived a mere five minute drive away.

"Maddie!" snapped Lindy, fishing out her car keys. "Get off your butt and go get them!"

"Lindy! I can't. It will take me—"

"Take my car and go!"

"Oh, all right, but I'm telling you—"

"Go—!"

Madelyn grabbed the keys and fluttered out.

Grimly, Lindy remained to guard her actor's costumes in the shared dressing room.

Damn Maddie, she seethed. She's been out to wreck my show from the start...

Ten minutes later, Malcolm showed up. Looking around, he raised an eyebrow. "Madelyn?" he asked.

Lindy didn't want to talk about it. "She'll be here."

"Where—?"

"She'll be here."

"Okay." Malcolm looked highly skeptical but kept further questions about Madelyn's whereabouts to himself. "What can I do?"

"Hang out by the theatre entrance and come tell me the moment Thom lets us in."

"Right." Malcolm made tracks.

Then Rochelle appeared, full of bonhomie. She tried to engage Lindy in conversation, but Lindy wasn't having it. She left her actor to prepare and went out to tell Malcolm that she needed a walk to clear her head. She passed the volunteer ticket crew at their table which was set up at the end of the lobby hall and punched the button to summon the elevator. When the door opened on the main floor, she met Darrick, Leo and Philippe heading in together. She told them she'd be back shortly and continued on to the Arts Court's front entrance. She pushed open the solid door and stepped out on the broad stone stairway, blinking into the late Friday afternoon sunlight.

It was now twenty after five. The show before theirs ended at five-thirty. They had to pre-set by at least five minutes to six. That's when the door would have to open. That's when any potential audience members would file in. Their first show was scheduled for six o'clock.

Six sharp.

That's when the theatre door would have to close. There'd be no more audience members allowed in after that.

They absolutely had to start on time.

If their show went too long, Thom would call a halt, bring up the house lights and usher the audience out. The next show was scheduled for seven-thirty and that company would be expecting that by seven-fifteen they'd get into the theatre to do their pre-set. If Madelyn didn't turn up with Darrick's suit in the next fifteen minutes, Lindy was going to have to decide whether to send him on stage in his jacket and whatever else he was wearing right now.

But that was okay, Lindy decided, because they weren't going to have their pre-set finished in time anyway...

She could see it all quite clearly. The spirit cabinet would stubbornly refuse to be built and a pressed back chair would fall apart in the rush. A leg would break off when the table was manhandled on to the stage. Essential props would be missing from their bins and no one would have a clue where they'd gone.

Malcolm was right from the beginning. Lindy had wasted her bequest. They should have named themselves 'The Friends of Chernobyl.' The show was a complete catastrophe.

The broad stone steps were littered with people whose attention was trained on their smartphones. A few were chatting in small groups. Some thumbed through copies of the Fimbria Festival program. At the foot of the steps, the French college student and her Papa from the night of the lottery were handing out flyers and inviting people to their show.

Heaving a desperate sigh, Lindy glanced up the street toward the parking garage. She'd forgotten her sunglasses so she had to squint into the sunlight. She blinked—and there was Madelyn! And, in a completely un-Madelyn-ish way, she was RUNNING!

And was she carrying—? Yes, she WAS—! And flailing towards the Arts Court like an angelic butterfly pursued by the Legions of Hell!

Quickly, Lindy scrambled down the stairs and, just as she got to the bottom, Madelyn came wheezing up holding a bag which she thrust at her friend.

"Bless you!" cried Lindy, snatching the clothes.

Too winded for words, Maddie sank in a diaphanous heap on the steps as Lindy raced up and away. She caught the elevator just as the door was beginning to close, rose to the venue's floor and scurried down toward their dressing room. As she swept by, volunteer ushers were opening up the theatre door and she nodded understanding to Malcolm, tapping his watch. She handed the costume pieces to Darrick, already half way through his make up. Then, with a word of encouragement, she left her actors to join Malcolm who was champing at the bit in the hall.

The previous show—a two-hander comedy by a couple of university kids—had apparently attracted a very sparse audience. Malcolm told Lindy that only about six patrons had wandered out and none had looked too pleased. The young comedians had a very small set, consisting of only a couple of stools, a lectern and an electric piano, so their tear down took only a few minutes. So at five thirty-six, by Malcolm's watch, Thom was inviting The Friends of Phyllis into the theatre to pre-set.

As Lindy and Malcolm raced backstage, all three actors, in costume and make up, strode across the lobby hall. Merrill and Hua, clad all in black, slipped in with their instruments through the back door. Energized with opening night excitement, The Friends of Phyllis Company threw themselves into lifting and toting, assembling and placing.

The pre-set was achieved in record time.

Then, while Thom checked his lighting and sound cues, the musicians began to tune up and the actors retired backstage to mutter, stretch and hum.

Lindy and Malcolm climbed to their seats at the back of the audience. Through the closed door to the lobby hall, they could hear an increasing babble of voices.

"Excuse me." A volunteer usher was coming up the stairs towards them. "Are you guys planning to stay there?"

"Yes," returned Lindy, a little confused, "is that a problem?"

"Well," said the usher, "it's just that the show has sold out, and we'll need both of those seats."

"Sold out—?"

Feeling like she was swimming slowly underwater in a waking dream, Lindy rose and floated down the steps to stand with Malcolm near the door.

Thom gave the usher the thumbs up, she opened the door—and a flood of people, chattering in enthusiastic anticipation, poured through.

Where the hell had they all come from? wondered Lindy, dazedly watching the patrons mill about the rows. On Monday night when she'd last searched the Fimbria ticket site, *Small Comforts* still had only a modest number of seats sold. What had happened in the meantime? The Fimbria Preview night? Was that enough to make this much difference?

Oh Dear God.

Just how well had her actors performed?

But here was the last audience member taking her seat. Here was the usher shutting the door. Here was Thom dousing the houselights. The musicians struck up, Bradley and Margaret Peever made their entrance, and the play was on.

As *Small Comforts* rolled past, Lindy couldn't quite put her finger on it, but she knew that, on the night of the Preview, Malcolm had been correct. The show she was watching wasn't what she could have expected from her rehearsals. Which was strange because, as far as she could see, the actors were making all the same moves and saying all the same lines.

But it wasn't the same show at all.

Not by a long shot.

For, instead of the grave and painful drama that Lindy had thought that she'd written and rehearsed, what now played out on stage was a vicious social satire, incisive and unrelenting in its ironic take on life. And so screamingly funny that the theatre shook with appalling laughter again and again and again.

Lines which Lindy had meant to be deeply serious were greeted with chuckles and groans. Dialogue from which she'd squeezed the ultimate pathos now ignited hoots and howls. Scene after scathing scene left the crowd teary-eyed with mirth.

When Rochelle and Darrick took their first bow, the audience roared to their feet, but, as Mary returned with the blackboard, Darrick waved them all back down. Pulling back Leo's lion hood, he humbly thanked the audience and proceeded to recommend other Fimbria productions worth their twelve bucks.

Then while Philippe, still performing as Mary, watched with rapt attention, Rochelle stepped forward and pointed at the chalked design.

"To get to your next venues," she announced impassively, "these are the routes that avoid the most dogs."

The audience erupted in ghastly laughter once more.

Afterwards, as they waited for the on-line critiques at a table outside the beer tent—this year tucked into a broad ground floor plaza at the west side of the Arts Court—the other Friends of Phyllis steadfastly ignored Lindy's subdued mood. They toasted and cackled and boasted around her in the warm June night, high on the riotous success of their play. Fellow artists kept dropping by to congratulate them, hoping, perhaps, that some of their precious SRO mojo would rub off on their own shows.

Then calling for quiet as she consulted her phone, Madelyn read the first reviews.

"A Pinter-esque triumph!"

"A terrifying farce!"

"A gut-busting whiz-bang-boom!"

Five stars! Five stars!! Five stars!!!

The company leapt to their feet to fling rapturous arms around each other.

Well, whoop-de-doo...

"Com'on, Lindy!" urged Rochelle, shocked to see her director just sitting there unmoved. "We're a smash! Where's that trademark smile?"

Even Lindy was suspicious of her weak reaction. Her actors had delivered a five-star hit, hadn't they? According to Malcolm, the rest of the run was already completely sold out.

So why did she feel so...disappointed?

Why did she, alone, feel so low?

Worn out with elation, the group began to break up. Merrill and Hua had to run for their bus. Madelyn, who'd been shut out of the packed theatre, pleaded exhaustion and trotted off with them. Philippe, Darrick and Leo headed to an old friend's new show. Besides Lindy, only Malcolm and Rochelle remained, nursing their beers through post-orgasmic smiles.

Then Rochelle shifted her gaze to Lindy and sobered. "You okay, babe?"

Lindy wasn't sure. "I guess so. Well, of course, I..." She flailed about for words to express her dissatisfaction. "It's just that...it's just that I thought...I hoped...oh, I don't know." She bit her lip, embarrassed by the tears that had started in her eyes.

Rochelle was confused.

"But, Lindy, we rocked your play. Don't you think?"

"Well...yes...yes and no." Lindy knew she was the only one who saw anything negative in the performance, and she didn't want to upset her actor, but..."The script doesn't really sound the way we rehearsed it at all."

"No?"

"Um, no, the message that I rehearsed you to tell—"

"I don't think you get it."

Was that anger Lindy detected in Rochelle's voice?

"Excuse me?" said Lindy.

"And I think you're being awfully selfish."

Definitely anger, then, and hurt as well.

Lindy's back went up. "I'm sorry, Rochelle," she said stiffly, "but the theme I wanted you to convey to the audience seems to have gotten lost in—"

"*Camme toé*, Lindy," Rochelle cut her short with a dismissive wave. "I don't think you realize what this show has meant to me. To us all!"

"Well, I—" began Lindy defensively.

Undeterred, Rochelle leaned in to confide. "Maybe you haven't heard, but for six years my husband, Jean-Maurice, and I ran our own theatre troupe called 'Faire le Clown.' Darrick and Philippe and a bunch of other talents were in it with us. We did English adaptations of Shakespeare and Wilde in the Ottawa parks in the summer, and French ones of Molière and Feydeau at a Gatineau playhouse in the winter. We had mad success, great reviews and loyal fans." Rochelle's voice darkened. "But then suddenly Jean-Maurice got really sick with cancer and, after he died, I was left to bring up our daughter, Ariel, all alone."

"Oh, I'm so sorry," said Lindy, ambushed by this startlingly melancholy information. "I didn't realize—"

Rochelle shook her head impatiently. "It's boring, but…I went into a real funk, you know? I gave up running our company. I gave up my union card, smoked too much weed and buried myself in a government contract for Agriculture Canada." Rochelle laughed at Lindy's blank look. "Yeah, an office job with the Feds. Can you see me compiling stats on Saskatchewan beef farmers?" Rochelle sniffed scornfully. "Frankly, Lindy, it was a tour of Hades, but it put food on the table for my baby and me." Rochelle's eyes dimmed and her mouth drooped, recalling life in the public service. But in a few seconds her face relit with a broad smile. "Then Ariel crashed her bike, and Serge the Orthodontist was the guy who put her teeth—and then my life—back together."

"Yes, you mentioned him when—"

"Serge had been a widower for years—" Rochelle shrugged, "—and there's always some sort of silver lining, right? My Ariel liked the idea of having Felix and Gabrielle for her brother and sister, and she wanted me to go for it. So, when Serge asked, I said '*oui*' and married him two years to the day after her Papa's last birthday."

Fruitlessly, Lindy cast about for something appropriate to say.

Rochelle's smile had turned wistful at a tender memory, but then she turned back to Lindy with a merry wink. "Being married to Serge gave me the opportunity to quit the Feds and dip my toes back into the theatre, but I wasn't sure I wanted to go professional again quite so soon. So when you gave me a role in your Fimbria show, I was super-pumped! Your play had so much potential, and then, amazingly, there was the chance to get Darrick and Philippe in on the action too—"

"Yes, about that—"

"—so now, along with you and your friends, my buddies and I have built a new Company." Rochelle grinned and shook her head indulgently. "I tell you, Lindy—rehearsing the show, feeling the camaraderie, hearing the laughter tonight—it's been a resurrection for us. And now you're telling me that none of that matters to you? Simply because your script doesn't sound like it did in rehearsal?" Rochelle laughed. "*Je m'en fous*, Lindy! Did you actually want us to just leave it there lying dead on the page? You should be thanking us from the bottom of your heart, babe, not moping around like Hamlet's Ghost!"

With another broad wink, Rochelle planted a kiss on Lindy's cheek and flit off to visit her friends at another table.

Shell-shocked, Lindy looked to Malcolm for support, but he was chatting with Chuckie the Clown—probably, she realized, another of Rochelle's former confreres—and hadn't heard a word that Rochelle had said.

I'm a failure, concluded Lindy, more of a failure than I was when I started this thing.

It was my show, and I bared my soul and raided my bank account to produce an honest drama.

But Dad and Greg were right all along.

I'm nothing.

I'm nobody.

And nobody cares what I'm trying to say...

CHAPTER FIFTEEN

Candide

People laughed. She was offended. That's how it was at every performance.

Although she had to publicly admit that the reviews were excellent, privately Lindy was furious that her actors had purposely hijacked her show. Simply reading those excellent reviews was maddening, too. Because the critics, while noting that the actor was playing under her married name, 'Rochelle Gagnon,' kept referring to Lindy's Friends of Phyllis as 'Rochelle Orangette's new theatre company.'

And, if that wasn't enough to drive Lindy completely crazy, while Rochelle's and Philippe's and Darrick's, and even Leo's performances were universally lauded—and his original score brought Merrill and Hua rapturous applause from the musically inclined—Lindy's writing and direction rarely garnered more than a casual nod.

In fact, it bugged Lindy to the nth degree that, although she'd been hoping to be taken seriously as the author and director of a perceptive psychological drama, all that the critics apparently saw was an hilarious social satire performed by local favourites.

As the Fimbria Festival whirled by and the number of their performances ticked down, Lindy felt more and more that her play, and by extension, her message about the hazards of seeking release from mental health problems, was deeply misunderstood.

Yet she couldn't publicly complain about being ignored. Rochelle and the others were always so careful to adamantly declare to the press and to fellow artists that Lindy was the real genius and guiding spirit behind their enterprise. Quitting the Company to sulk at home would have looked like the baldest ingratitude, so Lindy tried to keep her dissatisfaction to herself.

After the opening, there were five more scheduled shows on five separate days at five other times, and it was obvious from the first performance that the money they'd spent on posters and handbills had been wasted. Even though some of the shows were inconveniently late—Sunday's, in particular, didn't start until ten-thirty at night—every single one was packed to the rafters. In fact, one of the biggest complaints at the Festival was that Rochelle Orangette's new theatre company had been put into such a small venue.

Who was the moron who'd decided on that?

Trying to explain that Rochelle was just an actor who'd been cast in Lindy's show—and that, because they'd never attended outdoor plays nor French theatre, none of the original three Friends of Phyllis had had any idea of who she was—would have just made Lindy, Madelyn and Malcolm sound like idiots.

So Lindy kept her mouth firmly shut on that topic too.

When she wasn't on call for their performances, Lindy would sometimes go with Madelyn and occasionally Malcolm to other shows. Yet, even though as fellow artists they were almost always given the password to gain complimentary entrances, and even though the standards seemed as good or as poor as ever, the magic of the Fimbria Festival which had seduced Lindy last year was—for her—nowhere in sight. Instead, she saw the faulty mechanics of the performances, the cynical techniques of the actors, the rude failings of the writing. She rarely laughed, was never moved to tears. More often than not, she was bored. The shows blurred together in her imagination.

Lindy didn't cared.

Nobody cared.

It had all come down to nothing…

On the Tuesday of the second week, in the late afternoon before their eight-thirty show, Lindy matched her producer's signature at the Fimbria office and was presented with a fat cheque for their first three performances.

She'd promised equal shares to the actors and the musicians, so she was sitting on a bench in the main lobby of the Arts Court cutting cheques for the three performers when the kindly voice she'd heard in less salubrious circumstances said, "Hi there, sweetie. You're looking fine."

Lindy stopped mid-cheque and smiled up at the round middle-aged playwright, today featuring a yellow turban and bright red claws.

"It's nice to see you again," said Lindy. "How're the rehearsals for your Greek show going?"

"Oh, great, great! We're having some fun with the blocking but we'll get there." The woman plopped down beside Lindy. "And your show? How are your houses?"

"Okay—" Lindy hedged.

"Yes?"

"Actually, very good," Lindy allowed, but something in her tone must have alerted the other playwright that all was not well.

"So which one is yours?" she enquired, gently.

"*Small Comforts*," said Lindy, as lightly at she could. "Or, at least, I wrote it. It belongs to the actors now." She tried and failed to keep the bitterness out of her voice.

"Oooh," said the woman, impressed. "That's a big name here. You've got more wom than a parakeet. I had to sell my virtue to get a ticket. And it's your first script, I hear."

"Yes," sighed Lindy, "and my last," her lip trembled and, despite her best efforts at self control, she blurted out, "because I'm never putting myself through this again."

The woman leaned back against the wall and considered. "You know, sweetie, in the past twenty-five years, I've written about thirty plays—all different lengths and genres. But the first time I wrote a play, it was a comedy. I thought my choice of action and dialogue in the script had made that abundantly clear, but—" she smiled, "—the director who put it on—he was a fellow student at my university in Toronto—he didn't see it that way. He had his actors perform it as a serious drama. It was a disaster. And, believe me, sweetie, I was never going to write again either. But my professor, she said to me, Beryl, a playwright's script is like the root of the tree. It underlies everything else. The tree may grow from it tall and straight, or wide and shady, or stunted and gnarled. But that's not your concern. You put down your roots to feed whatever tree that grows, and the tending of that tree, well, that's up to others, not you—"

"But it still went ka-blooey—and all my ideas got lost—and I was my own director!" cried Lindy.

"Oh, were you now? With that gang from Faire le Clown in your cast?" Beryl snorted delicately. "I've known Rochelle and her boys for many years, worked with them too, and they may have taken blocking from you, but taken direction—?" Beryl chuckled as she heaved herself up from the bench. "Believe me, sweetie, if you've been able to keep them on script and on task, you've done very well. On message? That's probably impossible. But don't let it sour you into a has-been."

"Yes, but..." Lindy deflated into resentment again.

Beryl considered Lindy with a friendly eye. "I've heard plenty of chatter from people whose opinions I trust about the good scripting in your show. And word on the ground is that your writing shows potential for even better things. If Rochelle lets you go—and she'll be crazy if she does—you come see me and I'll introduce you around to some artists that I know. You're too gifted a playwright not to have options."

With another warm smile, Beryl waved, "Bye, sweetie," and disappeared toward the elevator.

"Bye..." Lindy watched Beryl go, the cheques she'd been writing laying forgotten in her lap. The friendly woman had given Lindy plenty to chew on. If Beryl, a professional playwright, believed that Lindy, a rank amateur, had 'potential'—but wait...hadn't Rochelle used that word?

Hadn't she said something about Lindy's play 'having potential?'

Okay, Lindy, she said to herself, what is going on here? These theatre people—do they all just use the same expressions? Or—hold on...didn't Beryl just tell her that she knew Rochelle and her company? And that she'd actually worked with them at some point?

Worked with them when? Lindy wondered.

Worked with them how?

Ottawa was not a large city. It wouldn't be difficult for Beryl and Rochelle to know each other very well...

Lindy didn't want to be suspicious of Beryl. She seemed like a kind and decent woman, and she told a fine story. But having dealt with some very slick theatre people for the last six months, Lindy wasn't sure. Why would Beryl care enough about someone whose play she hadn't even seen yet to offer to introduce her around to other artists?

"Lindy?" Rochelle was standing in front of her. "Why the long face?"

Lindy forced a smile and shrugged, "Just wool gathering. It's what we playwrights do. Oh, by the way, I have your first cheque."

She fished through the ones on her lap that she'd already written and presented Rochelle's to her.

Hey, *très cool*," laughed Rochelle, reading the amount. "That's a lot more than I was expecting."

"Everyone's getting the same."

"Yeah, I know. But I thought we had a pile of comps over the last few shows. Are you positive that your math is correct?"

"I took the amount the office gave me and divided it by three—"

"By three? Shouldn't it be by eight?"

"No. The two musicians opted for a flat fee, and Malcolm, Madelyn and I aren't taking a cut of the gate."

"You should. You're just as much a part of the Company as the rest of us."

Her bitterness resurging, Lindy forced herself to reply in an even voice. "Actually, we are the Company, Rochelle. Malcolm, Maddie and I are 'The Friends of Phyllis Theatre Company.' You and Darrick and Philippe are 'Faire le Clown.' We hired you to act in this show. Therefore, we are paying you. It is up to us whether or not we pay ourselves."

Rochelle's animated face had hardened. Without another word, she tucked her cheque in her tote bag and, as Lindy watched, marched toward the elevator. As Rochelle approached, the elevator door must have opened, because Lindy saw Beryl step into the hall. Rochelle confronted her. Lindy couldn't hear more than the occasional word, but, from the women's postures and the strident sound of their voices, the encounter was extremely frosty.

Lindy didn't want to meet up with either one of them right now. Gathering her paperwork, she stuck it in her tote bag and escaped to the exit.

Outside in the warm six o'clock sunshine, she paused at the top of the stone stairway, where the usual hangers-on loitered, to put on her protective sunglasses.

Lindy thought she might like to walk to the deli where they'd all eaten lunch after their technical rehearsal. She had plenty of time before tonight's show. There was no reason why she shouldn't wait in comfort with yummy food.

There were probably not going to be many dogs downtown that weren't securely leashed. Any owner would have to be nuts to let his dog run free in these busy streets. It was probably safe—

Or she could go just down the street to the Rideau Centre, under which she'd parked her car. She knew that there were never many dogs on that block and a half because the roads were so often clogged with traffic. And there should be no dogs at all inside the mall itself—

On the other hand—

"Lindy," Rochelle had come out to the stairway beside her, "let's go have supper at the deli. My treat," she smiled. "I just got paid."

Lindy was hungry and couldn't quickly come up for an excuse not to go, so she compartmentalized her anger with Rochelle and shrugged, "Okay."

Without further conversation, the women walked swiftly along dog-less sidewalks to the restaurant where they were soon settled into a booth by a large window. A harassed server took their order—Greek salad for Rochelle, poutine for Lindy—and quickly returned with their shareable half litre of the house's domestic white wine.

"Ah, Chateau de St. Catharines," chuckled Rochelle after her first sip, "refreshing like pop, but twice the buzz."

Lindy sipped her wine and managed a thin smile.

Rochelle measured her companion's mood and lost her grin. "Okay, you're still pissed. You've been pissed since we opened. And why? We're a hit, Lindy! The show's been packed. The audiences love us. The critics adore us! What the fuck have we done wrong?" She sat back with a scowl, impatient for Lindy to answer.

But Lindy had questions too.

"During rehearsals, why didn't you ever tell me or the others that you and the guys were members of your own theatre company? What is it with you and Beryl? And how come you think it's perfectly okay to cover up the real theme of my play with a bunch of cheap laughs?" she challenged.

Unexpectedly, Rochelle's face relaxed and she laughed. "*Ben là*, Lindy! Didn't we already cover all this? Well, not the Beryl thing, but that's pretty dull. She was my girlfriend for a couple of months before Jean-Maurice flew in from France, and, once I'd met him, I broke up with her *tout d'suite*. She's never forgiven me, I guess. Which is probably why she's been stalking you."

Lindy tried to be very twenty-first century and let the 'girlfriend' thing pass, but, "Stalking? A couple of conversations isn't—"

"Okay, I exaggerate—but I saw her giving you the 'we're both misunderstood playwrights' speech. Did she tell you about the roots and the trees and all that garbage?" Rochelle laughed at Lindy's guarded expression. "Yeah, it's one of her standard wheezes, the same one she used to score with me when I was trying to shop my first script. Did she tell you she can introduce you to her artist friends?"

Feeling totally out of her depth once more, Lindy nodded briefly.

"She's not lying. And after you go to her place to do that, she'll introduce you to a bottle of schnapps and her four poster bed. And then spend the next few months picking your brain for all your best material. You'd be surprised how much she got out of me before I ran for my life. Her next play was basically the one I'd been trying to sell, only set in Southern Ontario."

"Yes?" Lindy wasn't certain. Rochelle's tale certainly sounded like the truth, but, then again, she was an accomplished actor...

And Beryl seducing Lindy to steal her ideas? At her age? Who seduced grey-haired ladies? That seemed kind of far fetched. Although...theatre people...

Oh, yeah," smiled Rochelle grimly, "Beryl's a piece of work, for sure."

The harassed server finally plunked their food down, poured the last of the wine into their glasses and presented the bill.

"Do you mind paying now? I'm off shift after this."

True to her invitation, Rochelle ponied up the cash and the server shot away. The two women focussed their attention on their food for a while. The interruption gave Lindy time to think. She realized that Rochelle's story about Beryl had allowed her to avoid answering Lindy's other questions so, once her hunger had been assuaged, she asked them again.

"Okay, but your theatre company? And hijacking my play?"

Rochelle finished the last olive on her plate and sighed. "Our ex-company—that's right, Lindy, like I told you, Faire le Clown has been as dead as Jean-Maurice for the last two years—our ex-company hasn't hijacked your play. And we've used our talents to highlight your theme."

"By making Mary Yerst look ridiculous?"

"By making Mary look human. By showing that, as absurd as her fears may seem to the audience, they are obviously crippling to her. By forcing the audience to see that, because she can't find any real help, desperation has driven her to the Peevers' crackpot therapy séance."

"But the audiences laugh at Mary. She's not meant to be funny, and you guys make them all laugh at her."

"No, we don't. Not at Mary." Rochelle shook her head with finality. "At her struggle."

"But that's not funny either. I should know."

"Right, Lindy, I know about your issue with dogs, and I'd never laugh at you. Well, maybe a little—in private—with Serge," allowed Rochelle. "But, babe, you have to see, we're making the audience laugh at Mary's struggle to find relief from her pain, not because we're trying to make them see it as 'ridiculous.' We're making them laugh at it because—by magnifying it with humour—we're sticking it to them that they've been there too."

Rochelle moistened her mouth with the last of her wine. When her companion, still oozing skepticism, didn't comment, she threw up her hands.

"You know, Lindy," she said, earnestly, "it's like when you start smoking too much weed to self-medicate because your doctor just never listens to you. Or like when Darrick carries a dog around that's more scared than he is, so he can feel brave without the pills that make him too groggy to think straight. Or like when Jean-Maurice started mainlining that magical mushroom essence when the chemo didn't fuck his cancer." Pushing away her plate, Rochelle leaned across the table towards Lindy. "By making everything in your play gi-normous, we're making the audience empathize with Mary. We're forcing them to see that the ridiculous steps she's taking have been forced on her because fuck-all else has worked. And they laugh because they recognize themselves. Can't you see that at all?"

Lindy shook her head. "No, Rochelle, I can't."

"Well, come take another look then, Lindy. Check your preconceptions at the door, and come into the theatre tonight prepared to see what's really going on. Or try—at least try. Because we're breaking our balls for your play 'cause it's message is so important—and it's essential that we get it right. Okay? Can you at least do that? For us?"

"For Faire le Clown?"

"For The Friends of Phyllis," retorted Rochelle flatly. "That's our new theatre company. Your theatre company—yes, yours!—is our theatre company. Period. End of sentence. No fucking around. So give us your best shot. Okay?"

CHAPTER SIXTEEN

The Way of the World

Okay, thought Lindy, standing with the usher by the doorway as the house lights dimmed and the actors took their places.

I am here.

I am watching.

I am prepared to listen as openly as I can.

Rochelle, Darrick, Philippe—convince me that I'm wrong. That my play isn't lost. That you haven't clowned up *Small Comforts* just to amuse the groundlings...

It had been almost two days since their last show, which helped Lindy bring a fresh eye to the performance. Or else that supper with Rochelle tonight had knocked something loose. Because, although the laughter was just as long and loud, it didn't irk her the way it had in the last three shows. The actors did take a few liberties with her script, of course, but most of what she remembered writing was spoken. And, by concentrating on their performances—and not on her words—she came to the realization that the heart of her play's meaning was still there.

Yes, it was true, Rochelle and Darrick and his ludicrous 'cat' Leo had cunningly lowered the Peevers into comic book villains. And Philippe's Mary Yerst was escalated and stretched, her fearful reactions exaggerated into recurring gags. Yet Mary was never portrayed as the butt of a cruel joke. The actors were careful to never ridicule her essential anxiety nor did they excuse the Peever's wicked exploitation of it, and the honest emotional core of *Small Comforts* was still fully intact.

As she watched her play tonight, Lindy could definitely see that, if Rochelle's and Darrick's unspeakable Peevers were pond scum with fangs, Philippe's desperate Mary was an authentic tragic heroine, damaged but unbowed by her crippling distress. So, rather than feeling crushing resentment when the audience shouted with laughter at the blackboard finale, Lindy felt justified. People's hearty guffaws, she now acknowledged, were a cry of recognition that, in the end and forever, Mary Yerst was simply one of them as she tenaciously coped with an impossibly hostile landscape.

As the audience filed out, nattering like barmy squirrels, Lindy strode over to Rochelle to wordlessly envelope her in her arms. Philippe and Darrick made it into a vigorous group hug, which laughingly broke apart when Leo, squished, whined his distress. Then the four cheerfully joined the rest of the Company in tearing down the set so that the next show, a one-hander comic monologue from England, could slip in on time.

"Excuse me, mate," said the middle-aged brown comedian to Malcolm as they were leaving. "My director crashed his bike today, so could you with give me a hand with my set? It ain't heavy—just needs two blokes to hang..."

While Malcolm stayed to help in the theatre, Lindy went into the lobby hall, now filling up with ticketed patrons, to wait with Madelyn for the actors to bring out their costumes.

From out of the ladies' room, a multi-pearl-swagged Beryl bustled up.

"Sweetie! I finally got my bum in your seat tonight and I—" she started in, but Lindy had spotted someone much more important waiting to see her.

"Brittany!" she exclaimed, giving Beryl an apologetic glance, "it's great to see you! Did you see the play?"

"Absolutely," smiled Goldie's owner, "and it was fantastic!" She indicated a tall dark young man behind her. "This is my husband, John."

John stepped forward grinning. "That was phenomenal! I haven't laughed like that since university—and then I was usually drunk. You really are an amazing playwright!"

Brittany nodded enthusiastically.

Lindy blushed with pleasure. "Oh, I'm not really—"

"Yes, she's been hiding her light under a barrel for years," said Madelyn, stepping in. "Or at least at a desk in a Defense Department library. When Lindy finally blessed us with her gift, it was an epiphany for us all."

"So now the whole world knows," smiled Brittany. "Okay, we've got to run to our next show, but we wanted to congratulate you in person, because it was—" she laughed, fishing for a superlative.

"The goat," deadpanned her husband.

Everyone laughed again, although Lindy couldn't have explained why, then the young couple pattered off.

Lindy turned to Beryl who had stood patiently by all the while.

"So—any playwright to playwright tips?" she pleasantly asked.

"Sweetie, I wouldn't presume to tell you anything," said Beryl, fingering her pearls with a kindly smile. "Although, next time, you might want to cast some less frenetic actors." She pursed her lips and shook her head. "I could see that—out of respect for the material—Darrick and Philippe occasionally put a bit of an anvil on it. But I'm afraid Rochelle can never stop herself. She's so selfish. She takes her performances to a ridiculous level and then delights in upstaging every other actor on the set."

"I like the energy my actors bring to their performances," shrugged Lindy, bolstered by Goldie's owners' rave reviews. "I like how it connects them to the crowds..."

Behind Beryl's round figure, Lindy noticed Rochelle and Darrick peering out from the doorway to the dressing room. Rochelle ducked back inside but Darrick stepped briskly into the lobby.

"Of course, sweetie, but—"

"—and there's no way Rochelle's going to steal a scene from Leo," remarked Lindy, overriding Beryl's next criticism. "He's the star of our show, you know."

As Darrick handed over his suit to Maddie, Lindy smiled at the tiny dog, "Don't you agree, Leo?"

Leo, pleased to be out of his cat suit and into his summer-weight green vest, stretched out from Darrick's grasp and tried to lick her hand. Lindy smiled, let him touch her with his warm wet tongue, then scratched behind his soft ear and cooed, "Good show tonight, Leo. You really earned your biscuit."

Leo leaned into her caress and snuffled his joy.

"So, sweetie," Beryl smiled to Lindy, all sugar to hide her annoyance, "I guess you don't need any advice from me. I'll be off, then. I've got a ticket for 'Sammy's Sonata.' Word on the street is, it's a *bona fide* drama. The acting's supposed to be excellent. Perhaps you should try to get to it this week—just to see what proper casting can do for a play."

"'Sammy's Sonata?' Maddie and I saw that on Saturday," said Lindy evenly. "It was okay, but we thought the script was a little dry."

"Desiccated, hon," sniffed Madelyn, wrinkling her nose.

"Oh." Beryl dropped her supercilious smile, and bidding Lindy and Madelyn, but definitely not Darrick and Leo, a barely polite good-bye, sauntered away.

"Is the Queen of Filch gone yet?" asked Philippe, peeking around the dressing room door. He'd had a number of his original ideas turn up in Beryl's plays in the past, and he wasn't one of the well-connected playwright's fans.

"Philippe!" shrieked a very pregnant young blonde woman, who'd sat in the front row tonight, throwing herself at him. "*Tu etais formidable!*"

"*Merci, Adele!*" The pair bounced up and down together, then Philippe turned to Lindy. "This is my baby sister," he proudly announced, "Adele, this is Lindy. She is the Heart and Soul of The Friends of Phyllis Theatre Company."

"*Enchantee!*" bubbled Adele.

Lindy, her cheeks glowing pink once more, shook the young woman's proffered hand.

Rubbing a wrist that had gotten in the way of a steel pipe, Malcolm finally made his escape from the theatre.

"Is all of our Company assembled?" asked Darrick, as Rochelle and the musicians emerged from the dressing room too. "Shall we repair to the bar for a libation?"

"Sure," said Malcolm, "and I'm buying the first round."

Everyone was in a light, agreeable frame of mind. The players reported that weather outside the dressing room window had been perfect, starry and warm, so, as the volunteer ushers opened the venue for the Englishman's ten o'clock show, the entire Friends of Phyllis Theatre Company, plus Adele, headed for the beer tent plaza.

Madelyn had to drop off the costumes first, so she and Merrill detoured to her car, but very soon everyone was seated at a picnic table under the open sky enjoying a glass of beer, wine or soda, a selection of French pastries and several bags of veggie chips with, as Darrick declared, "a right good will!"

Rochelle grinned over at Lindy. "So you've decided to come back from the dark side?"

Lindy laughed. "Once I started to pay attention, it all fell into place. As you said, they really weren't laughing at Mary. They were empathizing with her predicament. Thanks for—what the heck is that—?"

At tables all around the plaza, people were posing the same question because, from deep within the halls of the Arts Court, a shrill fire alarm had begun to wail.

"It's probably nothing, my dears" said Darrick, shielding Leo's sensitive ears with one hand. "But, just in case it's not, I advise all of you to swallow your drinks. If they vacate the building, they'll send us off too." Darrick demonstrated his resolve by downing the last half of his beer in a generous swig.

"Will they actually vacate—?" started Lindy, but didn't need to finish her enquiry as a slew of audience members began to pour forth from the entrance to the smallest Arts Court venue, located behind the beer tent in the bowels of the old building.

Someone shut off the canned music that had enlivened the night, and a guy got on the loudspeaker to tell everyone in English and French that he was "sorry, folks, but you'll have to leave your alcoholic drinks on the tables and exit the beer tent plaza area immediately in a calm orderly manner, please."

All of The Friends of Phyllis drank down what they could, grabbed the rest of the snacks and rose to file out past the bouncers onto the quickly filling sidewalk. Once they'd elbowed their way to the corner, they could see that patrons were hustling out of every street level doorway of the Arts Court and streaming en masse down the stone staircase. Next door at the hostel, converted from a Victorian gaol in the nineteen-seventies, fleeing residents were joining the crush on the street.

Now, fire engine sirens could be heard screaming toward them from all directions, and the police had arrived to herd people to a safe distance away from the Arts Court. With onlookers already crowding every available clearing in the area, there was no use hanging around to see what would happen next. Shouting farewells, Lindy's Company split up to race to their cars or buses and make their way home.

Lindy, Malcolm, Madelyn and her teenage charges, Merrill and Hua, scurried down the street to the Rideau Centre parkade. The blare of the fire alarm was getting fainter to their ears, but "Oh my gawd!" cried Madelyn, who'd turned back for a last look at the Arts Court as they approached the door to the garage stairway.

As one, the rest of the group turned and gasped.

The edge of the Arts Court roof was engulfed in flames. Smoke belched from every crevice. They could see the old roof crackle and buckle in the heat. As they murmured to each other in dismay, a hot red glow began to pulse in the in windows of the third floor.

Oh Dear God, thought Lindy, the third floor is where our theatre is. Where our set is. Where our props are stored—!

"Wake up, guys!" suddenly shouted Malcolm, throwing open the garage stairway door. "We've got to get out of here before they rope off the streets!"

Through thickening traffic, Lindy managed to wheel her car onto the Rideau Canal parkway and slowly wend her way home. At one point, disruption from more speeding fire trucks sent her on to a less familiar route, but eventually she was able to turn down a street she knew better and confidently enter her neighbourhood from the east.

Once she pulled into her own driveway, Lindy called around to make sure that Rochelle, Darrick and Phillippe were safe and sound. Which everyone briefly assured her that they were, although Darrick confided that Leo was greatly distraught. Then, as she was about to call Maddie, she noticed Malcolm parking his car across the Avenue, so she got out to greet him.

"Madelyn's car got trapped in the garage," explained Malcolm. "So, she called me and I circled back to pick them up. The roads were pretty clogged but amazingly I spotted them and got her and the kids and the costumes over to Maddie's place. They were all stressed to the max, and I offered to drive Merrill and Hua home, but the kids said they were okay with hopping a bus from there."

He looked narrowly at Lindy, trying to gauge her mood.

"So—would you like me to stay tonight?"

Lindy sighed. "Yes—as Maddie would say—I think we'd both benefit from sympathetic society."

"No kidding," agreed Malcolm, so Lindy unlocked her door and ushered him inside.

Flicking on the television, the pair just managed to catch the story of the Arts Court fire on the local late night newscast.

Initial reports didn't sound good.

Originally built in the mid-1800's with thick outer stone walls, the Arts Court had been retro-fitted with fire doors and sprinkler systems over the years. However, as Lindy and Malcolm knew, it was full of nooks and crannies and its offices, meeting rooms, theatres and galleries were crammed with stacks of paper, varnished wood panelling, flammable fabric seating and combustible art.

Ironically, Lindy remembered, she'd seen a First Nation artist's birch bark sculpture in the main floor gallery entitled *Kindling*.

"I wonder if the artist will view the fire as an extension of his theme," she commented glumly to Malcolm.

"Maybe as a particularly brutal example of performance art?" was his equally grim response.

Lindy and Malcolm followed Twitter accounts of the blaze for an hour or so, then crawled into bed together to lie awake and doze and lie awake and doze for the rest of the night. By five-thirty in the morning, they were both up drinking coffee and wolfing toast and cereal, delighting Phyllis with an early morning breakfast. And at six, when the local morning show began, they moved into the living room to flip on the television again.

The breaking news was filled with graphic details of the tragic five-alarm blaze that had completely gutted one of downtown Ottawa's oldest architectural prizes.

Considering how antique and creaky the building was and how many people must have been in the Arts Court's rabbit warren of stages, dressing areas, restrooms, halls and lobbies at the time, fortunately—and against all odds—no one had been badly hurt. A few people had turned their ankles or wrenched their knees in the scramble to get out, and a custodian, a techie and a firefighter were suffering from smoke inhalation, but that was all the human toll. The equally ancient hostel next door had suffered smoke and water damage, but, thankfully, no one there had been harmed much either, and the building itself still stood intact.

It was five minutes to eight o'clock when Rochelle rang the doorbell.

"I knew you guys would be up," she said, handing Lindy a big bag of freshly baked bagels, a jar of Seville marmalade and a huge container of cream cheese.

At eight-fifteen, Darrick and Leo turned up with two dozen croissants, a couple of bottles of Prosecco and a large jug of orange juice.

And five minutes later, Philippe arrived in a borrowed car with a shell-shocked Madelyn in tow. He brought a tub of *cretons* and a whole wheat baguette and she, a boxed vegan quiche from her fridge which Lindy stuck in the stove to warm up.

While Malcolm and Philippe repositioned the television stand so everyone could see the screen from the dining room table, Lindy handled requests for coffee and tea. Darrick fixed mimosas in a glass pitcher and poured generous glassfuls for anyone who wanted an alcoholic cushion. Maddie sat staring into the middle distance and occasionally dabbed her eyes.

Then everyone settled in to share the food and drink and watch as the local colour-commentators interviewed the Fire Chief and the Arts Court General Manager and various eye witnesses to the tragedy. With fire crews still mopping up, the interviews were conducted beside the Rideau Centre parking garage, the remains of the Arts Court squatting in the middle distance, a reeking stone hulk surrounded by yellow hazard tape.

In a rare show of empathy—or possibly because she witnessed Leo being fed a doggie snack—Phyllis leapt up onto Lindy's lap, accepting a soft petting with a quiet purr.

For a while, except to ask politely for the marmalade or the cream cheese or a slice of quiche, nobody said much. At ten, the morning show wound up and Malcolm flicked off the television. He took a final helping of *cretons* and concentrated on spreading the pate on the last piece of baguette.

Lindy looked around at all the solemn faces.

"So..." she said in a small voice, "you guys figure we've lost everything?"

"Not everything," said Rochelle with a huge sigh. "We're all still here..."

"Yes," allowed Darrick, cuddling Leo safely in his lap, "if the conflagration had occurred an hour earlier, it might have been a much greater calamity."

Everyone nodded gravely.

"I've got the costumes..." quavered Madelyn uncertainly.

"But the set, the props, my folk's dining room table?" Lindy asked hopelessly.

"Well," said Malcolm sadly, "as much as I can't imagine anything fierce enough to destroy that damn spirit cabinet, I'm afraid it's all gone. Sorry about that, love. Maybe, just in case, somebody should go down later and check it out. But you know, Sarah and Jamie are flying in early this afternoon, so it won't be me."

"Um-hm, that's fair. But, geez, Greg and Nan were planning on driving to Ottawa on Friday to see the nine o'clock show and stay over, too," worried Lindy. "I wonder if they'll still want to come up now?"

"My mother didn't even get a chance to see Mary," chimed in Philippe wistfully. "She's seen every role I've ever played..."

"I know, babe," commiserated Rochelle. "Serge and the kids had tickets for the Sunday matinee. And Jenn was coming then too." She blew out another huge sigh. "*Merde!* I used to think the worst thing that could happen was a thunderstorm before intermission." Impatiently, Rochelle dashed stubborn tears from her eyes.

Wordlessly, Darrick offered to pass Rochelle the mimosa pitcher so she could pour herself another hit. With a tremulous smile, Rochelle waved it away. Straightening her shoulders, "What's the Fimbria Director saying on the web?" she asked Lindy instead.

Lindy gently passed Phyllis' limp slumbering body to Madelyn. "Yes, I guess we should suss it out."

She climbed the stairs to retrieve her laptop from her bedroom and returned to the dining room to pull up the site.

The message was concise.

Due to unforeseen circumstances, it said in a red outlined box, the destruction of the Fimbria office and Arts Court venues had forced the cancellation of the rest of the Festival, including those shows scheduled for the University and Bring-your-Own venues. Updates would be posted as soon as further policy was determined.

That was all.

No cause of the fire, no alternate information site, no emergency phone numbers.

Madelyn was puzzled. "Why would they cancel all the other venues too? Most of them are nowhere near the Arts Court."

Lindy shook her head. "I guess the office computers went up in flames too, so—"

Madelyn frowned. "—they've lost all their records?"

"No," answered Malcolm for Lindy, "I assume all that crap would be in the cloud. But they've probably lost their paper trail. You know, the permission letters, the producers' signatures, stuff like that."

"Do you think that means they've lost all the cash too?" said Philippe.

Lindy grimaced. "Most producers would have picked up their weekend cheques on Tuesday, like I did, I guess. But the cash ticket sales from Tuesday on?" She shook her head.

"Yeah," agreed Malcolm, "that's not looking good. Any cash from last night's performances, for example—unless it was in a majorly fire-safe box..." He grimaced and displayed a double thumbs down.

"That's dismal," sighed Darrick. "My professional colleagues live off their ticket sales. And I wonder if disappointed patrons with passes will want their money back?"

Malcolm shrugged. "Probably the lost pass policy will cover that. Probably. But who knows? This is going to be a shit storm for the Festival, no matter how you slice it."

"It would suck to be an international company doing the whole circuit," commented Rochelle, soberly. "Some of them blew off Montreal to do Ottawa. And I guess there won't any Best of the Fest performances. Damn, I thought we were a shoe-in this year."

"And what about the Fimbria Awards?" added Philippe. "And the Prix Bytowns? I was hoping—" His voice broke, the enormity of his loss too overwhelming to contemplate. He covered his eyes and bowed his head.

Sniffling back a tear, Darrick tenderly patted his gentle friend's shoulder.

Everyone sunk into the deepest gloom.

Phyllis jumped out of Maddie's arms, making her tear up too.

Lindy took a sip from her tea cup and put it down. It had gone stone cold.

Malcolm pulled the laptop over to him, searching for pictures of the Arts Court fire in a desultory way.

Darrick took final gulp of mimosa, draining his glass.

Leo whimpered as Phyllis stalked him from the sideboard. Lindy pursed her mouth, shaking her head at her irredeemable cat.

Then Rochelle chuckled out loud. Instantly, she had everyone's attention. "Aren't we a sorry crew," she said, stretching luxuriously in her chair.

"But Rochelle," began Madelyn, mournfully, "this year's Fimbria—"

"Oh, fuck this year's Fimbria!" grinned Rochelle, sending a shock through her tablemates all 'round.

"Fuck...?" echoed Madelyn faintly.

"By which I mean to say—*ben là*, Friends of Phyllis, enough melodrama! It's time to forget *Small Comforts* and move on with our lives!"

Lindy shook her head firmly at Rochelle. "Maybe for you, guys. But I've lost my shirt on this deal. My entire investment has been burnt up—"

"For the first time," interrupted Rochelle, flatly, "and probably not the last." She favoured Lindy with one of her trademark winks. "Babe, we're artists, aren't we? And we'll all survive, *n'est-ce pas?*"

Lindy's face remained clouded, but Darrick's and Philippe's lips began to crack into smiles. Rochelle laughed again and nabbed Phyllis for a robust petting as she pussy-footed by.

Malcolm lifted an eyebrow and shrugged to Madelyn, "The show must go on?"

"That's what I've always heard," she shrugged back at him.

Then, letting fully ruffled Phyllis bounce back to the floor, Rochelle turned her attention on their still frowning Playwright and Director. Her grin tempered into a sympathetic smile. "Okay, Lindy—*c'est vrai*. You've spent a boatload of dough on this year's show. And we're all grateful, we really are. But the blaze of glory that was *Small Comforts* is reduced to ash and cinders. And now it's somebody else's turn to bankroll. I'll tell Serge the Orthodontist," she shrugged. "He won't mind. I'll make sure of that."

Rochelle grinned wickedly. Darrick and Philippe nodded conspiratorially. Leo yawned a smile.

Evil felines, every one of them, despaired Lindy. A clowder of narcissistic, preening, selfish cats. Even Leo, that most feline of dogs. Poor Serge, she drily reflected, amusement beginning to make an inroad on her sorrow, he'll never stand a chance. I wonder whether he knew what he was marrying into...?

But Rochelle wasn't finished yet. "So, babe," she continued, diabolically, "what're you planning to write for us next year?"

"Next year?" repeated Lindy, startled out of her reverie.

"Yeah," said Rochelle, grinning confidently, "next year...outside...in the parks..."

"In the parks?" Lindy looked wildly about at the rest of The Friends of Phyllis, every one of whom was regarding at her with encouraging smiles.

"We know you've got the talent to do it," nodded Malcolm.

"And you know that you can count on me for artistic support," declared Madelyn.

"A new theme, I think, but one with the same weight of import?" suggested Darrick.

"I'd like another breeches role," specified Philippe.

"Well, that's settled," grinned Rochelle. "So cry 'Havoc!,' Lindy, and let slip the pups of your creativity!"

Everyone laughed.

Except Lindy.

Oh Dear God and All Angels, she thought, shaken to her soul. Me write another show? A play for the parks? Outside in the open air? With millions of dogs running around?

Oh, damn...

She could see it now...labs and collies...mastiffs and boxers...Rottweilers and pit bulls ...jaws and fangs and claws...blood on her clothes...blood on the grass—Crack! Crack!!

But no, Lindy's mental elastic band wasn't working and her panic was mounting high. She might have bested her fear of Leo, but she was nowhere near addressing the roots of her terror of all things canine. Deep in the back of her mind she could feel the nasty voice stir. If she was going to slow her heart rate, to regain any degree of calm, she'd have to decompress in the usual way.

"A doggington bark," Lindy began to loudly intone, to all but Phyllis' surprise. "A doggington woof. A doggington growl..."

"Steady on, old girl," urged Darrick, alarmed.

But her mantra was working, so Lindy ignored him. "A doggington ruff. A doggington snarl. A doggington howl..."

"Playwrights," shrugged Rochelle.

The Company dissolved into laughter once more. Then Malcolm sobered and, with a fond glance at his daffy ex-wife, addressed the rest of the group. "So," he asked, cheerfully, "where do we go from here?"

Steadily chanting, Lindy wondered too. Her Company seemed to be sweeping her relentlessly down a hazardous path which would require a level of courage and grit that she'd never dreamed that she might possess.

Just how far have I grown in these last ten months? she questioned herself. Am I ready to move on with my Company? Ready to be that...somebody?

Or were Dad and Greg right to restrain me—a little nobody—from disgracing myself?

With her heart rate slowing to normal, Lindy was able to cease her soothing chant. I've done okay so far, she reminded herself. I put on the Fimbria show that I said I would—and it was pretty much a success. But a summer theatre troupe? Out in the wide open world?

Do I have that kind of gumption? mused Lindy. I know that I didn't used to—but do I have it now?

Can I become a professional playwright? Can I write another good play? Can I face down the Infernal Hounds of the Ottawa Parks?

Lindy wasn't sure what the answers might be. Yet—as she listened to her Company eagerly debating the pros and cons of renting an alternative foul weather playsite—she knew for certain that she desperately wanted to find out...

CHAPTER SEVENTEEN

A Flea in her Ear

So much had conspired—a good word to choose considering with whom she was dealing, thought Lindy sardonically as she gussied up in her bedroom before catching the bus to this evening's playsite. Yes, so much had conspired since *Small Comforts* had literally gone up in smoke in the Arts Court fire.

Rodent-gnawed electrical wiring in the attic's wooden rafters had turned out to be the cause of the blaze. And so it seemed that *Small Comforts*—and the future of last year's entire Fimbria Festival—had been doomed by an ill-starred mouse.

But that was then and this was now. The world had moved inexorably on, and now, as Lindy choose a light but modest cream tee-shirt for the hot July afternoon, she mulled over the events of the last twelve months.

First of all, she considered, pulling on a pair of khaki capris, there were the births.

After a lot of discussion—and an occasional shouting match—by the end of July the defunct companies of The Friends of Phyllis and Faire le Clown had been reborn as a new traveling theatre troupe. Named 'Excursion

Theatre,' it was a not-for-profit professional outfit with fine accoutrements like an artistic mandate, a high school apprenticeship program and a charitable organisation registration.

"All of which should ease our tax burden considerably," Darrick had blandly assured Malcolm.

Lindy, Malcolm, Rochelle, and Darrick were on the Board of Directors, along with Leo, of course, and also Philippe—who, to his gratification, had won 'Best Performance by an Actor' for the role of 'Mary Yerst' in the Prix Bytown Awards at the end of last year.

Rochelle's wealthy Serge the Orthodontist had been easily tapped for start-up as well as initial production funding. And so, projected budget in hand, one of the Board's first actions had been to hire Jenn Lundehund as interim Website Builder and Publicity Manager.

Lindy thought that Jenn, preparing for a year's maternity leave from her government job, had welcomed the opportunity to keep a foothold in the arts. She'd been sadly disappointed to give up her leading role in *Small Comforts* last spring, but Jenn's spare body had simply refused to gracefully accept its nurturing role, and her pregnancy had soon become just one hugely awkward nauseous nightmare.

"I just couldn't stand the smell of eggs or toast or coffee," she'd confessed to Lindy, "so I couldn't eat breakfast at the deli or darken a Starbucks' door for almost an entire year! And it's true, you know—the Chateau Laurier hotel does have the loveliest ladies' rooms in town—and the Sears at the Carlingwood Mall has the worst!"

Jenn's evolving friendship with Rochelle had been an enormous help, however, as she'd plodded through the last five wretched months. Like a mother cat who'd adopted an orphan duckling, the actor had accompanied Jenn on her doctor visits, found her an excellent midwife and coached her through her pre-natal exercises.

Rochelle had gotten Lindy to do most of the driving, of course, but, as the actor had blithely remarked, "Since you don't have to suffer the ouch, Lindy, you should be glad to contribute to Jenn's sterling effort to increase the population of Canada."

"Although I might be happier to contribute," Lindy had privately grumbled to Malcolm, "if Rochelle ever saw fit to bestow a little cash on my constantly expanding gas tab."

All the same, when Jenn's full-term healthy baby, Harriet Pearl Lundehund, had been born at the end of November, Lindy had rejoiced along with the rest of the company. Baby gifts and heartfelt blessings had flowed, making it obvious that the pretty child was going to be surrounded by a goodly number of ersatz uncles and aunts.

Lindy, Maddie and Malcolm had chipped in to buy Shaker design baby furniture.

Darrick and Leo had showered the newborn with Kate Greenaway nursery art and a soft chihuahua stuffie.

And Philippe had bestowed delicate woolen hats, booties and sweaters knitted by his Maman and sister, Adele, which Jenn had immediately decided were far too lovely to use—and carefully stored away in acid-free tissue paper as an heirloom for her future grandchildren.

Meanwhile, Rochelle had given Jenn kindly tips about breast-feeding—with which Jenn had struggled, yet scrupulously persisted in—and good advice about how to cater to and comfort a tiny child. She had also generously volunteered her capable teenage step-daughter, Gabrielle, for babysitting. And, at Malcolm's request, his daughter Sarah—a great source of single parenting lore—had begun to regularly skype with Jenn from Calgary.

But Jenn had never heard a word from Terence Harrier.

In fact, even before *Small Comforts* had held its geriatric Preview last May, Terence had scarpered back to his American college. Malcolm and Darrick had surmised that the little man had made the mistake of still believing the old '500 Mile Rule' which stated that indulging in personal flings far from home would never have any heavy consequences. So, when his Canadian one night stand had resulted in an actual pregnancy, he'd panicked and rejected his paternity. As soon as possible, he'd made tracks for the border—and 'goddam jerk' was the kindest name that Malcolm ever called him for abandoning all responsibility for his child.

However, Jenn, her tears long shed and dried, had now become quite comfortable with this state of affairs. Everyone agreed that placid little Harrie was nothing like her abrasive daddy, in either looks or temperament. And Jenn, having accepted the others' dim view of Terence—and being reluctant to engage in a bitter cross-border child-support war—had been relieved that he'd taken himself so thoroughly out of the picture.

No longer in the throes of morning sickness—and with a lamb-like baby who'd made her better socially connected than she'd ever been in her entire life—by late February Jenn had put the cherry on top of Excursion Theatre's new website and moved on to her publicity management duties.

So then, mused Lindy—as she pattered downstairs to her front vestibule for her new pink sandals—in early March the Excursion Theatre Board had been able to advertise for high school apprentices and techie hires. They had called for auditions in April and had been ready to post a firm summer schedule by the beginning of May.

Glancing in the antique mirror at her recently trimmed greying bob, Lindy remembered that she'd worried a lot about going head-to-head with other more established summer theatre companies—particularly the famous one she'd heard that Beryl was again writing for—but her associates had pooh-pooh her fears.

"We're mainly going to set up in parks that no one else is visiting," Darrick had patiently explained.

"And when we're not, we've tried to leave at least a week or so between us and the other guys," Malcolm'd added.

"And, if we haven't—well, the more, the merrier," Rochelle'd laughed.

Until Excursion Theatre was up and running, Lindy recalled—as she checked that her front door was firmly locked—the Board had agreed that Rochelle and Philippe were free to take commitments elsewhere. So, while Producers Malcolm and Darrick spent the fall and winter dealing with sponsorship proposals and government grant applications—and the usual purchasing, hiring, scheduling and booking—the two actors had auditioned for theatre and other media roles.

Predictably, Rochelle had been awarded a major speaking part in a local professional show playing in early November—which had allowed her to get her union card re-instated—and had picked up a lucrative job making

French tapes for a language instruction start-up in Kanata. At the same time, Philippe—with his teeth attractively fixed by Serge—had been cast in a pair of Montreal-based television ads for winter vacation packages in Quebec. This had led to a minor role in a made-for-television movie, filming in late February in a small town on the outskirts of Ottawa. By the end of March, however, both actors had been back full time with Excursion Theatre, helping with supplementary auditions and publicity and gearing up for rehearsals to begin in mid-May.

So much for the births, thought Lindy, deciding to trust the weather forecast that said she wouldn't need her umbrella tonight. Next, there were the weddings and celebrations.

To everyone's shock—including her own, chuckled Malcolm—in September, Madelyn had abruptly married props builder Andrea Spitzer's charming Uncle Jasper Lowchen. He'd then whisked her off to live in his deluxe ocean-view condo in Victoria, British Columbia.

Which had been lucky in some ways, Lindy now realised—settling on taking, but not wearing, her cream sunhat—although she quite often missed her flighty friend.

On the other hand, with his arch rival Maddie married and gone, Malcolm had become firmly wed to his retirement career of producing Excursion Theatre and now favoured Lindy's home and bed much more frequently.

So there was a balance in the universe.

Madelyn's nuptials had been celebrated by a select group of close family and friends under the climbing ivy in Darrick's classy townhouse garden. As maid of honour in a definitely un-Lindy-ishly lime green sateen frock, Lindy had held Maddie's heavy bouquet of Olde English roses. Darrick had been best man and, on a specially sewn lace cushion on the back of his dashing tux, Leo had carried the rings.

A flower-bedecked Hellmutt had also been slated to be part of the ceremony. But, to Madelyn's sorrow and Lindy's undying relief, Maddie's dear friends, Cynthia and Ricardo, who had volunteered to drive the doggington growl out west to rendezvous with the new bride in Victoria, had been forced by a family mix-up over a borrowed van to depart two days before the wedding.

"Thank God for small blessings," Lindy had murmured to Rochelle, as she tugged up her off-the-shoulder lime green sateen sleeves. "All Maddie's big day needed was for me to dissolve in a puddle when Hellmutt glanced at me sideways—"

Then, with the knot firmly tied, the happy newlyweds had treated a much expanded list of guests to a tasteful cocktail reception at a swanky downtown boutique hotel, a mere half block away from the burnt-out core of the Arts Court ruin.

With Hellmutt being driven inexorably westward, reflected Lindy—polishing her sunglass lenses—on the morning after the celebration, she and Malcolm had dropped off the oldster newlyweds at the airport.

There, Maddie had been deeply affected by Lindy's warm farewell and had fervently invited her to visit as soon as she could.

"You must shake off the dust of dreary old Ottawa, hon," The Empress Madelyn had trilled—as Jasper coped with the extra charges for his new wife's overweight suitcases—and then graciously added, "and Malcolm might benefit from making the journey too. Oh yes, my friends," she'd carolled with mounting enthusiasm, "both of you must come see us in the bracing sea air of our spacious inner harbour abode!"

Which the pair of them had subsequently done in late October when, with Lindy's newly-issued passport in hand, she'd spent the remainder of Dad's bequest on the last minute booking of a posh balcony suite for a fortnight round trip cruise from Vancouver to the Hawaiian Islands.

"I'm up for Hawaii," Malcolm had approved. "Lots of volcanic activity there."

Malcolm had paid for their flights from Ottawa to the West Coast, their ferry rides to and from Vancouver Island and their rental car. He'd also good-naturedly shelled out for six nights in a hotel room during their visit to Maddie and Jasper in Victoria since, with Hellmutt in residence, the condo hadn't turned out to be nearly as 'spacious' as advertised.

So Lindy had felt that splashing out a little on her first attempt at ocean travel with Malcolm had been well justified.

The cruise line hadn't allowed pet dogs, the seas had been calm, Mount Kilauea had been erupting and it had only pelted rain for three of the seven days that they'd been in Victoria so, all in all, Lindy considered—as she hunted through her living room for her purse—that she and Malcolm had enjoyed a very pleasant three weeks indeed.

"Italy next year," Malcolm had happily suggested on their flight home. "I'll see if one of my Neapolitan colleagues can get us in to see the Campi Flegrei before it blows up."

While Malcolm had been away, Darrick was supposed to be minding the shop, but a death in his Toronto family had called him and Leo away for two of the three weeks, and so there were lots of production pieces to pick up after both his and Malcolm's planes had hit the Ottawa airport tarmac on successive days mid-way through November.

Then, as December rolled around again, Lindy recalled—as she finally located her purse in the living room and proceeded to off-load her bus pass and credit cards into her roomier tote bag—she'd felt a bit lost without Madelyn around to share a tipple or a festive holiday meal. And she'd missed Malcolm, who'd flown to Calgary for two weeks to visit Sarah and Jamie.

But, on the weekend before Christmas, Philippe had driven Lindy across the Ottawa River to his mother's Gatineau ski chalet to meet Adele's baby girl at a lively Franglais carol-sing. Lindy had been very pleased to be included and, after a lot of fussing over what would be appropriate as a hostess gift for a French Canadian dinner, she'd decided to bring traditional iced shortbread stars and snowflakes from a Bank Street bakery.

However, Philippe's pianist Maman, a *Québécoise* with smiling Irish eyes who worked for the Feds at Export Development Canada, had been more interested in the music than the menu. Instead of the *tourtière* and *ragoût de boulettes* that Lindy had expected from her internet search, Maman had simply ordered in heaps of fragrant Chinese, Malaysian and Thai food for her culturally diverse crowd.

There hadn't been many sweets, however—just a co-worker's box of Laura Secord chocolates and the iced cookies she'd brought—so, to Lindy's complete satisfaction, the shortbreads had disappeared almost the moment they'd been set out.

Next, Darrick and Leo had invited Lindy to be one of the five artsy guests seated around their glistening board for a sumptuous Christmas dinner. After smoked salmon rillettes, roasted beetroot salad and cranberry glazed Cornish hens with wild rice stuffing, Darrick and Leo had paraded in their masterpiece—a lush chocolate mocha cream yule log festooned with meringue mushrooms and white chocolate pinecones.

Despite the lavish dessert, Darrick had also graciously plated and served the traditional iced shortbread that Lindy had brought in a plastic container. Unfortunately, the cookies had immediately provoked an energetic argument among his brandy-soaked friends about whether or not unsalted butter was essential for a tender crumb.

Appealed to as the presumed baker of the treats, Lindy had guiltily muttered something about Mom's old fashioned recipe from the sixties. Which had resulted in the youngest and loudest member of the salted-butter-faction blustering, "And was unsalted butter widely marketed to the housewives of the mid-twentieth-century? I think NOT! Thereby proving irrefutably that we are correct!"

Lindy hadn't had any idea who was right. She'd never baked a batch of homemade cookies since her eighth grade home economics class. But she'd worried what sort of verbal explosion might happen if the other guests had found out, so she'd simply requested another slice of Darrick's and Leo's delicious cake and kept that information to herself.

And last, but definitely not least, having deposited their shih tzu, Gérard, in a cushy kennel overnight, Rochelle and Serge the Orthodontist had invited Lindy and Malcolm and the rest of the Excursion Theatre gang to a lavish New Year's Eve soiree at their exquisitely decorated Georgian-style home in the old-money neighbourhood of Rockcliffe Village. Planned as a bang-up occasion for the Gagnons' family and friends, the opulent entertainment had come complete with a groaning seafood buffet, a decadent sweets table, a midnight champagne toast—and fireworks twinkling above their snowy garden terrace.

Lindy had had her doubts when she spied the tower of *macarons*, the *tartes au sucre* and the platters of artisanal donuts and *éclairs*. But Ariel, Felix, Gabrielle and their young cousins had merrily gobbled up the iced shortbread cookies that she'd brought on a festive dollar store plate. So she'd been pleased that Rochelle had squeezed her hostess gift in among the densely packed desserts after all.

As Lindy had later confessed to Malcolm, with multiple seasonal delights to attend, she'd never once regretted opting out of her sister-in-law Nan's bland Yuletide invitation. But on Christmas Day—as she now remembered, stashing her cellphone in her tote bag—she'd phoned Greg to touch base and insist that he and Nan plan a trip to Ottawa in early July.

Because thirdly—and most significantly for Lindy— there'd been her new play.

For, while Excursion Theatre had still been in its nascent form, Rochelle had begun to coax, wheedle and finally strong-arm Lindy into writing their next show—and it had to be a full evening of theatre this time around. So, bulldozing her enormous heap of self-doubt aside, Lindy had begun to write again…

Entitled *A Tale My Father Told Me*, the two act script which had resulted was meant to be a sombre domestic drama about a mean father who meets his comeuppance for his unkind treatment of his daughter.

Rochelle, Darrick and Philippe had been enthusiastic. But Malcolm had looked a little uneasy at the Company meeting where Lindy had initially sketched out the plot.

"Are you sure you want to go there?" he'd asked her privately afterwards. "You know, you and your Dad—" He'd winced and shaken his head.

"Well, it's what popped out of my brain," Lindy had sighed, "and I guess I'll find out…"

And—at first—it had seemed as if Malcolm had been absolutely right to fret.

For several long weeks the nasty badgering voice had brutally disrupted Lindy's every attempt to rest. But, as the details of Lindy's plot and her heroine's character had grown stronger, the jagged string of milky-tea-and-peanut-butter-cracker-television-nights had only served to thicken her skin and shore up her resolve to explore the essence of her pain. In fact, the act of writing the heart-shredding play had seemed to diminish rather than intensify her anxiety and, as the long winter had slogged by, Rochelle's bossy voice had become the dominant one in Lindy's head, urging her to get busy editing another scene.

Despite its stubborn demand that she minutely explore endless tracts of harrowing emotional terrain, through her early drafts, Lindy had rather enjoyed writing a drama again. But, to her annoyance, she now had real theatre professionals critiquing her dialogue. So her script had undergone at least eleven revisions before Rochelle and Darrick had deemed it ready to produce and, by the time the baby squirrels were digging up the tulip bulbs in Lindy's front yard, she'd been heartily sick of every line.

In Rochelle's opinion, however, Lindy's primary blocking and direction couldn't be beat as a basis for later improvisation. So, in mid-May, Lindy had once more met her Company for rehearsals at St. Jude's church hall and, flipping her hair behind her ears, begun to direct her playscript as well.

As she'd listened to her actors at the first read-through, Lindy had decided that she was pleased with how her casting had turned out.

Philippe, of course, played Emily Ryste, the bullied but increasingly defiant daughter and Rochelle was Judith Seever, her canny next door neighbour and willing accomplice. On Rochelle's advice, Chuckie Calamansi had been awarded the meaty role of Albert Ryste, the domineering father, leaving Darrick and Leo to perform as Albert's vile toady, Roger Cane, and his evil dog, Ned.

The small roles of the lawyer, the accountant, the banker, the doctor, and Albert's and Emily's other neighbours were capably shared between two university theatre students who, on first hearing, had seemed well up to the job of delineating each secondary character in a memorable way.

With four professional actors and two gifted theatre students in the cast for the entire six week rehearsal period,

Lindy had found her directing tasks slightly easier. She'd been able to do table work or block or honestly criticize performances without anyone making rude remarks or stomping out in a rage.

Even so, she'd been forced to put her foot down several times when script interpretations or egos clashed. And keeping the focus on the principal actors in each scene had swiftly become her greatest headache.

"I'd prefer it if you'd give each other a little more room to act," Lindy had gently urged her talented actors early on.

"Please stop attracting attention away from the speaker," she'd later sharply reminded her inconsiderate cast.

"Quit stealing each others' thunder!" she'd finally squawked at the selfish bastards. "You too, Leo! I saw you making those puppy dog eyes!"

There was a reason why 'generous actors'—those who give others the time and space to perform on stage—are so appreciated by their fellow artists, Lindy thought wryly as she slipped a couple of throat-taming mints into her tote bag for tonight. Without Maddie there to kibitz, she hadn't known the exact theatrical term, but she'd soon realized that unless she insisted that they behave, her players— professionals and amateurs alike—would frankly sabotage each others' performances with devilish regularity.

On the designing side, Darrick's clear sketches of his roaring twenties set and costume designs had been a huge help, allowing Lindy to visualize an actual performance of the final production. He'd also come up with an enticing poster and eye-catching programs—and charmed competent Jenn into sewing much of their wardrobe.

"We did so enjoy perusing the photos of your nephew in his zombie pizza get-up—" Darrick had begun and, although her days were already jammed with feeding schedules and press releases, Jenn just couldn't say 'no.'

Maddie's nephew Merrill hadn't been available for the show—he was jetting off to the Czech Republic to perform in his second cousin's chamber orchestra for the summer—but they'd paid him to compose another original score and engaged Hua and her sister, Lei, to play it live at the performances on the flute and violin.

Meanwhile, as naturally thrifty Philippe had helped Rochelle make the rounds of the second hand shops to source whatever hand props they could find, the actual construction of most of the set pieces, as well as of the props that they couldn't buy, had been frugally handled by Lindy and Malcolm. Only once, on the day of a rather complicated build, had Designer Darrick attended one of their 'cut, glue and paint' sessions in Lindy's basement.

The set piece in question was a high-backed garden bench with a trap in the back through which an eavesdropper could access a hiding spot under the seat. Darrick had wanted some very particular dimensions and, having seen how Malcolm had botched up the spirit cabinet, hadn't trusted him to build it unsupervised.

Leo had joined them downstairs for a while, but the sawdust had made the little dog sneeze and he'd seemed disturbed by the smell of the glue. So Darrick had deposited him upstairs on the living room sofa in his comfy 'backstage bed' which his owner had brought along just in case of such doggish sensitivities.

Thus, Darrick had been predictably huffy when he and Lindy had come upstairs to get some coffee only to discover that Phyllis had bullied Leo out of its lovely fuzziness, so that now his little companion was curled tightly at the opposite end of the sofa in ignominious defeat.

"I see that Phyllis has not taken her titular demotion in our theatre company lightly, my dear," he'd sniped as he'd unceremoniously dumped the cat out on to the floor and restored Leo to his cozy bed. "Perhaps you should make it clear to her that, as a Board Member and a Leading Actor, Leo now far outranks her in importance and talent and, therefore, is much more deserving of First Class treatment in every way!"

"I'll have a word with her," Lindy had said, hoping to placate her incensed colleague. Eyeing her cat severely, she'd scolded, "Mind your manners, Puss, or there'll be no tuna tonight!"

Darrick had nodded with grim satisfaction. "Well spoken, Madame Director."

However, silver-grey Phyllis, unabashed, had licked her paw and bided her time. And, as soon as the humans had returned to the basement with their hot drinks—taking a leaf out of Rochelle's playbook—she'd nonchalantly booted poor Leo out of his bed once more.

Wonderful techie Thom Mudi from last year's Fimbria had been contracted for the summer to run their sound and lighting board. And Lindy blessed the day that Stage Manager Extraordinaire, Jessie Bergamasco—eldest born in a large Italian-Canadian family—had been hired. With her iron will and velvet gloves, the green-eyed woman made it look easy to shepherd the cast and wrangle the technical crew through even the most chaotic situations. No actor, no floodlight, no costume could ever go astray under her calm supervision.

The professionals respected Jessie.

The student actors bowed to her.

The high school apprentices adored her…

Malcolm had quibbled a little about paying their union salaries but Lindy had insisted that the Company had to find room in the budget. Thom was already a proven marvel and, from the moment she'd walked into the rehearsal hall, Jessie was worth the combination of everyone else's weight in twoonies.

By mid-June, *A Tale My Father Told Me* had begun to take on a life of its own. And this time—Lindy had thought with burgeoning confidence as she watched her actors animate her script in the direction that she'd chosen—this time I've got it right. This time, she'd preened, I'm the truly the queen of my show. Take that! you uppity cats..!

Yet, inevitably, by the time the solemn social drama Lindy had wrung from her anguished soul had stood on its feet beneath the towering pines of a downtown park for its first July Preview, her troupe of commedia dell'arte schooled players had morphed it into another hilarious farce.

"Damn," Lindy had grumbled to herself, as the story unfurled, "Rochelle and Philippe, Darrick and Leo—you've scammed me again!"

Still, while the show had been howlingly funny, Lindy had to admit that once more her engaging actors had managed to preserve her basic theme and confidently sell it to the diverse crowd. Their emotional appeal and skillful technique demanded unqualified attention—and got it in spades.

Which wasn't so simple when lost toddlers hollered for their moms...

Or when bats insisted on skimming through the set...

Or when approaching rain clouds forecast a stormy commute home...

In the final scene, browbeaten Emily revealed to her contemptible father that, with the aid of clever Judith and her associates, she—his only child—was the true architect of his financial and social humiliation. The revelation—an open secret with the audience—and Albert's resulting impotent fury was always greeted with shouts of delighted laughter and satisfied applause.

For Davida had defeated Goliath.

The fool had hoodwinked the tyrant.

The loser had trounced her vanquisher.

Oh, how the mighty had fallen!

And Lindy's actors made damn sure that their audience cared profoundly that Emily arose triumphant in the end…

The critics had praised the sassy play and the weather so far had been kind. By this point, including the two Previews, Excursion Theatre had performed eight well-attended shows in five different city parks.

One of which Beryl had attended two nights ago.

"Sweetie, I'm so sad for you," she'd crocodile smiled. "Once again you've allowed Faire le Clown to undermine your perfectly adequate script. You really should let me introduce you around to some artists that I know..."

So Beryl had liked it too.

And I have to be content with that, Lindy supposed, as she petted Phyllis good-bye, donned her protective sunglasses, locked her side door and headed across the Avenue to await her bus in the hot July mid-afternoon sun.

I wanted to put on one show and now I've put on two. That's a great accomplishment for a retired old lady.

I wanted my friends to help me produce and direct. Now I've got a whole lot more friends to drive me out of my mind.

And I can't be a selfish cat about where my actors take my scripts. The audiences eat up their schtick.

Still, mused Lindy, as her bus turned the corner and stopped for her to clamber on, I really wish somebody would take my dramatic writing seriously sometime.

But then again, she had to admit—sinking into a window seat near the back door—I'll be lucky if Greg doesn't go completely berserk when he catches me seriously parading our family woes in front of the Great Unwashed while he and Nan watch my play tonight...

CHAPTER EIGHTEEN

The Homecoming

As promised, the kids were waiting for Lindy at the Bank Street bus stop. Along the broiling sidewalk and down the cool stone steps they led her, away from the traffic's dirt and noise, into the green oasis of the Glebe's Central Park.

Lindy's fear of dogs was still troublesome—well, not with Leo, who wasn't an actual dog, per se—but the Company had become highly sensitized to her need for safety, and great precautions were taken that, at every open air performance, she was actively shielded from doggington pounces and doggington jaws.

On their way to the playsite, eight-year-old Ariel turned cartwheels through the fresh summer grass, but fifteen-year-old Felix stuck close beside Lindy, prepared to defend her boldly against all doggington passersby.

There were a couple of dogs who got Lindy's attention, a bouncy white terrier and a gloomy basset hound, but both were securely leashed and walking briskly with their owners on another pathway. Trusty Felix made a show of placing himself and Ariel in between Lindy's nerves and the canines, so she just pushed her greying bob behind her ears and walked on.

As Lindy and her lively escort approached a shaded dell, Malcolm looked up from his folding chair and waved a sheet of paper at her.

"The Ontario supplemental arts grant came through. We might be able to keep the lights on this week."

Sitting beside him, Serge Gagnon, a clean-cut balding white Franco-Ontarien man in his early fifties, smiled and said in lightly accented English, "Don't kid yourself, Malcolm. You're running a theatre company. There will never be enough money. It's like having teenagers who'll never move out."

"True," allowed Malcolm, as Lindy plunked into a chair on his other side and smilingly dismissed her guards to find amusement elsewhere, "but if I think about that too much, I'll never sleep at night."

From the perspective of her lawn chair, Lindy checked out tonight's site. It was a rather nice one—grassy, treed, and fairly private, well away from traffic noise and with no children's climbers anywhere. Much more secluded than the one they'd loaded into yesterday at a crowded park in the city's suburban south end. There, during their first few scenes, they'd had to compete with the hubbub of an early evening soccer game on the next field.

Which actually turned out to be a good thing, reflected Lindy, because the audience had swollen with curious soccer fans as soon as the game was through. Some of them stayed to watch the rest of the show—and the bigger the crowd, the bigger the buzz. And the bigger the buzz, the bigger the take when the actors affably passed the hat after the performance too.

Beneath a stand of lofty catalpa trees, several high school apprentice techies—Serge and Rochelle's seventeen-year-old Gabrielle among them—had just finished setting up the low banked stage and were now unfolding the painted scenery cloths to hang at the back on its pipework scaffolding.

In the audience area, the university student the Board had hired as Front of House Manager was supervising two more teenage apprentices who were laying down bright yellow ropes to keep patrons back from the edge of the stage and out of a central aisle.

On stage, Stage Manager Jessie was consulting with Techie Thom about positioning the portable lights.

Behind the stage, members of the cast were warming their voices and gossiping as they limbered up.

Across the grass, Felix was tossing a Frisbee to Ariel.

In the trees, a hidden songbird warbled to its mate.

At this moment, all seemed to be right with the world.

But, as Lindy knew only too well, appearances could be deceiving...

A number of audience members who had brought their suppers began to position their chairs and lay down picnic blankets. Some brought doggington companions whose distracting scuffling and joyful woofs Lindy obstinately forced herself to ignore.

She had enough to worry about tonight without subsiding into full panic mode.

As Lindy listened to the men chitchat about Company business and watched the crowd grow, her cellphone rang. Her brother had texted her that he and his wife had made it to her house and let themselves in.

"That Greg and Nan?" asked Malcolm.

"Yes, they got here okay," said Lindy, pursing her mouth in concentration as she texted her brother back. "The plan is, once they get unpacked and have a munch, they're coming to the park to see the play tonight."

"Nervous?" Malcolm, who already knew the answer, swatted away a fly.

"Oh, yeah," sighed Lindy, stuffing her phone back in her tote bag. "I'd be happier if they'd seen *Small Comforts* first, but there's nothing anyone can do about that."

"No kidding," sympathized Malcolm, heaving himself up out of his chair. "I've got to get away from these trees. They're just bug magnets. Coming, guys?"

Serge agreed, mainly because it was time to feed his kids, so Lindy went along too, and the three moved their chairs closer to the audience area. Then, while Serge doled out chicken sandwiches and fruit flavoured waters to Ariel and Felix from a small cooler, Rochelle, Darrick and Philippe rambled over to touch base.

Lindy was, as always, fascinated whenever she saw Serge, the quietest and most self-effacing of men, and his roguish wife together. Even though Rochelle blatantly used him for childcare and a steady bank account, Serge, a solid rock amid the heaving ocean of her artistic life, adored her unreservedly. As Lindy now observed, Rochelle's mere presence had the power to set Serge's ears and, she assumed, his heart aglow.

"Hey Lindy," grinned Rochelle, her page boy dyed a fetching electric blue for the show, "I hear that Felix and Ariel gave you the authentic VIP experience this afternoon."

"They were perfect," smiled Lindy, allowing the kids to look extremely pleased with themselves—white knight Felix nodding courteously and Ariel's impish grin the picture of her mother's own.

"I've just taken Leo for his stroll, but I must go walkies myself now," announced Darrick. "Will you kindly lend him your patience for a few moments, Madame Director?"

"Of course," Lindy readily agreed, gently receiving Leo unto her lap. As Darrick strode off, the dainty chihuahua, panting softly in his summer-weight vest, settled happily into what over the course of the last year had become unremarkable territory.

"My friend Xander can't come tonight," reported Philippe sadly. "So we don't need to save him a space..."

"Maybe on the weekend?" sensitively suggested Lindy.

Rochelle kept her and Malcolm updated on the constant disaster that was Philippe's social life. As Darrick had once observed, if there was a scoundrel or a cad within five hundred kilometres, you could be certain that they'd dated, drained and ditched poor Philippe.

"He said he had to be in Montreal," Philippe mournfully shrugged.

"Maybe for your birthday party next week?" offered Rochelle, no less kindly.

"He couldn't say. And I wish you hadn't planned anything," sighed the actor. "I'm going to be thirty—*fuck ostie!*—and I'd rather not think about it..."

Soon Darrick returned for Leo, and they and Philippe headed backstage. Rochelle gave Serge a distracted kiss and, serenely self-absorbed, wandered away to finish preparing for her performance. Then Malcolm jogged off to buy iced coffees and snacks from a nearby coffee shop, leaving Lindy to hang close to Serge—who soon got called away—and Felix and Ariel, who enthusiastically obeyed their Papa's parting instructions to move Lindy's and Malcolm's folding chairs into the audience area.

Under Lindy's direction, the kids positioned her and Malcolm closest to the stage—or at least, furthest away from most of the dogs. But that didn't really matter, because Lindy's plan was to reserve the front row space where they were situated as seating for Greg and Nan and then find somewhere else for her and Malcolm to watch the show.

Not too far back though. Not on the outskirts where most of the doggingtons lurked...

The kids made sure that Lindy was comfortable and then loped off to watch Serge and the university student Front of House Manager marshalling her volunteer ushers to distribute programs to the picnickers and the newly arriving spectators.

Abandoned largely to her own anxious thoughts, Lindy felt the muscles in her jaw spasm.

What if Greg got really stroppy about her limelighting their personal hassles with Dad? What if he tore a haughty strip off of her at intermission in front of the whole audience?

What if she lost her cool and screamed back?

Crack!—she snapped her mental elastic band and scolded herself, Stop it, Lindy! It'll be all right, you fool...

Maybe Greg isn't as controlling as you remember him.

Maybe he'll be glad to see some touchy family issues aired out in the open.

Maybe he'll have undergone a one-hundred-and-eighty-degree personality change in the time since we co-executed Dad's will, she sighed.

By the time Malcolm returned to sit beside Lindy, the audience was thickening. The play had great buzz, and the upper crust Glebe was full of habitual theatre patrons. There were fashionable couples, modern families with their trendy kids, and sundry groups of millennials concentrating on their smartphones—all accompanied by a plethora of dogs.

Big dogs. Small dogs. Well-bred dogs. Mutts…

The park resounded with their jolly barks and whines as they chased tennis balls and played tug-o-war with their leashes.

A doggington romp. A doggington frisk. A doggington stray…

What was keeping Greg and Nan? fretted Lindy.

She took a tiny sip of her iced coffee, usually her favourite summer treat, and put it down beside her chair. It was cloying on her taste buds today, oversweet and thick. She opened the paper bag and looked at the cranberry muffin that Malcolm had brought her.

"Here," she said, handing it back to him.

"Don't want it?" he asked, surprised that she wasn't hungry. Lindy usually gobbled down the pre-show snacks he brought her like an agitated goldfish.

"Thanks, but no. And you can finish my coffee," she said, handing the paper cup to him as well. "I'm not feeling too peckish today."

"You're sure?" asked Malcolm, with a frown, but readily took the proffered drink.

The audience had swelled in a gratifying way—and Malcolm had scarfed down both of their snacks—when Greg and Nan finally arrived toting their folding chairs.

Standing to stretch out a leg cramp, Lindy spotted her stoop-shouldered brother and his tall elegant wife as they took programs from an usher at the back. She waved vigorously to get their attention. When Greg nodded that he had seen her, Lindy signaled that they should come up to the front row where she was seated.

Instead of coming around the side or down the centre aisle to reach her, however, Lindy was surprised to see her relatives ponderously weave their way through the center of the crowd. Other patrons muttered, clearly unhappy with the disturbance, but Greg forged obliviously ahead with Nan trailing impassively behind.

"There you are," declared Greg when they reached Lindy's side, as if she and Malcolm had been purposely making themselves difficult to find. "Malcolm," he added with a curt nod, but didn't offer to shake hands.

Lindy saw Malcolm smother a grin. "Hey there, Greg!" he said heartily and stuck out his hand so obviously that Greg felt compelled to make contact.

"Hello, Lindy. What a nice evening for your little show," said Nan, accompanying her chilly greeting with a vague air kiss.

Lindy noticed the slight, but she was too frazzled to take umbrage right now.

Nan insisted on sitting with her sister-in-law, but there wasn't room for four chairs in the informal front row space that Lindy had carved out. So, to everyone but Lindy's relatives' considerable annoyance, Greg pushed through the same group of inconvenienced audience members and made them all wedge into a small, clear and, thankfully, dog-free spot that still gaped just behind the mid-row.

"How was the drive up?" asked Lindy as nonchalantly as she could manage once they'd all unfolded their chairs and—after many humble apologies from Malcolm and Lindy to their neighbours—sat down.

"Nobody knows how to operate a car in this country anymore," groused Greg.

"You can say that again," agreed Malcolm cheerfully, and for the next fifteen minutes the two men enjoyed griping about feckless drivers, heavy traffic and lousy highway maintenance. Every once in a while Lindy or Nan would add a brief comment, but it was mainly the men who carried on. While Lindy sat tensely counting the minutes to curtain, Nan indifferently checked her phone.

No one would guess from the informal greeting and casual conversation between Lindy and her brother and sister-in-law that the trio hadn't actually seen each other in the flesh for almost two years. Separated in age by only seventeen months, Lindy and Greg had still never been close siblings and, when the Arts Court burned down more than a year ago, Greg and his wife had gratefully decided not to come up to visit his little sister in Ottawa after all.

On the other hand—as she'd recalled this afternoon—although Nan had extended her usual dry invitation, Lindy hadn't chosen to travel to Oshawa to visit them last Christmas either. And, judging by the even tone of his voice when she mentioned not seeing them last December, Greg had long forgotten that she'd ever been expected in the first place.

Lindy was just about to burst a blood vessel when—finally!—Jessie hopped up on the stage to welcome the audience and ask that all phones and beeping things be turned off—which most of the audience proceeded to do. Then, with nerves taut as a tightrope, Lindy took a deep breath, counted to ten, snapped her mental elastic—Crack!—and the show began.

Through her protective sunglasses, Lindy surreptitiously watched her brother's reactions to the first act of the play. Like his younger sister, Greg had experienced a very stressful childhood—Dad had required absolute respect and obedience from any son of his!—and Lindy had spent many recent sleepless nights chewing over what would happen when Greg actually witnessed the connections between her script and their lives under Dad's brutal sway.

How upset would he be? she wondered.

Would he be enraged?

Would he blame her for using their family dystopia as fodder for a comic play?

But, to Lindy's bewilderment, Greg seemed to be snickering when the rest of the audience guffawed and listening with composed attention the rest of the time.

He didn't seem angry.

He didn't seem uncomfortable.

He didn't seem even vaguely dismayed.

And, eventually, Lindy came to the stunning conclusion that Greg must not be aware of any link between the despotic father on stage and their own.

This was confirmed at the intermission when, as the generous applause died down, Greg turned to his sister and said, "Good play, Lindy. Really funny. I can't believe that you wrote it. Where do you get your ideas?"

Where—?

Lindy was too gobsmacked to think of an answer but, luckily, Greg's question appeared to be purely rhetorical. Instead of waiting for an explanation, he immediately stood up and, saying that he needed some exercise, quickly strode away.

Nan coolly praised her sister-in-law's dramatic efforts as well—"It's quite a good show, Lindy. Very entertaining..."—and then excused herself to stand in line at the portable restrooms.

Malcolm asked Lindy if she wanted anything from the refreshment stand—"No thanks"— and then, spotting a friend, invited her to meet his jogging university colleague, Luke, who was giving his husky a bit of a run in between acts.

Lindy gave him a bemused head shake, so Malcolm went alone, and she was left sitting by herself.

Lindy was baffled by her brother.

Had Greg genuinely not seen anything in the play that reminded him of Dad? Was his experience so very different from hers? Was he just covering up his real feelings out of pride? Out of loyalty to Mom? Out of—what?

Lindy knew that Greg had not shown grief over Dad's death. At the funeral, he hadn't choked up when he gave the short elegy or been seen to shed a single tear.

Of course, she reminded herself, her brother had never been prone to emotional display. Even at Greg's and Nan's wedding, the photographer had mentioned to Lindy that he'd never dealt with such an unruffled groom before...

Still, she'd assumed that Greg's sangfroid at the funeral home had resulted from the same emotions that she'd been feeling.

Mom—who'd once informed Lindy that she couldn't be faulted for what happened with Dad because she'd "had to take it too"—had, nonetheless, been genuinely mourned by her children when, at seventy-six, her ravaged body finally gave in and she faded to black. With her long history of thyroid, breast and ovarian cancers, she'd always been 'the invalid,' always in need of Greg's and, especially, Lindy's kindness and care.

In fact, Lindy supposed, over the years Mom had kind of devolved into a rather demanding family pet and, as such, had been insulated from taking too much blame for her kids' daily pain.

Therefore, Lindy had mourned Mom.

But Lindy hadn't been able to mourn Dad.

For Lindy, Dad's death had been a liberation. For her, there'd been personal release from a lifelong burden. After nearly sixty years, she'd finally been freed from that carping Napoleon who could never be pleased. Who'd run roughshod over her every hope and dream. Who'd savagely lashed out to enforce his own beliefs and choices on her life.

But maybe Greg hadn't felt that way.

Maybe her brother—"Aaahh—!"

Gabrielle had quietly come up behind Lindy to tap her on the shoulder and apologized—"Sorry, I didn't mean to scare you!"—when Lindy, startled out of her dark musings, tensely recoiled from her light touch.

Apparently, there was a problem backstage in need of more hands. Gabrielle had been sent by Jessie to ask if

Lindy could take over safeguarding the secondary props table, located behind the final line of spectators, until the end of the intermission.

Lindy knew that her stage manager would never ask unless there was a serious glitch screwing up something, somewhere, somehow. And at this point, she prayed, any remaining dogs would be securely leashed…

Therefore, stiffly rising and throwing her tote bag over her shoulder, Lindy shelved her broodings and made her way to the props table.

Trying not to scan too closely for doggingtons of any sort, Lindy replaced the apprentice techie, who quickly ran off, leaving Lindy alone and vulnerable at the very edge of the last audience row.

So, with ears and eyes sharply alive to every unforeseen noise or sudden movement from the intermission crowd, she stood uneasily awaiting the techie's return…

CHAPTER NINETEEN

Pygmalion

Lindy was still wearing her protective sunglasses, but there were shadows amidst the patches of glare from the setting sun. Despite her best intentions, she peered suspiciously about her as she waited protectively beside the secondary props table for the apprentice techie to come back.

She saw Greg sit down, and then Malcolm, and finally Nan. But she couldn't leave the table to rejoin them, and they were chatting together and didn't seem to be looking for her. A bell rang to announce that the intermission was over, and Jessie reappeared to ask everyone to mute their phones. The actors quietly took their second act places and the play resumed.

Still, the apprentice techie didn't return.

Rochelle made her first entrance from the back of the audience, but it was not cool to interrupt an actor in character to ask a question. So Lindy simply made sure that Judith had her watering can and got out of her way.

The play continued as usual and, after about five more minutes, the apprentice techie finally returned to the props table. Mutely signaling her thanks, she indicated to Lindy that she could go.

Lindy didn't want to disturb the audience by barging back through it to her chair, so she stayed standing where she was for a while. But she worried that she would mess up the actors' normal sequence of entrances somehow, and so she gradually faded toward the trees where she had originally sat in the shade with Malcolm and Serge. Doffing her sunglasses in the waning light, she kept a wary eye out for doggington roamers but, as the play rolled on, none appeared and she began to think she could relax.

By the end of the show, however, when darkness had fallen and the stage was lit solely by the Company's portable lights, Lindy had edged her way back to the side of the apprentice techie at the secondary props table. Then, after the standing ovation that the play always earned—and while the actors spread themselves throughout the audience to genially pass the hat—she went to find Malcolm, Greg and Nan.

Unfortunately, she had trouble wedging her way through the scrum of patrons, who were busy folding up chairs and gathering their scattered coolers, blankets, kids and dogs. When she at length arrived where her group had been sitting, all four chairs and her three companions had totally vanished…

Suddenly, in the midst of all the pandemonium, a couple of rival doggington woofs near Lindy decided to have a terrifying scuffle, snapping and snarling and trying to sink their teeth into each others' throats.

Lindy felt her pulse begin to race.

A doggington fight. A doggington chomp. A doggington slay…

Her heart thudding through her tee-shirt, Lindy stumbled away from the battling dogs and ended up in a mass of people flowing back to the stairway that led up to Bank Street.

She knew she should go back to look for Greg and Nan, but, even though the dogs had been eventually separated by their owners, she was afraid to return to where they had scrapped. Without meaning to, she found herself climbing the stone stairway and was soon standing on the Bank Street sidewalk again.

Observing that there were no dogs in her immediate area, Lindy shuffled over to a low fence and, pulling her cellphone out of her tote bag, called Greg. She wanted to explain that she was already out of the park and to ask where he and Nan had left their SUV, but her brother didn't answer her call. So she texted him that she'd meet them at home, crossed Bank Street and found the nearest bus stop.

Her bus came quickly.

Lindy hopped on, crossed the Rideau Canal and traveled along to her usual stop in her neighbourhood.

It was a dark and starry but moonless night—and she needed to be alert for sidewalk, yard and porch dogs—so she decided that she'd postpone checking for texts until she'd navigated the run home and was safely locked away behind her own solid side door.

Along the familiar two and a half blocks to her house, she sped like a thief hustling swag to her lair.

But the neighbourhood looked far different under the pooling light of the infrequent streetlamps than it did during the day. Her way was pocked with shadowy gardens, dim paths and haunted laneways…

When a frenzied yapping broke out, Lindy froze, her heart agallop—until she could locate the Pomeranian tottering on the back of a sofa while it hurled warnings at her through a sturdy front window across the street. Then—reassured that the doggington yelp was securely corralled—she ducked her head and fled on.

Why didn't I stay at the park until I found Greg? Or maybe gotten a drive home with Malcolm? Why am I always such a total dingbat? she lamented to herself.

Turning the final corner, Lindy thankfully scurried up to her house. She noticed that Greg's SUV wasn't in the second parking space at the end of her driveway, so she supposed that he and Nan must still be en route.

It was all good.

She'd get in touch with her brother once she was inside.

Lindy had forgotten to put on the outside light at the side door before she left this afternoon—and she was on her last nerve from her various doggish encounters—so it was a bit of a fumble to find the keyring in her tote bag…

Eventually, however, she managed to stuff her key into the lock and was gratefully turning the door knob when her hyper-vigilant ears discerned a far bark—then a closer bark—then a cascade of frantic barking and snarling—and the bloodthirsty racket was tumbling down the stairs inside her house—!

Lightning-scorched, Lindy dropped her hand from the doorknob.

Oh Dear God.

Paulie the Doberman.

Greg and Nan must have brought him with them...

Now Lindy could hear the furious dog's fierce growls as it body-slammed itself against the other side of the door. Somewhere in the recesses of her mind, she knew Paulie couldn't knock through its sturdy wooden boards, but every atom in her body was screaming, Run!

RUN!!!

Which, shamelessly, she did.

Down her driveway to the sidewalk, down the sidewalk to the cross street, across the cross street and down the further sidewalk Lindy hurtled.

Fleeing from lethal peril—

Fleeing for her life—!

Then half way down the second block, she spotted it.

Brittany's porch.

Safety at last!

Up the stone walkway, up the stairs she sped and collapsed again, blind with fear, in her secure hideaway behind the brick post.

Her eyes might be blind, but Lindy's other senses were heightened. Particularly her sense of hearing. Now, from a window behind her, open to catch the breezes on a warm summer night, a conversation flowed.

"Oh my goodness, it's happened again!" exclaimed Brittany's voice. "Put Goldie in the kitchen, John."

"Well, okay. But don't you think it's kind of odd that she'd be afraid of Goldie? I mean, she might snuggle her to death, I guess, but otherwise—"

"She's an artist, honey. A playwright. We saw her play at the Fimbria last year. The one about the girl who goes to the psychics? Remember? Just before the fire started?"

"Oh, yeah, that was great! The best Fimbria show we've ever seen, actually—"

"And I told you that we should go to Windsor Park this month to catch her new one?"

"Yeah, I'm on board with that. But it's still odd. Goldie—"

"She's a theatre person, honey. They're all odd. So—go stick Goldie in her bed in the kitchen, and I'll invite Lindy in for tea."

"Okay," said John with a vocal shrug, and a few seconds later the door opened behind Lindy's shrinking form and Brittany's pleasant voice said, "Hi there, Lindy! It's nice to see you again. Why don't you come in?"

Deeply embarrassed, Lindy slowly unwound from her crouch. "I'm sorry—" she croaked.

But Brittany cut her off with a warm smile, "We've got air conditioning, but it was too nice to use it today, so we're a little tropical. I hope you don't mind."

The younger woman was holding her front door open in such an inviting manner that, without thinking, Lindy scooted inside and was soon established on an ancient comfy sofa in a toddler-toy-cluttered living room. When John returned to greet her and take a seat in a beat-up old armchair, Brittany went down the hall to the kitchen to fetch them all a snack.

"So, tell me," asked John, with sincere curiosity, "what happened to your play after the fire last year? Did you get to put it on someplace else? Or did it just go up in flames with the Arts Court?"

By the time Brittany reappeared with at tray full of iced tea and cheddar cheese and crackers, Lindy and John were deep in conversation about the perils of weather for an open-air theatre troupe.

"We've had great skies so far," Lindy was saying, her heart rate normal once more, "but my actors tell me from experience that we can expect to lose at least a few performances to rain-outs. Unless you have an alternative indoor venue, which we haven't managed to get this year— we were hoping to book one, but it fell through—you'll never get a perfect season in the parks."

"Sounds challenging," commented Brittany. "Iced tea?"

"Thanks," said Lindy, accepting a glass, "but would it be okay if I went to tidy up a bit?"

"Of course," smiled Brittany. "Upstairs, first door to your right."

She pointed back up the hall toward the kitchen.

Lindy followed instructions and was soon coming back down.

Unfortunately, while she'd been busy upstairs, Goldie had decided that her owners couldn't have possibly meant for her to stay in the kitchen when there was food on offer elsewhere in the house. So, as Lindy turned the corner on the landing, she saw the gentle retriever nose her way out of the heavy swinging kitchen door and wander speculatively into the hallway toward the living room.

Lindy tried to step back out of the dog's sense field, but the wooden landing creaked and Goldie looked up to see who was coming down.

Lindy froze.

Spotting the strange human female who always smelled as frightened as the rabbits Goldie sometimes surprised at the park, the friendly dog's face split into its usual welcoming smile.

Hello, Goldie's soft brown eyes said. How nice of you to visit me.

Despite the obvious differences in breed, there was something about the dog's trusting expression that reminded Lindy of the way that Leo often looked at her now. So, summoning all the courage that she had, Lindy wet her lips and forced herself to speak quietly to the doggington mild.

"Hi Goldie."

Goldie's plumey tail wagged softly. How nice of you to talk to me.

"Sit, girl."

Oh, the frightened one wanted to play a game. Smiling wider, Goldie plopped her rump onto the hardwood floor.

"Now, lie down."

That was an easy one too. Goldie stretched out happily.

"Good girl."

The frightened one knew her other name. How nice. Goldie grinned and thumped her tail again.

"Now, Goldie, you need to stay, because I'm going to—"

Lindy's concentration was interrupted by large grey tabby cat who scampered past her down the stairs. Reaching the bottom of the steps, it walked straight up to Goldie to touch noses—Hello dog—Hello cat—and then padded away, tail held high, towards the living room. Goldie seemed to take this as an invitation, because she immediately got to her feet and, with a cheerful glance at Lindy, followed the cat down the hall.

"Oh, there's the dog," she heard Brittany exclaim. "No wonder Lindy didn't come back. John, get hold of Goldie and don't let Whiskers near the cheese. Oops, there you are—"

Brittany, who had leapt up to go check on her guest, ran straight into Lindy, who had descended and was cautiously coming into the living room from the hall.

"Everything okay?"

"Oh yes," Lindy sank back onto the sofa and picked up her glass of iced tea. "Goldie and I were just having a chat. She's a very friendly dog."

Wagging her tail, Goldie slipped out of John's loose grip to throw herself with a contented groan at Lindy's feet.

"If you're not comfortable with her there—" began Brittany, concerned that Goldie was pushing their sensitive guest too far.

But Lindy shook her head, "No, it's fine."

Experimentally, she reached down to stroke Goldie's silky head.

The dog closed her eyes and smiled.

Lindy smiled.

Brittany and John smiled.

The grey-striped cat took advantage of being ignored by hopping up on the coffee table to paw at the cheese.

"Whiskers, get down!" chided Brittany as soon as she noticed. She swept the cat onto her lap and laughed. "If you want to be loved, get a dog. If you want to live with a pirate, get a cat."

"I know," laughed Lindy. By now she was scratching Goldie's ear and the dog was leaning into her hand just like Leo did. "My cat is exactly the same. But she's not too good with dogs. It's kind of nice how your two animals get along."

"We bought them at the same time from the breeder," said John. "She had both puppies and kittens for sale so we—"

Lindy's cellphone rang.

"Oh, sorry," apologized Brittany, "we forgot to tell you that, while you were upstairs, you had a call."

"Oh, please don't worry," said Lindy. "It's probably nothing important..."

With a low whistle, John called Goldie to him so that she could retrieve her cellphone from her tote bag.

"Hello?" she answered the call.

It was Greg.

And he wasn't happy.

When he and Nan lost track of Lindy, he explained in a testy voice, they assumed that—like Malcolm, who was in charge of the cash in the hats—Lindy had stayed to help her Company decamp. Because he was at the play, Greg continued—without letting his sister reply—he had turned off his phone and it wasn't until they had ordered a nightcap at a Bank Street bar that he'd checked his messages and realized that Lindy had gone home. So, instead of lingering in the pleasantly air-conditioned bar, he and Nan had downed their drinks, got into their SUV and gone home too. But, obviously, Lindy hadn't—because they were in the house right now and she wasn't there. So where was she? Unless he was catching up to her at the Civic Hospital emergency room, he warned, she'd better get her butt home right now—!

Behind her brother's peevish voice, Lindy could hear Nan baby-talking to Paulie, who whined and whimpered in reply. The sound filled her with cold fury, and as Greg wound up to his final demand, Brittany and John saw Lindy's face go hard.

"I'm at my friends' house," she told Greg stiffly, "because I couldn't enter my own."

"What? Why?" returned Greg. "Oh, I guess you mean because you were too chicken to face Paulie. For Christ's sake, Lindy—grow up. He's just a dog."

"You never told me you were bringing him."

"So what? The dog sitter fell through. What were we supposed to do?"

"Ask me if it was okay to bring him? Let me know that Paulie was with you?"

"Lindy, if you can't even deal with a friendly dog like Paulie, you need serious psychological help—"

"He's not a friendly dog, Greg. I know friendly dogs," said Lindy nodding at Goldie and thinking of Leo, "and your stupid Doberman isn't one of them. Listen to me, Greg," she continued, overriding his scornful response, "if you guys want to stay at my house tonight, you leash that nasty dog in the basement by the laundry. That's what Maddie always did with Hellmutt when she brought him over. It won't hurt Paulie—and I deserve to sleep safely in my own bed without worrying that some evil mutt is about to leap on me and rip my face off."

"We're not banishing Paulie to the basement, Lindy," stated Greg. "In fact—"

"And," interrupted Lindy, relentlessly, "if you and Nan don't want to do that, you can take your dog and go sleep in a motel tonight. Got that, Greg? As they say—it's my way or the highway. Do you understand?"

"Oh, you bet, I understand!"

With a rare loss of emotional control, Greg cut off the call.

Lindy shook her head grimly at her phone.

"Well done," said Brittany with quiet approval, as Lindy put her cellphone back in her tote bag. "You can't let people treat you like you're a nobody or pretty soon you'll start believing it yourself. Can I serve you some cheese and crackers?"

When, thirty-five minutes later Lindy arrived back at her house, Greg and Nan's enormous SUV was just pulling out of her driveway.

Nan rolled down her window so that Greg could lean over his wife to tell Lindy in a snotty voice, "We got tired of waiting for you to come home to apologize."

"I don't need to apologize."

"Well, then, you've got your wish, Lindy," he announced, haughtily. "We're leaving."

"Fine by me—"

"And there'll have to be a major change in your attitude if you ever want us to come back."

"Not gonna happen," said Lindy steadily and stepped around his bumper.

Unnoticed, across the darkened Avenue, a car pulled in to park.

Lindy reached her side door and began the ritual of looking for her keys at the bottom of her tote bag.

Unexpectedly, Greg threw the SUV back in drive and rolled up beside her.

Safety-harnessed in the back seat, Paulie the Doberman glared at Lindy and growled low in his throat.

Lindy noted that the window was up and the harness looked pretty solid. So, although her pulse quickened and her internal alarms began to sound, she decided to ignore Paulie as best she could. She was about to ask Greg what else he wanted, but her older brother headed her off.

"You know, little sister," declared Greg through his open window, as Nan sat sourly in the passenger seat, "Dad would be ashamed of you. Throwing your own brother out of the house he grew up in—"

"Dad was ashamed of me for just standing there," retorted Lindy. "He was hateful and meanspirited—"

"Because he was a little critical?"

"Because he was cruel—"

"He wanted us to be our best. He tried to instill a little discipline in us—"

"Discipline? He beat us—"

"Only to toughen us up."

"He whipped us with the dog's leash!"

"Yeah, well, those were different times. At least he was never a namby-pamby like those fathers you see pushing baby strollers down the street. Dad was an old-fashioned disciplinarian and it was his rigorous expectations that made me into the man I am today."

An insufferable prig? thought Lindy, but asked instead, "And who would that be?"

"A success," sniffed Greg. "Something that you, Lindy, with your fake phobia and flaky plays will never be. I'm not stuck in the past whining about how hard I had it as a kid. I've had a very successful career, and a very successful marriage, and now I'm enjoying a very successful retirement. You, on the other hand—"

"You're right," interrupted Lindy evenly. "I, on the other hand, am a complete nut case who had a dull government job and a broken marriage. But my pension's pretty decent and I've got some savings in the bank and, believe me, Greg, my retirement's shaping up a treat. I've found an art that I'm good at. My plays get rave reviews. I've found friends and colleagues who like and respect me, who forgive my fears and protect me from my insanity. And I've got Malcolm who loves me. And a car. And a house. And a cat. Not too shabby for a complete failure, I'd say."

Lindy made to turn away to stick her key in the lock, but her brother wasn't finished with her yet.

"Well, good luck with your 'art' and your 'pension' and this crummy old house," he scoffed. "And good luck with your bottom line, because those deviants you think are your 'friends' will probably have you sucked dry in no time. And Malcolm?" he snorted. "Dad managed to save you from that dirty womanizer when he first tried it out on you. But I guess there's no fool like a homely old—"

Lindy nipped around without counting to ten.

"Go away, Greg," she hissed. "Move you and your snooty wife and that vicious dog off of my property right now!"

"Oh, we're going, Lindy," grimaced Greg, "and, like I said, we won't be back."

"Good!"

"But someday soon we expect to hear from you."

"Not likely—"

"Someday soon you'll be crying to us on the phone," Lindy's brother smirked down at her. "'I'm out of money, I'm out of friends, and Malcolm's screwing around with some blonde bimbo.' Oh yeah, we'll be hearing from you, little sister," he sneered.

As Greg self-righteously reached to put his SUV back into reverse, Malcolm popped out of shadows where he'd been eavesdropping to lean over beside Greg's open window and laugh, "Well, those that can, do, Greg. But I've always preferred LBJs—"

A wee bit startled by her ex-husband—who she hadn't spied lurking about—Lindy laughed along with him. "Liar," she said, shaking her head affectionately. "You've had your share of blondes. Now, say 'good bye' to Greg and Nan..."

"Bye now," grinned Malcolm, letting himself into Lindy's house with his key.

Somewhere up the Avenue, a car door slammed.

"Don't let me keep you, guys," smiled Lindy, preparing to follow her ex inside.

"Oh, you're so selfish!" finally snapped Nan, leaning across Greg to skewer her surprisingly forthright sister-in-law.

Paulie responded to his owner's hostility with new aggression but, despite the rush of adrenalin the dog's guttural snarls produced in her, Lindy refused to be cowed.

"I'm an artist," she boldly declared. "A playwright. Selfishness goes with the territory."

"Yeah, she's here!" came Rochelle's voice, ringing out to someone further up the dark Avenue. "Hey Lindy," she called, as two more car doors slammed, "we've got amazing news!"

"Now you guys better go," firmly urged Lindy. "My deviant friends are arriving and I wouldn't want you to insult them too."

"Bitch!" Nan threw herself back into her seat. "Get us out of here, Greg!"

Paulie gave a sharp bark.

"Oh, shut up!" snarled Nan at her dog, and Paulie's voice died to a whimper.

Smiling sweetly, Lindy raised a dismissive hand. "Bye Greg. Bye Nan. Bye Paulie."

With a grand show of indifference, Greg refused to respond to his sister's sarcastic farewell. Raising his window, he hit the gas to back inexorably away from Lindy and her misguided life. The effect of this dramatic exit was somewhat dampened, however, since Greg had to stop for a group of people who were walking up Lindy's driveway. They were an odd-looking set—a blue haired woman, a slight young fellow and an older graying man who carried a chihuahua in the crook of his arm.

The actors from Lindy's little play.

Greg revved his motor and lightly tapped his horn, expecting them all to jump out of the way. But the actors just waved amiably as they strolled casually around his SUV and up to Lindy as she opened her side door.

What a bunch of freeloaders, mused Greg, when he finally gained the Avenue. Lindy will soon regret casting her lot in with those freaks!

Smugly, Greg wondered how long it would be until his little sister came crawling back to plead for his financial help. Once it happened, he'd be stern and exacting, yet ultimately forgiving, he decided. He really wouldn't need an entire pound of Lindy's flesh to be fully satisfied...

For now, though, he was just going to send his sister the bill for tonight's bar tab and accommodation. So, as Nan confirmed on her phone that they were expected at a pet-welcoming moderately-priced suburban motel—with parking and continental breakfast included—Greg abandoned Lindy to her grievous fate and drove his lovely wife and friendly dog sedately away.

CHAPTER TWENTY

All's Well That Ends Well

Greeting her Company warmly, Lindy ushered them into her home.

While Malcolm and Rochelle organized coffee, beer and wine, and Philippe and Darrick set out nacho chips and cobbled together ham and pickle and salmon salad sandwiches, Lindy attempted to catnip Phyllis down from her living room refuge on top of the highest bookshelf.

But Phyllis wasn't having it.

She flattened her ears and hissed.

Her queendom had been invaded for hours by a ravening wolf and she was making it perfectly clear that she wasn't going to forgive Lindy any time soon. Spotting Leo coming into the dining room, she let loose a bloodcurdling "Yyyaaarwlll—!!!" that raised the hair on the back of everyone's necks and sent the teensy doggington arf diving for sanctuary beneath Darrick's armpit.

"Exactly how you felt about that Doberman, I'm sure," grinned Rochelle to Lindy.

"Paulie is not a friendly dog," said Lindy flatly. "Okay, Phyllis, you stay up there 'til you feel safe coming down. That's definitely what I would do."

She entered the dining room and looked at the spread of food and drink with approval.

"I've got frozen cherry cheesecake you can thaw in the fridge for dessert. Pour me a beer, will you, Malcolm? I just need to toddle upstairs for a minute and then you can spill the good news Rochelle was talking about..."

When Lindy came downstairs again, the Company were already sating their 'great-performance-gang!' sharpened appetites around Maddie's antique table, which continued to dominate Lindy's dining room with its lumbering bulk.

"So, what's the big news?" asked Lindy, seating herself where Malcolm had left her beer glass and grabbing a salmon sandwich triangle. "Malcolm already told me about the grant..."

"Yeah, I'm glad we got that," nodded Malcolm, "but this is something else. You know how I had trouble finding an alternative indoor site for rainy days?"

"Oh, did you find one?" asked Lindy, hopefully. "Next week's supposed to be pretty damp."

"Nope," grinned Rochelle, "but this is better."

"Super-cool," nodded Philippe.

Darrick just smiled archly and stroked Leo's ears.

What is this cadre of cats up to this time? wondered Lindy, uneasily. "So, what—?"

Malcolm looked to Darrick. "Do you want to tell her or shall I?"

Receiving a modest shrug from the actor, her ex continued, "Well, I will then, if you don't mind. Lindy—"

"Am I going to like this?" muttered Lindy.

"Oh, definitely," laughed Rochelle.

"—not only are we going to have a place to play when the weather's crappy. We're going to have a permanent theatre space right downtown near the university!"

"Whoo-hoo!" crowed Rochelle and Philippe, slapping a high-five.

Darrick smiled benevolently upon his excited confreres.

"That sounds...nice," returned Lindy, cautiously. "How are we going to manage that?"

"Okay," said Malcolm, grinning, "I can see that you're a little skeptical—"

"Not so much skeptical as—"

"But it's really going to happen, and I'll tell you why." Malcolm took a final swig of his beer and prepared to update Lindy on this evening's unexpectedly exciting events. "First of all, you saw me go talk to my friend Luke. You know, the guy I sometimes jog with who owns the husky?"

"Ye-es..." Lindy wondered if she should have opted for something stronger than beer.

"Well, yesterday I ran into Milda—the Theatre Department secretary I dated a couple of times?—and she told me that Luke owned a little old stone chapel near the university that had been reno'd into a fitness studio several years ago. Unfortunately, his tenant's yoga business had suddenly gone tits up and he'd flown the coop at the beginning of June. Milda was pissed about that because she'd just signed up for summer classes and it looked like the guy had walked off with everybody's money—"

"Which the blackguard undeniably did!" grimly clarified Darrick.

"Anyways," continued Malcolm, "Milda thought that Luke was having trouble finding a new renter. So tonight I asked him if he'd consider letting us use the space occasionally for the rest of the run. But he said he'd just sold it to someone else and I'd have to talk to them."

"Okay-ay..." Lindy could see that both Rochelle and Philippe were actually hugging themselves with delight.

"So I asked Luke for the name of the new owner—and it turned out to be—"

Rochelle and Philippe performed a drum roll on the tabletop—

"Darrick Kinnow!"

To most of the Company's enthusiastic applause, Darrick leapt up and thrust Leo above his head to wave the startled pup around like the Stanley Cup.

"Thank you! Thank you, my friends!" he exclaimed and, restoring Leo to the crook of his arm, swept them all a gracious bow. Then, resuming his seat, he turned to Lindy who sat dumbfounded by Malcolm's tidings. "I assume that, once you are over your considerable surprise, dear lady, you will be as elated as the rest of the Board?"

Gathering her wits, Lindy stammered, "Oh, of...of course, Darrick. Why—? I mean, how did you—?"

Darrick smiled benevolently at his unsettled friend.

"For the last three years, Leo and I were members of that yoga studio in that restored chapel which is, after all, a mere block and a half from our townhouse. We had recently re-enrolled in a yearly plan and so we were, indeed, two of the owner's unlucky victims." Darrick shook his head sadly. "He's absconded to parts unknown with our fees."

"The bastard," Rochelle commiserated, while Malcolm and Philippe nodded in accord.

"He preached self discipline, simplicity and universal love," sniffed Darrick, "but in the end the lure of filthy lucre must have overpowered his—but, I shall not dwell upon it." Darrick thrust away his contempt with a sweeping hand.

"That's wise, Darrick," solemnly agreed Rochelle, hiding her wicked smile.

"Yes, that river has flowed on. For, as the sage propounds, the river that one steps in is never the same water twice and one should never dwell. So—where was I? Oh, yes," Darrick pulled himself together and resumed. "Thus, the yoga studio is now vacant. And Leo and I were out having our walkies yesterday morning when we encountered Malcolm's colleague, Luke, standing outside of the chapel with his real estate agent trying to decide whether to rent—or 'sell the damn place.'" Darrick shook is head in disapproval. "His words, not mine. So Leo and I stopped for a bit of a chin wag and, by the time we ambled on, we had an appointment to view this morning."

"That was quick," worried Lindy. "Are you sure you had enough time to—?"

But Darrick just smiled. "Oh, Leo and I didn't just fall off that turnip truck, my dear. We brought along our old friend, Andrew, who's a civil engineer and knows all about things like joists and plumbing. He gave the place a once-over that Sherlock Holmes would have been proud of—and then gave us the thumbs up. So Leo and I checked our bank accounts, called our realtor friend, Trena, and put in an offer around three o'clock. Then, just ten minutes before curtain, we got a text from Trena that our offer had been accepted and—bing, bang, boom—Leo and I are now theatre owners!"

To more heartfelt applause from Malcolm and their fellow actors, Darrick and Leo stood to style a second extravagant bow.

"That's—that's great, Darrick," hedged Lindy, as the actor resumed his seat. "But how did you get a mortgage that fast?"

Darrick chuckled gently. "Oh, my dear Lindy, I'm not going to saddle myself with a mortgage this late in life. Not an intelligent move for an artist exiting his middle-age years, wouldn't you agree?"

Lindy figured Darrick was well through that particular exit, but that was beside the point. "So how did you—?"

"Do you remember our journey to a family funeral in November?" enquired Darrick. When Lindy nodded, he continued, "Ghastly time for my uncle to choose to shuffle off this mortal coil, of course. Late autumn in Toronto is unspeakable—all grey skies and naked branches. But the trip was not without its fiduciary benefits. Uncle Whitaker was most kind."

"Ah..." Lindy remembered the wealthy neighbourhood in Toronto where Maddie had said that Darrick had been raised, recalled the expensive bronzes and oil paintings in his luxurious townhouse—and decided she probably didn't need to worry that he'd overspent his inheritance on the purchase. "But I thought you said that it was a yoga studio?"

"It was, yes, but Andrew says that, since the place has already been used as a commercial establishment, all of the most important work has already been done. He assured me that it has enormous potential for an inexpensive conversion into a theatre space. Here, I've got some photos."

Passing the relevant images on his phone to Malcolm, Darrick began to list off all of the property's best qualities.

"As you'll see, it's a charming little old stone Victorian chapel with beautiful wood wainscoting, wide plank floors and a sublime ceiling that soars to the angels on high."

"So it'll be a cinch to hang the grid," smiled Rochelle, "and we might be able to fly some of our sets."

"And there'll be wonderful acoustics," nodded Philippe.

"Maybe we can pad our bottom line by bringing in live music when we haven't got a show on," mused Malcolm, swiping through the photos. "You know, folk singers or jazz combos or—I don't know—rap poets?"

"Maman has lots of musical friends who are looking for gigs," offered Philippe.

"There's a main floor lobby that's already fitted with a juice bar—" listed Darrick.

"Oh, yeah? I wondered what that was." Pleased with this excellent news, Malcolm passed Darrick's phone to Philippe. "Do you think we could get a liquor licence?"

"I don't see why not," said Darrick. "It just might take some time—"

"Then we could open the bar an hour before every show—" plotted Rochelle.

"—and sell craft beers and wine," nodded Malcolm.

"Now, as you'll note, the main hall is basically a box like our last Fimbria venue," Darrick continued, "but there's a flat elevated stage area where the altar used to be—"

"We could build in a rake," suggested Rochelle.

"—and there's stairway from the lobby to the choir loft which was used as an office space, but we can also fit it out for our technical booth to call the shows."

"What kind of natural light does the main hall get?" Philippe wanted to know, passing Darrick's phone to Rochelle. "Will it be dark enough for matinees? Those are awfully big windows."

"We can easily mask them," shrugged Darrick. "Permanently, if we so wish. It was a Methodist chapel so there's no stained glass and, as the property was a yoga studio, there are no pews left. We'll have to invest in seating. And probably risers to set them on, as well."

"What about restrooms?" Malcolm inquired.

"There's three—one's for handicapped—and a high dry basement with a large open space for a workshop and storage."

"So I won't be building any more spirit cabinets in Lindy's basement."

"No, those days are over, my friend. And Luke assured me that the wiring, plumbing, furnace and air conditioner were all upgraded just five years ago."

"How about parking?"

"There are two parking spaces for the Company, as well as street parking and a public parking lot not far away."

It all sounded too good to be true to Lindy. "But doesn't the place belong to you, Darrick, and not to the Company?" she objected.

"Yes, but you see, Leo and I are willing to rent it to Excursion Theatre for a very low rate, just to cover the taxes," explained the actor, patiently. "And, like most renters, the Company will pay for all the utilities."

"Don't worry, Lindy, I'll be sure to check out the legalities and watch out for our bottom line," smiled Malcolm.

"But is it ready to use for rain dates this summer?" Lindy refused to have her concerns so easily dismissed.

"Yes," Darrick assured her, "in limited bring-your-own-chairs, forgive-our-deficiencies, we're-using-our-portable-lights-and-sound-board kind of way."

"At least there'll be no bats," laughed Rochelle, handing Darrick's phone to Lindy. "And no dogs. That ought to make you happy, babe!"

Lindy put down the phone without even a glance.

What was the use of looking at photos? She'd probably just see problems, but her Company seemed determined not to notice any downsides to this permanent theatre plan...

Darrick shrugged. "Of course, once *A Tale* wraps in August, we can swiftly accomplish the rest of renovations. I'll give you all a tour on Monday when we're dark, and you'll see why Leo and I are confident that we can have our first show up by late fall."

"That sounds perfect," grinned Rochelle. "We should decide on our playbill right now—although, Darrick and Leo, you bought the theatre for us, so maybe you prefer to say what show we should stage first?"

"Well, since you leave the decision to us—and Leo and I have been mulling this over—in our considered opinion," announced Darrick, "if we want to have a show up and running before Christmas, it would be easiest to remount *Small Comforts*."

"*D'accord*!" exclaimed Philippe. "I won the Prix for that role. I love Mary, you know."

"And I loved you in that role," admitted Lindy, grudgingly.

"But then we think we should produce an expanded version of my inheritance play, *Entitled*, as our winter show," continued Darrick, "and Lindy can serve as co-writer and direct it too."

"Darrick, are you sure that show is worth—?" began Lindy, recalling Darrick's last limp Fimbria attempt.

But Rochelle rolled her eyes and snapped, "*Tabernac!* Here we go again! Why is it that your first instinct is always to be so fucking selfish, Lindy? You're not the only playwright sitting at this table, you know."

"Yes, don't be stingy, Lindy. We're all experienced at plying our quills in some form of the art," sniffed Darrick. "Malcolm excluded, of course. We can't all be artists," he added, courteously excusing Malcolm's perceived failing, "but his pecuniary talents seem to have kept us afloat."

"Damn straight," grunted Malcolm, getting up to retrieve the cheesecake and some clean plates.

Pretty certain that Rochelle and Darrick ought to know a thing or two about selfishness, Lindy nonetheless wondered if her actors were right. Was her knee jerk reaction to Darrick's suggestion simply in self-defence of her blossoming reputation as the author of two popular shows? And how much of that popularity could actually be attributed to the actors' interpretation of her script?

Wasn't theatre always a collaborative art?

So, why shouldn't she serve as the co-writer on Darrick's script? Would it hurt to expand her theatre resumé into 'Orwellian dystopia?' Maybe her input would freshen and enliven the awkward play she remembered from the Festival—

Suddenly Lindy realized that all her actors were watching her musings with tense expectant faces.

And it dawned on her that it actually mattered to these odd theatre people what she thought and what she did.

That's amazing, reflected Lindy. What I told Greg about them respecting and caring for me? Those weren't just words. It's the honest truth!

And I absolutely owe them equal support.

"Well?" asked Malcolm, cocking a quizzical eyebrow at Lindy as he returned with the cheesecake. "Are you going to hang with the gang?"

"Positively!" she declared, pushing her greying bob behind her ears. "The grandmother was another role that I loved Philippe in..."

As one, Darrick, Rochelle and Philippe heaved a great sigh and relaxed. With a stealthy wink to ex-wife, Malcolm divvied up the cherry cheesecake, and everyone accepted a good, if still partially frozen, slice.

"So that's late autumn and winter decided," said Darrick, reaching into his pocket for a plastic baggie from which he retrieved an organic jerky treat for Leo. "What shall we do in the spring to round out our bill?"

"We could do a Molière that we've done before," suggested Philippe. "Perhaps '*Le Médecin Volant*.' We had good houses for that."

"It's not a bad idea to establish ourselves early as a bilingual company," agreed Darrick, "and simply re-staging one of our French farces will give Lindy breathing space to edit—"

"—and then we'll head back to the parks with Lindy's next play in the summer," grinned Rochelle.

"Lindy's next play?" chuckled Malcolm, licking cherry topping off his fork. "She's only just sent *A Tale* out into the world."

"Yes, but," Lindy slowly allowed, handing Darrick back his phone, "I think I do have another show in me. In fact," she confessed, "I'm already planning it out now. It's a drama—no, who am I kidding?—it'll end up being a farce—but it's based on the Scandinavian fairy tale *East o' the Sun, West o' the Moon.*"

Her actors' ears immediately perked up.

"What's it about?" they chorused.

"A plucky young woman who, nevertheless, loses her love because of her fears. But then, with the aid of a bunch of new friends, she seeks him out and finds him again."

Lindy strove to ignore the glint of amusement in Malcolm's eyes.

"That sounds like a good plot," approved Rochelle. "It's got lots of potential..."

"Will I be cast as the heroine?" asked Philippe. "I've got a beautiful braided blonde fall I could wear..."

"And I'm sure you'll write another substantive role for us," nodded Darrick.

Leo, chewing happily on his second jerky treat, said nothing but gazed confidently up at Lindy with liquid brown eyes.

Perhaps having a bricks and mortar theatre won't be such a bad investment with this gang of narcissists, Lindy decided. They're always going to be playing something somewhere. It might as well be in our own space with Malcolm and me.

Shortly afterwards, with all the food and drink polished off, the actors blithely took their leaves.

Malcolm helped Lindy tidy up and then, yawning, excused himself upstairs to get ready for bed.

With all the ugly canines cleansed from her realm, Phyllis finally deigned to allow Lindy to lure her down from her living room aerie and followed her into the kitchen.

"And the great thing about us having our own indoor theatre—" Lindy explained to her impatient silver-grey cat as she opened a tin of her favourite tuna, "—is that we get to say whether anyone can bring in their dog..."

* * * * *

Six months later at Excursion Theatre's newly converted chapel playhouse, deep in rehearsals for the remount of Darrick's vastly revised play, Lindy's temper was wearing thin.

Philippe's sore throat was getting so bad, she could hardly hear his lines.

Malcolm was loudly debating over his phone with Jenn about the price of printing their next programs.

And the roof repair guys had placed their ladders right where she always liked to put her director's chair.

Irritation piled on irritation until—

"Rochelle!" Lindy finally snapped. "Tie up your damn shih tzu! Gérard's trying to hump Leo again, and I've already tripped over him twice today—!"

Right.

Stay with the tour, Lindy.

In for a penny, in for a pound.

A doggington arf. A doggington yip. A doggington play...

Final Notes And Acknowledgements

The plays I have used as subtitles at the beginning of each chapter are the twenty theatrical performances Lindy attended before she went to the Fimbria Festival. They are all either comedies, farces, romances or theatre of the absurd. Her understanding of theatrical form, therefore, has largely been shaped by comedic, farcical, romantic or absurdist structure and rhythms, character and dialogue, and it may make a bit more sense to the reader that, despite her serious intent, Lindy never has much luck writing tragedy or drama.

Also, it must be noted, the 'Arts Court' of my imagination is based upon the building as it appeared over a decade ago and is not meant to represent the thoroughly renovated, modernized and entirely fire-safe Arts Court that exists in Ottawa today. And, of course, all of the rest of the places, events and characters portrayed in this novel are entirely fictitious, with any similarity to actual locations, occurrences and people, alive or dead, completely coincidental.

I was inspired to write this optimistic social comedy by my retired friends who have bravely embarked on challenging new adventures in their sixties—Jill who rented a studio for her art, Sandy who walked in the steps of Spanish pilgrims, Bev who helped build a school in Central America—and so many more who have used their retirements to achieve ambitious personal goals.

A huge thank you is due to my patient readers and editors, Alison, Kevin, Angela, Laura, Brenda, Bev, Lara and, of course, Lorne. Your comments were extremely helpful and all the awkwardness and mistakes remaining in this novel are purely mine.

Thanks to all the people I've met and worked with in student, amateur and semi-professional theatre, especially Lorne and Kevin, Alison and Rick, Al and Wendi, Lori Jean, Mathieu, Jodi, and Sean, Prof. Doug and Cedric at Carleton University, my professors and fellow students at Queen's University, many dedicated drama teachers and students from the Carleton and Ottawa District School Boards, and the tireless staff members, helpful techies and enthusiastic volunteers at the Ottawa Fringe Festival. Over the years, my adventures in and around numerous performances have been some of the most delightful, stimulating and, yes, frustrating experiences of my life.

And, finally, humble thanks are owed to both of my cats, silver-grey Leila and grey-striped George, whose doppelgangers feature in this novel and who share my fascination with and sometime fear of the neighbours' friendly pet dogs...

Lightning Source UK Ltd.
Milton Keynes UK
UKHW010632210919
350180UK00001B/93/P